# ORBS

## and the Attack of the Hair Spiders

PEACE

MAGIC

ANGER

MIRROR

## A . M . RICHARDSON

First published in 2019

ISBN 978-1-9160643-0-0

**Printed and bound in Great Britain**
00 10 20 30 40 50 60 70 80 90 100 110 120

www.chronospublishing.co.uk
www.am-richardson.com

Acknowledgements

Sue Mitchell

The Fen Country - by author Christopher Marlowe M.A. 1926
(Werewolf of Dogdyke)
Roger Parsons

*for Stephanie, the one who makes my life worthwhile,*
*and for Diani and Keyan, who never fail to make me smile.*

# CONTENTS

THE REALM OF
THE SIRENS

THE REEF OF RUIN

REEF
GAP

● TILÖS

GREAT EASTERN
REEF MARKER

GREAT WESTERN
REEF MARKER

GIBRALT

PORT OF
MÜR

THE GREAT PURPLE
CRYSTAL MOUNTAINS

● CASTLE
HORN

HABERDASH

THE ANCIENT
FOREST

SPITWIND CLIFFS

DRAGON
TEMPLE

BRICKABRACK

TICKLEPENNY
LOCH

CHERRYBERRY FOREST

● NO MAN'S FRIEND

LANG
MAR

CRIM

HARÚK

ADMAR

ANGRIB

THE SIBLING ISLES

# TETHERA
## The Realm of Magic

AR POINT

BELTANE'S SPEAR

MOGG'S EYE

THE PLUNDERTOFT MINES

THE GREAT WALL

THE FAERY HILLS

DOGDYKE

RICK SHES

WIGTOFT

RYM

N

W

E

S

PEACE

MAGIC

ANGER

# Prologue

The forest was cold. A forgotten darkness had crept back into the world. The once green trees now groaned with hunger, starved of sunlight and poisoned with infertile soil. The birds had stopped singing for fear of disturbing the silence. But something rustled through the undergrowth; hurried feet crunched leaves and snapped twigs before coming to an abrupt stop.

'I'm here,' began a confident voice.

'Are you alonesies?' replied a little grunty one.

'Yes, for now. But they aren't far behind and my broom is getting tired.'

'How many?'

'Two. One red, the other white as you requested.'

'Good my youngsy friend,' came the grunty little voice again. 'You must use the coin and let them follow.'

'I will, though I'm not altogether happy about the arrangement.'

'What worries you youngsy?'

'I'm worried that I'm not up to this task.'

'Youngsy. You are the only person being ables to do this task. No one else is having the skills or powers you have. Besides, you are being the best for taming dragons.'

'Yes well, so far that's been mainly down to luck. I'm surprised I haven't been eaten yet and I still don't understand why having a red and a white chase me was so important.'

'You will my youngsy, you will. Now be off, we's being shortsies on time.'

'Okay, right yes, off,' said the first voice, now sounding less confident.

'Youngsy, you *must* be off, this task will not waits for you,' implored the grunty voice.

'Okay. Okay. I'm going. Oh and Orbulous, what's with all the "youngsy" talk all the time? I am over a thousand years old after all.'

'Well that is being very youngsy compared to my ages. What would you prefer I be calling you?'

'My name of course – Merlin.'

# CHAPTER ONE

# Smoke and Mirrors

The Town of Brickabrack was quiet as it had been for months. None dared venture out at night. Doors were bolted tightly and no windows were left on the latch, for something cruel visited the town after sunset, as the darkness crept in.

Nithelda Nutton (more often referred to as Nanny Nutton) had just set her cup and saucer down on the small oak table by the fire as her loyal, scruffy-looking owl hooted twice to let her know her final batch of mushroom scones were ready to be taken out of the oven.

'Ooh thank you Phidias,' she said fondly, patting the old bird on the head, 'but I do wish you'd use English and save your hooting for your feathered flock of friends.' She hobbled into the kitchen with Phidias perched on her shoulder, meandering over to the cast-iron monstrosity that was her oven. Some years back she had bought it from a surprisingly kind giant who had thrown in a free pair of old and well-worn oven gloves to 'seal the deal' as it were, for Nanny Nutton was quite the negotiator. Of course, despite her renowned negotiating skills the kind giant had failed to mention that this particular oven was rather fond of cremating everything.

She always baked scones late into the evening as not only was she the town's button shop owner, she was also a retired headmistress of Pendragon's School of Magic and, for her sins, still offered private tuition to some of the brighter youngsters of the town. She would teach them more advanced spells and treat them to scones and cherryberry jam, sometimes even pickled newt livers if they had been particularly well behaved.

It was late and as she lay the latest trays of crusty, blackened mushroom scones to rest, a familiar sound caught her keen ears.

She stopped as the room fell silent. Listening, she carefully pulled her frail hands out of one of the enormous giant's oven gloves (that were each roughly the same size as a dwarf's sleeping bag) as another low rumble wavered from the other side of town.

'Oh no! He's back,' she whispered loudly, shuddering until her knees began to knock.

Phidias scuttled off from the kitchen back into the lounge, squawking, hopping and frantically flapping towards the mantelpiece before settling down and turning into solid gold.

'Huh! Charming! It's times like this we need to stick together. Would your father have left Merlin at the first sign of danger? Well?'

The golden statue of the owl did not budge.

'Well, there'll be no more squeaky-mouse scones for you my feathered friend. You had better hope we are not on his list tonight,' she said as she went about dousing candles and dimming the lanterns throughout her rickety old house.

The relentless rumbling grew closer. Nanny Nutton could now hear that with every rumble an almighty crashing noise followed soon after.

*

Silence filled the air once more as a trail of thick black smoke meandered down streets and along passageways before settling on Eastgate. No curtains twitched nor doors creaked ajar for a glimpse of the terror lurking in the gloom. The townspeople simply lay in their beds as they had done every night for months; petrified, breaths held tight, hoping they weren't next.

The rain was falling heavily on the town, trickling down sewers and pitter-pattering its own eerie tune on shabby rooftops and rusty cast-iron guttering. Oddly, the rain was also splashing off the trail of smoke rather than travelling through it – almost as if it were a solid form. It twisted here and writhed there; this was no ordinary smoke, this had both purpose and desire. It slithered from Eastgate onto Broadbank as if searching for something.

The Brickabrack guard ran past the Archway to Nowhere and pressed himself tightly against the wall of the Imperial Guards' quarters. His knuckles turned white as his grip tightened on his spear. The smoke slithered towards him hungrily. He watched as it coiled and thrashed wildly before resting as a deep black puddle on the ground. The puddle then rippled and spattered as a hand suddenly emerged from it. Pale and sinister it menacingly grasped for the air. Upwards it travelled until a figure, cloaked in shadow, surfaced, stepping boldly onto the damp grubby cobbles.

'YOU?' the guard spluttered.

'ME!' the creature replied.

'I thought you was the beast! Coming to get me. I very nearly killed you with me spear!' The guard spat angrily.

'What beast?' the creature replied, smiling.

'The beast! The one that's been stealing people for its supper and destroying our town.'

'How do you know I'm not this beast of yours?' asked the cloaked creature.

'Ha. You're no beast. I mean, you've looked better but the one I'm talking about has horns and nasty teeth and all the other vile things people say they seen.'

'Tell me guard – have you seen this beast?'

'Well, no, but others have. Why?' the guard asked, scratching his head.

'I'm afraid they're liars, every last one of them!' the creature chuckled mockingly.

'What makes you think they're lying?' the guard barked in protest. 'Have *you* seen the beast when it comes at night? Besides, what are you doing out this late anyway? You know no one's advised to roam the streets come nightfall. And what was all that magic about? The smoke and funny-looking puddle? What other things can you turn yourself into?'

'I can turn myself into anything I choose to,' the creature said mysteriously, 'just as I can turn you into whatever I choose!'

'Wh-WHAT?' the guard gasped.

*'Morphidius Mdudu!'* the creature shrieked.

The guard's spear, along with his armour and helmet clanged loudly as they hit the ground. Moments later a lonely worm squelched its way from under the guard's helmet and made for the nearest slop-filled gutter. Insane laughter consumed the street's silence and then thundered its way around the entire town.

Next, the figure raised its exhausted hands and wearily aimed them at a modest five and a half storey property.

'Do it!' the creature hissed to himself. 'No. This isn't me,' he replied back to himself. 'This is *all* you are now, now DO IT!' The creature turned with teary eyes back to the property. *'Oblitundo!'* he wailed as the force of ten dragons demolished the house in one fell swoop. Bricks showered down onto the cobbled streets. Another piece of the town had fallen victim to this mysterious villain. Once the debris had settled cries of distress erupted along the surrounding streets. Then silence.

Shiny black lips smiled wide to reveal brittle-looking teeth. The cruel creature spun about and stepped from the street back into his deep black puddle, splashing out of sight. The puddle then hissed and bubbled as if it were boiling. Black steam rose from the cobbles and moments later the puddle, along with the smoke, had vanished.

There were more bricks and screams to follow before a puddle appeared on Cannon Street. Nanny Nutton could see him limping awkwardly down towards her house, as if he himself were both tired and in pain. The hood of the creature's cloak concealed its face in shadow.

'Quick Phidias, he's coming, you'd better go and hide.' She said sarcastically to her ever faithful but ever frightened pet. 'I sometimes wonder if your father really was Archimedes. You simply are the worst protector I have ever had. And I don't like golden owl statues cluttering up my mantelpiece either so I'm afraid you are neither use nor ornament to me. The apple has fallen well and truly far from the tree you useless waste of plumage, and furthermore…'

Nanny Nutton's rant was suddenly interrupted by a garbled collection of words from the desolate grey streets below. She paused and listened as her tightly bolted shop door downstairs swung open.

The cloaked figure ambled inside to see shelves of every shape and size covering all the walls. There were shelves on shelves and even some on the ceiling. A large oak counter and lots of odd-looking ladders with wobbly rungs occupied the remaining spaces. More impressive than this were the jars and baskets, all of them full to the brim with buttons. There were buttons that sparkled invitingly like precious gems, buttons that glowed as if made of fire. Some were like snowflakes, others like oozy snakes that wriggled. Some smelled like wild roses while others made pretty melodies. They were all mesmerising and highly desirable to the vile intruder.

'So many beautiful buttons!' the figure said loudly with a sinister chuckle, 'but where to begin?' He grabbed fistful after fistful and rammed them into his large pockets until he sounded like some oversized baby rattle. He jingled and jangled as he fumbled through the shop stealing more and more buttons.

'Enjoying yourself?' asked Nanny Nutton in a well-rehearsed, retired headmistress tone, her arms folded tightly.

'Actually I am,' the cloaked figure replied jovially, without even turning to face her. 'Amazing things really, buttons -' he paused, stuffing another fistful down his trousers.

'How so?' Nanny Nutton quizzed.

'Well, not only are they quite lovely on their own but they hold things together, help us maintain our dignity, you know, a bit like…'

'Good manners?' Nanny Nutton interrupted.

'I was going to say "women" actually,' the cloaked figure replied, now turning to face her.

'What are you?' Nanny Nutton asked authoritatively, 'and what do you want with my buttons?'

'Be quiet crone, I am not here to listen to the nonsense of an old lady,' the cloaked figure spat. 'I'm tired of your words and your buttons!'

'Then leave. Have you not caused enough pain tonight?' Nanny Nutton said coolly.

'Ha ha ha har. My dear woman, the night is young. I've not even started!' he snarled, his eyes wide with rage.

'Why are you doing this?'

He paused and blinked as if he had just sobered from a drunken slumber. 'I d- I don't know?'

'Then stop,' the old woman said, stepping from behind the enormous counter and placing a gentle hand on his unnaturally cold forehead. He closed his eyes and let out a deep sigh. Nanny Nutton smiled as the fright she had been hiding eased somewhat.

But this wasn't to last. His body suddenly jolted. With his eyes still closed his face began to flinch with pain. He opened his eyes, now returned to their wide, furious state.

'Are you trying to trick me?' he roared at her.

'No dear.' Nanny Nutton whimpered, stepping backwards.

'YOU WILL NOT TAKE THEM FROM ME!' he shrieked in a somewhat confused manner.

'Keep the buttons dear,' she said with a forced smile that she hoped would conceal her fear.

'They're mine crone!' he thundered. 'This town is mine!'

'Okay dear, there's no need to get upset,' she said trying to reason with the dark villain.

'Yes, yes you're right,' he muttered under his breath. 'I was right though, buttons are like women. You see when a button becomes old it has no use. No one misses an old button, they just replace it with a shiny new one. Old buttons just disappear. So with that in mind...' the cloaked figure paused and grinned wickedly. He raised his gaunt hands and aimed them directly at her.

'NOW!' Nanny Nutton yelped.

In an instant several jars fizzed and popped. Buttons pinged off in all directions and all of a sudden several people were stood in the shop. Men with long beards and peculiar hats stood alongside women dressed in glorious gowns of shimmering greens and purples. As the storm of buttons ended the cloaked figure looked up to see numerous wands and staffs aimed at him.

'Do not move,' spoke a familiar voice to the creature.

'Ah Luther! How lovely to see you and after so many months. Tell me how are Lizzi and the children?'

The group of Witches and Wizards looked baffled at each other but none more so than Luther.

'You leave them out of this!' Luther thundered, wondering how the creature knew his name. 'This ends tonight, you can either surrender and be offered a fair trial or we finish you.'

'Hmm. Now that's a toughy,' the cloaked figure said mockingly whilst smirking under the shadow of his hood. 'How about I let you all know tomorrow?'

'I believe you seriously underestimate the gravity of your actions beast. We will have no choice,' Luther said gruffly.

'It's just a few buttons,' the cloaked figure replied, shrugging his shoulders like a scorned child.

'What about the destruction of our town, the disappearances, the murders? Those will not be viewed as lightly as some ill-gotten fashion accessories.'

'If you think I'll stop, you're dead wrong my old friend. I will never stop. Not until this town and its folk are nothing more than rubble and ash.'

'Remove your hood so we can all see you,' the old Wizard said, raising his staff and pointing it directly at the creature's head. 'If you do not cooperate then you leave us no choice,' Luther added. He thrust his staff forwards, bellowing: *'FACTU –'*

'On second thought...' interrupted the cloaked figure before pausing.

He slowly raised his pale hands to his face and drew back the hood of his cloak. He shuddered as the cool night air struck his puce skin and his wide eyes began to narrow. He began panting as if he had been holding his breath for a long time. Then he gazed up to the room full of people whose mouths were wide with disbelief.

'What's going on?' he asked with a puzzled expression smeared across his face. 'Luther, what are you doing here?'

'The question we need answering my lad, is what are you doing here?'

'I don't know.' the cloaked figure answered.

'It's a trick Luther. Finish him while we have the chance!' hissed a scrawny-looking Wizard with a long faded ginger beard.

'Wait!' the cloaked figure pleaded, 'I – I don't even know my name.' he said, rubbing his face with trembling hands.

'Well my lad, your name is Griffin and we are your friends.' Luther said calmly.

'Griffin?' the cloaked figure said staring blankly back at the group.

'Here perhaps this will help,' Luther said softly, offering the cloaked figure a mirror.

The dark creature took the mirror and gazed deeply at his reflection. 'I have no memory of this face. I…' he paused again, unable to finish his sentence. He shuffled and squirmed uneasily before fainting in a heap on the button shop floor.

'I can't believe it!' Nanny Nutton gasped. 'All this time! All this time it was Griffin.'

'Yes, it appears we were all wrong. He hadn't been taken like the others. He *was* the very evil we thought had taken him too.'

'What do you mean? What are you saying?' commanded the ginger Wizard.

'Why isn't it obvious Fonzo?' Luther said coldly staring at the unconscious creature on the shop floor. 'Griffin *is* Blackmouth!'

# CHAPTER TWO

# The Rise of Blackmouth

'A Warlock, by definition, is *a man who practices black magic, an oath breaker,* and it is here in this Chamber that I declare that you, Griffin Marcavious Larry Black should now be recognised as one,' barked the elder from his pale and unnecessarily tall marble pedestal.

The elder, twisting his faded orange beard around his withered, boney finger, turned to address the large audience that was quickly gathering.

Now, on an average day the High Council Chamber Two within the Town of Brickabrack could hold several hundred people, creatures and beasts in one sitting. However, on this particular day it seemed more like several thousand had turned out to see the extraordinary events that were to unfold within its thirteen walls.

The rows and aisles were packed so full that those lucky enough to be sat on the cold marble benches actually had others perched precariously on their knees and shoulders, which made the lucky ones rather unlucky really. This was fine in some instances, like where Mr Proofgrease the local bacon grinder had sat his young, awestruck son on his knee, but not so fortunate for a pot-bellied dwarf by the name of Captain Shiverrs.

'You'll not see me perched like a faery on some foul beast's knees! I've not battled me way through fire and death to be a knee-percher!' he snorted disdainfully to a frail old lady as she was about to sit down and who he rather harshly belly-bounced away. It was only moments later that Captain Shiverrs was unpleasantly surprised to have an eight foot rock troll by the name of Skrolly decide he wanted to sit somewhere. Mistaking the Captain for a brightly coloured and rather plump-looking cushion he delicately, and quite carefully, placed himself down like a lady at a tea party so as not to disturb those around him. You see, rock trolls, although appearing quite terrifying with their lumpy hard skin, enormous hands, not to mention their blunt teeth and fingernails, are actually some of the more pleasant creatures that live within the old Cherryberry forest on the borders of the town. Also, being a rock troll and hard of hearing (due to the large amounts of rock wax that gather in their small ears), he failed to recognise the muffled wails coming from beneath him nor the two short, stumpy legs kicking frantically from under his grey, boulder-like bottom.

'Order! Order I say!' boomed Councillor Fidrib. 'This is High Council Chamber Two, not some half-witted market stall. Why, some of the greatest Wizards, Witches and powerful beings of our time have sat where you are. It is a powerful and exceptionally magical place and it will not be made a mockery of!'

The chamber fell utterly silent. Even Captain Shiverrs had quietened down – whether this was because he was listening intently or he had run out of air remains a mystery.

Wide-eyed and full of energy the Elder began.

'We have all witnessed the disturbing occurrences that have been taking place in and around Brickabrack; people, even some of our precious children, snatched in the night never to be seen again. Entire properties demolished in a single blow. Great fires ravaging large sections of the old forest and then – puff – gone without a trace leaving a ghastly trail of death and destruction.' He paused and heaved in another large breath between his cracked, wrinkly lips. 'My good people, we have our answers and more importantly – we have our evidence!' The crowd were overwhelmed, clapping and cheering – the elder may as well have announced that he was giving a free pot of gold to everyone.

Clearly enjoying the attention he stood, dazed and with a half-cocked smile on his face, almost forgetting Griffin, the accused, stood in front of him.

'Throw him in the dungeons!' cried a large, round Witch from the audience that had clearly spent too much time in Mrs Macrocker's Pie Potions Shop.

This drew the elder out of his glorious daydream and he quickly changed his expression from that of a bedazzled schoolboy back to the sincere, stern Council representative that he was.

'Innocent until proven guilty!' promptly came a deep, manly voice. A tall man, good looking with a top hat and cane, was stood at the very front of the hall. 'And if you spent more time thinking and less time eating, yes, I'm talking to you, Patty Pigswill, then you would see that he is innocent! And furthermore…'

'SILENCE!' interrupted the Elder. 'We all know where your loyalties lie Fineart, but I'm afraid your efforts are wasted. We have enough evidence to put him away forty-seven times over!'

'Evidence? Evidence you say!' said Fineart sharply. 'What evidence do you think you have?'

'I, my friend, have the kind of evidence that will put this evil master of the dark magic, this Warlock, away for an age beyond any of us. Why, by the time he is released my great, great, great, great grandchild's, child's offspring will have been dead two hundred and sixteen years.'

'You can't be serious!' replied Fineart who was now clearly concerned. 'Fonzo…' Fineart continued, at which the audience chuckled.

'How *dare* you address me by my first name in this chamber!' snapped the Council Elder who had from a young age resented his parents for their quirky name choice and lack of forethought.

'Councillor Fidrib, you know this isn't right,' Fineart contested. 'The Bottle-snare charm is reserved for murderers and demons,' he said, standing up to address the untidy mass of creatures and the townspeople, 'and as we can all see Griffin has neither a knife nor horns.'

Raucous laughter filled the chamber, which displeased the Elder so much that he chomped down hard on his own tongue. Moments later, as the fit of giggles continued, he drew his gold staff from behind his unnecessarily tall pedestal and aimed its purple crystal tip straight at Fineart. The crowd gasped in disbelief as the cowardly Council Elder began ranting and chanting behind Fineart's back.

Fineart's body jolted and he suddenly found himself locked to the spot. His feet felt as heavy as the very marble slabs he was standing on. He fought it but it was useless. Then from behind him came the deep, droning voice of Councillor Fidrib.

'Your mockery is both time wasting and disrespectful. This Warlock has been brought before us today to be tried for murder, destruction of public property, destruction of ancient property, performing black magic spells without reason or authorisation and stealing from Nanny Nutton's button shop.' He sharply thrust his staff a quarter turn to the right and Fineart, who was unable to speak or move, spun around. The beautiful cane that was still in his hand screeched in a perfect circle on the cold floor, like cutlery on crockery.

'I take it you have nothing more to say on the matter?' asked the Elder, a patronising tone in his voice, knowing only too well that Fineart couldn't reply. 'Good. And now my fine beings, we seriously need to address this issue so I take it there will be no further...*interruptions,*' he said, spying a few unsavoury characters in the audience before turning back to Griffin, who, out of respect and knowing the inevitable outcome, had remained silent throughout the whole ordeal. 'Griffin Marcavious Larry Black, I have viewed Master Agar's truth orb and I have seen the events that you were involved in. We, the people of Brickabrack trusted you. You were well respected here yet you turned your back on us. My people, the truth I'm afraid is too horrific to witness and quite frankly unsuitable for minors.' Mr Proofgrease's son, still awestruck, sighed with disappointment. 'However, there will be a public display of Master Agar's orb at the Gatehouse next Tuesday night where you may view privately for the small sum of one Guilder-Groat.' He paused, rubbing his gaunt hands together while sporting a greedy grin. 'Griffin Marcavious Larry Black, it is here, today, that you have been found guilty by seven of the thirteen Council Elders of all of the aforementioned crimes. How do you plead?'

Griffin stepped forward.

'Councillor Fidrib and all creatures and people here today, I'm afraid I do not know if I am guilty or not as I have no memory of the past few years.' He paused and shrugged his shoulders. 'You know, I remember a time when Brickabrack was a better place, its walls strong and its people compassionate. "The place any being would feel welcome" – that's what they used to say. Better were the days when music and warmth enchanted folk from far and distant lands. Talk was of a town that shared, not stole from its visitors, a town where children could play freely in the streets and rivers. A better time, when even the Great Well served a purpose and was not left a tattered relic of a better past.' He paused again staring blankly at the stark chamber floor. 'But then an evil stirred through these very streets like some unstoppable disease. Corruption amassed, grog fuelled the depressed and lonely to rage and before long the once peaceful place I called home became a prison. That same evil may have stirred in me.'

'LIES!' exploded the Elder. 'Where were you? I want to hear you say it. I want the truth!'

'That is the truth!' insisted Griffin. 'I can't remember how I came to be this way. The only glimmer of memory I have from these past years is of darkness and tormented trees, like those of the old forest – the section where no one visits anymore.'

'Slightly convenient don't you think – that you should suffer a memory lapse during this particular period of your life.' The Elder went on, 'Griffin, this all began did it not, when you disappeared. And it was only when you disappeared that the deaths and crimes began to take place. Two years you've been missing and now you turn up on our doorstep, looking rather ill, and instantly, like a sudden change in the wind during a storm, the murders stop, the crimes stop. Now, we have a signed account from your wife stating what happened around the time of your disappearance. Can you confirm the following to be true?'

Griffin stood silently for a moment. He had barely had time to even think about what his family must be going through.

*A Warlock, an oath breaker.* Fidrib's words would haunt him forever.

And this is what Griffin had become. Although he had not always been this way, in fact he had been quite a pleasant character, a good listener and someone who could always be relied upon for comfort and understanding. He prospered from a will to do good, had lots of friends in far and distant places and was

Councillor Fonzo Fidrih

well thought of by a great many people. He married a young and beautiful woman of his home, the Town of Brickabrack. She too was very well respected and many a bachelor had revelled in her company, but ultimately lost their prize to him. She was a lady, a natural beauty with a warm face and a warmer heart. She had auburn unkempt hair that danced fiercely in the slightest breeze. Her name was Lizzi Agar, youngest daughter of Master Agar, a powerful Wizard and Griffin's old mentor.

Councillor Fidrib pulled a multi-coloured glass orb from the sleeve of his orange cloak; the faded golden pleating of his sleeves shimmered like a dusty old trophy that needed a good gob of polish. He held the giant marble aloft and with his powerful yet dulcet tone stated, *'Agarictum Orbis, Lizzi Blackeus,'* which pulled Griffin's gaze back to the cold marble floor of the chamber.

In a burst of mesmerising colour and flashing lights the orb emitted a picture that filled the room. At first glance the image was hazy, like staring through dusty spectacles, but then, like rippling water on a mill pond it settled and the image became clear. It was Griffin's house, tall and rickety, lying on Westgate by the Tipsy Toad Inn. Fonzo Fidrib's eyes turned pure white, glazed over like two freshly boiled eggs and as if in a trance he began to narrate.

'This is Lizzi Black's account of her husband's disappearance.'

You see, whoever holds the orb and requests it to show something becomes its puppet for the duration of the show. And during the show the puppet, or in this case Councillor Fidrib, will have no idea what he has said or done.

And so he continued.

'One Autumn's eve upon arriving back to their small brick home in the centre of town, lying opposite the Tipsy Toad Inn, Lizzi met an odd sight. Broken wood lay strewn on the damp cobbled street. It was what looked like the remnants of their front door, which was no longer on its hinges. It lay in tatters, with most of it appearing to have been smashed to small splinters. Lizzi, knowing only too well of her husband's antics and his experimental nature, assumed he must have done it accidentally. She entered the house, calling out for her husband.

"Oh Griffin? Is there something you want to tell…" she stopped abruptly mid-sentence. It was only then as she stood in the silence that she noticed something that sent a shiver trickling down her spine. There were large tear marks on the back of his favourite, and quite weathered, red leather chair that sat by the open brick fire. She teased some of the cotton padding out of one of the tears.

"Griffin!" she shouted, waiting a moment for some form of response.

"Mother, what's going on?" spoke a voice from high above her. She gazed up to see a gangly thirteen year old boy with scruffy black hair and sharp elbows stood on the landing four stories up, rubbing his eyes as if fresh from a deep sleep. He had a strong jaw and deep-set eyes, a dark ring around each. His clothes rarely fitted him as he was constantly growing and his pyjamas were no exception, the trousers stopping halfway down his shins.

"Oh…Garad…it's you. Have you seen your father?"

"No, I've been asleep, it's late and…" Garad paused taking in the full view below him. "Mother, why is the room in such a state? It looks like a tussle of trolls has had a furniture throwing competition down there."

"I don't know why it's like this, where's your sister?"

"I think she's still in bed but…"

"Well go and check please," Lizzi interrupted, her concern mounting with each passing moment.

"But Mother, what's going on?" Garad impatiently asked.

"I don't know Garad – now go and check on your sister! Griffin Black you come out this minute!" Lizzi ordered while trying to contain her emotions. "I think it's just one of his crazy experiments, yes, that's it, a magical whatja-macallit gone wrong, yes that's got to be it." She tamed her long auburn locks, placing them neatly behind her ears, wiped a lonely tear from her pale cheek and smiled up at where her son had just been standing almost in some last attempt of reassurance. But deep down she was scared; she knew that this was unusual – even for her ever accident-prone husband. Something bad had happened here. There was no fire, no light. All the flickering of the many candles had been extinguished and the room was full of blues and greys. Deep down, she was sick with worry.'

The crowd in the Council Chamber were transfixed. Some had never witnessed the power of the orb before but for those who had, this viewing was somewhat disturbing. Even Skrolly the rock troll was on the edge of his seat, which had thankfully allowed Captain Shiverrs enough room to breathe.

Councillor Fidrib went on, his eyes glassy and dead.

'He had altogether vanished. Lizzi spent that night scouring the streets, checking every archway, drain and armoury store, and all the while fearing the worst. Three months passed with no sign or clue as to his whereabouts. Initially, Lizzi had called on the whole townspeople to set up regular search parties but they soon dwindled. People just assumed he had either accidentally blown himself somewhere distant in an incantation gone wrong or that he had been taken by the infamous Ticklepenny Loch monster.'

The Elder stopped, his eyes returning to their normal, unnaturally electric shade of blue. The orb dulled and floated downward like a feather. Councillor Fidrib reached up and grasped it with his pale, claw-like hands.

'So, now that we have that side of the story, can I trouble you for your account of what happened that night, and no lies please, they won't wash with me...' he paused, 'or the orb.'

The Elder, using his staff that was also still controlling Fineart, whisked the orb through the air like a bubble in a breeze across the chamber to Griffin. He opened his hand and it fell gently onto his palm. A rush of anxiety pulsed through his body like electricity, unnerving him.

He knew that this meant the truth he couldn't remember would be revealed through him. Worse still was the notion that, because he would be unaware of what he was saying, the whole of the room would know before him what had actually happened and this thought scared him immensely.

'Griffin Black repeat after me, *"Agarictum Orbis, Griffin*

*Blackeus.*"

Griffin stood afraid. While under the orb's control anything could happen. He was being accused of murder along with all sorts of other terrible crimes. What if one of the crowd became angry and attacked him? What if the ogre on the sixth aisle decided it was lunch time? What if the redrump dragon hanging from the rafters sneezed? Worse still, what if old Nanny Nutton decided she wanted her buttons back and Griffin ended up with no clothes on, cold and embarrassingly unaware.

'Say it!' demanded Fidrib.

Griffin turned to his silent, statuesque friend Thomas Fineart, smiled and whispered, '*Agarictum Orbis, Griffin Blackeus.*'

Two freshly-boiled eggs now stared out to the audience and the orb shone brightly once more. Then Griffin began to speak – he was narrating his own story.

'In fact none of these rumours or beliefs are true.

Griffin had been indeed, sat in his favourite oxblood red leather chair, smoking his cherryberry hardwood pipe and indulging in a little light reading. Being a keen writer and quite the poet, Griffin usually read several books at once. On this particular day he had six books on the go. The one he was carefully ingesting was called *Odd Creatures that do the Oddest Things* by Claude Mitoes. It sat resting neatly in his palm while the other five floated in a clean line in front of him, bobbing up and down as if floating peacefully along an invisible babbling brook.

These included: *Dragon Snacks* by Nora Lottabones; *Noises of the Night* by Owlyn Hoots; *The Art of Fire Potions* by Roarus Blackburn; *The Art of avoiding Fire Potions – Volume 3* by Bernie Bits and *12,003 Uses for a Stick* by Iva Stampatoo.

You see although he had stacks of books, Griffin only had the one bookmark. A single bookmark, slender and incredibly long, made of old dusty silk that weaved its way through all six different shaped and coloured books that swayed weightlessly in front of him, holding its place in each of them.

He had just turned to a page about a fish in a skirt that danced in a bowl of soup when, without warning, the blazing fire in front of which he was sat suddenly died in an almighty puff of smoke. Why, it was as if the very flame had been ripped from the burning wood and all that now remained was a glowing log covered in grey ash.

He sat bolt upright, his gaze transfixed upon the fireplace. He was totally vexed by this and leaned forward to investigate further.

He crouched to the ground and laid his book to rest, at which the remaining five suddenly thudded in unison upon the faded red faery-woven rug complete with scorch marks and black soot stains. On all fours he crawled forward and slowly placed his head under the chimney breast; his face now hung, suspended as if waiting for a guillotine blade in the space where the fire had been blazing.

He blew the log which fizzed and hissed bright orange, resembling lava between the cracks of the perished wood. He twisted his body and cocked his head to one side, peering up slowly to see…nothing – just a peek of the midnight blue autumn sky and the odd star dotted here and there.

A sigh of relief gushed from deep in his chest and he felt a great weight or should I say fear lift. It was only then, when Griffin was feeling quietly comfortable again that something caught his eye – a dark shape, mysterious and eerie, reflecting in the brass mantel surround. It was stood behind his red chair, staring intriguingly at him. He made out no features at this point, only a shadow with burning green eyes. He froze, his skin tingling with fright.

He swung around and let out a deep manly howl but there was no one there. His head spun in all directions, his eyes frantically scanning the room, searching past all the oddities that filled it; floating books, upside down furniture (for any necessary upsidedownness parties), bubbling potion-making apparatus, the old talking dragon skeleton that Lizzi's Uncle Hector had given him, shelves of different coloured liquids in different sized vials, tubes, glass jars and demijohns. Pumpkins, plants, a queer looking rhombus-shaped magnifying glass. All this, and no dark apparition. Nothing.

His gaze fell back to the chair which now had deep claw marks carved into the leather, the discoloured white cotton stuffing oozed out of the fresh wounds.

An epiphany hit him like a brick to the head. He spun round in a flash, fell to his knees and once more gazed at the brass mantel surround. Leaving no time to even gather his thoughts the piercing green eyes, shrouded in shadow, leered over his left shoulder.

He screamed before everything faded to black and he passed into darkness.

*

He woke in familiar surroundings but it was not his home. He quite oddly enough was in the middle of the old Cherryberry forest some thirty miles from Brickabrack.

"What is this trickery?" he said, scratching his head and quickly checking himself for injuries. "Hello?" he inquired. A somewhat apprehensive tone to his voice. "Is there anyone there?"

A bone-chilling cackle echoed through the trees. Woodcock, roosting ravens, pie-eyed pigeons and all manner of birds left their comfy perches to avoid the shrieking sound that resonated from all over the forest.

Griffin was only too familiar with that sound.

"Show yourself Hexen!"

His teachings at school had covered the topic of the *Hexen Witch's Cackle* although he had never had the displeasure of meeting an invisible Witch let alone endure the shrill he was now being plagued with. For this is what Hexen Witches were renowned for; invisibility, insane cackling and a love for all things sinister and dark.

"Recite the song and you will see," came a voice from not a few feet in front of him.

"No games Witch. Show yourself and explain the purpose of my capture," insisted Griffin.

Silence.

"I mean it Witch, I'll have your head for this oath breaking!"

He raised his hand, his long, elegant fingers outstretched. But something was different. He was unable to conjure his magic. Uncannily resembling the fire in his home, it was as if his very soul along with all his energy and magic had been ripped from his body. You see Griffin, unlike the majority of other Witches and Wizards, didn't need a wand or staff to summon and focus his magic. His flowed through him more freely than the blood in his veins.

"Aha ha ha ha ha ha!" came the same chilling cackle. It came nearer until it rang in Griffin's ears. As he winced at the deafening pitch, something grabbed his arms and pulled and pushed.

His body writhed as if he was dancing a painful waltz with an invisible partner.

He closed his eyes, holding his head trying desperately to guard his ears from the cackling.

Suddenly, the soft mossy ground disappeared under his feet. Had a great crack formed in the forest floor Griffin pondered? Was he falling into a bottomless crevasse? He opened his eyes to actually see the floor moving further away from him. Trees whizzed by in flashes of burnt oranges, reds and browns. Upwards he flew, hitting several branches on his way up through the seemingly endless canopies, his speed still increasing. The dark of the forest thickened as he climbed higher and higher. The warm colours he had seen not a few moments past had now turned to shades of blue and grey. He yelped as the battalions of branches and thorny thicket began their attack. And just as all the world's light had disappeared and he could no longer see his own hands outstretched in front of him he broke through the last canopy. Small branches, twigs and loose foliage floated up with him into the cool midnight breeze.

His eyes burned as the sudden moonlight struck his pupils. His body twisted and turned, like a worm on a hook, dangling high above the forest roof. Finally he stopped, suspended upside down in the black sky like a lonely wisp of cloud. The blood rushed to his head.

He thrashed at the space between him and the sea of leaves below but he was unable to move. His body became weak and just before he was about to pass out once more, the invisible force then released him.

He hit the forest hard, his head taking several blows before he was spun by the sheer force of the fall, from here every branch was like taking a blow from a bull ogre. His body was bent left, then right as he smashed his way through branch after branch.

About halfway through his descent he hit a large stump protruding like a limb from one of the old cherryberry trees. With his last vain effort he scrambled and hung on, the bark rough on his soft skin. His fall had stopped and for a moment he was able to draw breath and fully appreciate the pain that his body had just endured.

Weeping and sobbing with fright he hung on to his stump, suspended hundreds of feet from the forest floor. Nothing but a vast expanse of darkness, and inevitably more pain, lay between him and safety.

With the cruellest of intention, the invisible force returned. It grabbed Griffin by the ankle and heaved, trying to pull him from his perch.

"Why are you doing this to me?" Griffin screamed with anger, spitting a few broken teeth out at the same time.

"Recite the song and you will see." came the voice again.

"What song? Who are you? Let go! LET GO OF ME!" Griffin implored, shaking his leg furiously, trying desperately to free himself from his see-through kidnapper. Hanging on to his stump with both hands the force grew stronger. It was like dangling with a piano tied to one leg. "Please don't! I have children. You'll kill me. I HAVE NO MAGIC." Griffin pleaded but his captor's lust for his demise seemed insatiable. With an ear popping cackle the invisible force gave one last tug and Griffin's hands left the stump. Large fistfuls of sharp mossy bark cascaded down after him into the abyss.

All he could see was blackness and as his speed increased and the inevitable sudden stop drew nearer a voice whispered into his ear, as if floating freely next to him: "Die Griffin Black!"

The ground hit him like a clap of solid thunder and a column of pain skewered his body. The shin bone of his left leg snapped and peeped through the layers of muscle and skin surrounding it. Onwards the searing pain travelled as his pelvis clove itself in two...'

Griffin stopped. Something that had never before happened mid-flow during an orb recital.

The rows of people and creatures gazed on in utter horror, half of them already feeling both guilty and uncontrollably full of pity for Griffin.

A milky tear streamed down from one of his pure white eyes, and he went on.

'No one person should have to endure so much pain. He lay there among the mushrooms, the dimly lit roomushes (which are essentially giant upside down mushrooms that glow different colours at night - most handy in a dark forest come nightfall), flowers and rankwart thicket, screaming and writhing in agony. His last thoughts before his eyes closed were of his children and his beloved.

*

He awoke to a duller pain in his body and an odd muffled conversation. It was still dark. One voice he recognised as his captor's, the other was dark, deep and sinister.

"This was my reward! My very own little bit of treasure! What is the point of favours if rewards do not follow in equal measure?" screeched the Witch in a ditty-like fashion.

"Use him, turn him, make him hurt forever!" replied the new voice.

"He is a no good Wizard from a no good history of Wizards and I want him dead as you promised." the Witch challenged.

"Your lack of obedience I find disturbing," came the deep voice again. "Do not forget it was I who allowed you back here and granted you power. If you would prefer the alternative…"

"Err, no, no sir, Lord of mine…it's just this has been a long time coming! A bittersweet revenge."

"Revenge can wait, trust my judgement. This feeble excuse of the magical world will be our greatest accomplishment. Now turn him, make him feel the pain, use him."

Griffin closed his eyes and with the batting of an eyelid opened them again to a new dawn and a new sight. He awoke in a small clearing. A little of the morning light was given clemency to glimmer its way through the endless leaves, casting polka-dot shadows on the mossy carpet before him.

He sat upright, only then realising he was caged; a small wooden prison made of bulrushes, wicker and willow now encased him like some foul beast. He struggled but it was magically sealed with a strange green light that wound its way around the tightly woven structure. It was only moments later that he noticed his pain had dulled further and he could feel his legs again.

"Oh, you're awake then," came a voice from behind him that was riddled with disappointment. "Of all the cursed things to happen, you miraculously survived, how did you not die, falling from a height that would have killed a giant!"

"What are you going to do to me?" Griffin asked hesitantly.

"I have a more prudent question," spat the Witch. "What are *you* going to do for me?"

"What do you want Witch?"

"Recite the song and you will see."

"What song?" Griffin wailed with frustration. "Which song do you speak of?"

Griffin sat for a moment, thinking hard.

"Song, song, which song?" he said to himself, a puzzled expression cast over his face. "Of course, that's it – witch song! - the Covenantium Chime – the Witch Hunter's song!

Is that the song you speak of?"

Griffin was answered with silence.

"Oh how does that confounded song go, I haven't sung it for years – erm, now then:

> *A Witch you are, a Witch you were,*
> *Show yourself, dark and pure,*
> *With foot of hare and sting of bee,*
> *Bring this Witch before me.*

> *A Witch you are, a Witch I'll see,*
> *With tortured soul and hate aplenty,*
> *With a sprig of Monk's and some Ivy,*
> *Bring this Witch before me.*

> *A Witch you are, a Witch you've been,*
> *Stirring all those who are unclean,*
> *With a broom of wood and eyes of green,*
> *Bring this Witch before me.*

> *A Witch you are, and now we'll see,*
> *The black of your soul so expect no mercy,*
> *So with courage on side and power with me,*
> *Bring this Witch now, before me.*

A great wind howled through the trees and the whole forest shook from its roots up. And then with implausible strength the very air in front of Griffin began to bend and contort, shaking furiously like a child's doll being jerked from side to side.

An almighty implosion of dark mist materialised and began to spiral into a violent vortex, black lightning bolts forked out in all directions, scorching several trees on the edge of the clearing.

A deathly wail came, as if someone was screaming their last, which was finally surpassed by a giant explosion of green sparks that sent Griffin's cage rolling some several feet into the distance with him still inside being tossed around like a fresh summer salad.

As the silence ensued Griffin turned his head to where the explosion had occurred, but before his gaze reached the distance his eyes focused on a pair of well-worn cloth boots standing right next to his cage.

He scanned upwards, seeing a youthful hand reach for her pocket and pull out a black feather with a ruby crystal tip. She aimed it directly at him and before he could look up to see her face she screamed, *"Lipso Noctumbra!"*

A green flare emitted from the tip and beamed straight to his mouth – his lips burned and cracked.

"AAAAARRRGH!" Griffin screamed, his mouth wide open with agony. The Witch watched with grim satisfaction as he writhed around on the floor. Within moments his once pale pink lips had turned to treacle-black, shiny and evil.'

Griffin had stopped narrating though his eyes remained purer than fresh snow. The image from the orb froze and began to flicker wildly as both the audience and Councillor Fidrib gazed on with uncertainty. Suddenly a new image fluttered into life; it was of Griffin but he appeared much younger.

He was at school, sat alone in an old stone stairwell, wearing a smart cloak, the likes of which most Wizards would wear to a ball or dance.

He looked sad, his face still and weary. He quickly looked up and forced a smile before a pretty girl wearing an elegant ball gown sprang into view at which point he began narrating again.

"What's wrong Griffin? Feeling woozy after all your dancing?" the pretty young Witch asked as she sat on the step next to him.

"No, it's not the dancing, it's *her*. She's meddling with my feelings again. I don't understand it. She seems to crave the attention I give her, but then won't commit to a relationship."

"Don't worry Griffin," the girl said, "there are always others you could consider."

"Oh yeah, like who?"

"Other girls that might have feelings for you."

"I doubt anyone will ever want me – an orphan with no prospects. Abandoned as a baby. Left on a doorstep by my kind mother with nothing but a few quickly scribbled words on a piece of parchment, a dirty doll and her tatty old wand."

"Well at least she left you something, besides there's nothing wrong with orphans – we do alright don't we? Oh that reminds me, we have a chess tournament next week so we had better practice together again soon." She said, nudging him fondly.

"Yeah I suppose," said Griffin.

"Oh Griffin you'll be fine and…"

"Fine! FINE!" he snapped, "I will not be fine, besides, what do you know of it? NOTHING! I don't need you. You're not my friend. I don't even like you – in fact I wish you were dead!" Griffin pulled his wand from his robe and thrust it forward at the school girl.

"Griffin what are you doing? GRIFFIN!"

He stared blankly ahead with piercing eyes, as if he was staring straight through her. A tear welled in each of his dark eyes before he shrieked, *"FACTUMORTIS!"*

Griffin's eyes returned to normal, he was back in the Council Chamber and Fonzo Fidrib held the truth orb firmly in his hand.

'How you managed to change the truth to one of your memories is a mystery to me and has never happened before,' Councillor Fidrib snarled angrily.

'What did I say Fonzo?' asked Griffin.

'Let's just say there are some things that are best left unsaid and not proclaimed for a large audience to mull over – we wouldn't want people getting any wrong ideas now would we?'

Griffin turned to the audience who were sat in utter silence, shocked and unsure.

'Tell me, please, what did the orb show?'

Councillor Fidrib, who was again playing with his beard, stared back at Griffin. He shook his head, sighed loudly and said, 'I think it best we have a little chat, you and I.'

*

By the order of Councillor Fidrib, Griffin was led by several larger-than-normal guards from the thirteen-walled Council Chamber to a smaller chamber where three familiar faces waited anxiously.

'Father!' his young daughter Pereé squealed with uncontrollable emotion as she ran forward throwing herself at him.

'Hello pumpkin,' Griffin sobbed as tears welled in each of his exhausted eyes, 'the last time I saw you, you couldn't even walk.'

'Mother must've taught me then, heeee-la-di-dah' she finished as she went joyously skipping off round the small chamber with her arms flailing.

Griffin smiled, turning from her to his son Garad.

'So you're here then.' Garad said coldly.

'Yes son I'm here, Griffin said stepping forward to hug his eldest. 'I missed you my boy.'

'We missed you too – and even though everyone said you were dead, we never stopped believing.'

'I'm glad you didn't Garad,' Griffin said sadly, 'and I'm sorry I've missed so much, but thank you for being strong for your mother and Pereé.'

Griffin embraced his son again, squeezing tighter this time, before turning to Lizzi.

Her normally warm, care-free expression was gone, she looked tired, even withered, like a flower with too little water. And tiredness soon turned to a look of disappointment and anger. Lizzi paced suddenly to Griffin and slapped him firmly around the face.

'YOU LEFT US! YOU LEFT ME!' She wailed, breaking down into a fit of tears that had been saved and hidden from the children for two years.

'I didn't leave you,' Griffin retaliated, his cheek throbbing, 'I was taken! Don't believe me? Watch the truth orb viewing.'

Before Lizzi could respond the chamber door swung open and Councillor Fidrib entered quickly followed by Master Agar, Lizzi's father.

'Right then,' began Master Agar, 'we haven't much time. Outside this chamber, right now, is a town full of curious, scared and some might say angry people wanting answers. Unfortunately, following the truth orb recital we do not have those answers but we need to reassure them whilst keeping you all safe.'

'Until we prove he is the murderous Warlock after all.' Councillor Fidrib added.

'Until we have investigated what happened during the orb recital, thank you for that Fonzo,' Master Agar said shunning the unhelpful comments of his ginger colleague.

'Why are they angry?' Lizzi asked her father with concern.

'Well, memory loss or not Lizzi, Griffin is responsible for the deaths of several people and they just want answers, wouldn't you? So, Councillor Fidrib here and I have just discussed a suitable plan which needs to happen immediately. You shall be escorted through the town to the gates after which we shall explain more.'

'But Father…' Lizzi began.

'Sorry Lizzi, we have no time, we must be going now. Hold tightly to one another, be brave and you will all be fine.'

'Councillor Fidrib, you wanted a chat with me?' Griffin said openly to the ginger wizard.

'Chats can wait,' Master Agar interjected, 'we need to get you all to safety and disband this rabble outside, come, we'll go back through Council Chamber Two. Do you know I think I saw a dragon climbing the library tower earlier – the town's gone mad!'

— CHAPTER THREE —

# Creepies, Crawlies and Old Wizard Stories

The sun was setting. Griffin, along with his family, were led by the Imperial Brickabrack Guards from the great Chamber down its beautiful if not pointless stairway. One hundred and sixty-nine steps darted from left to right; some small steps in groups, some big steps alone, some perfectly straight, some tapered at the edges. One section had a raised platform with plants and trees running through the middle, so the steps were split in two. Once they were at the bottom of the stairway, they were prodded through the North Western archway past the old well; the monkshood with its lovely purple bell-shaped flowers meandered up the stone pillars that supported the domed roof.

Once in the centre of the marketplace swarms of the townspeople started to gather. They booed and hissed all manner of unnerving comments. Lizzi held tightly to Pereé who wept loudly for the nasty people to go away.

'Go back to the forest Blackmouth!' one old hag spluttered, her mouth in no greater condition than Griffins.

'Yeah and take your stinking, cursed family with you!' joined in another.

The family continued, all of them too afraid to lift their heads. Lizzi, once hailed as *Citizen of the Year* for her immaculately trimmed gobblestop verges (a sturdy bush peppered with multicoloured berries) and popular cauldron parties, began to cry. A gaggle of finely dressed ladies who would queue to attend her parties, and who she thought were her closest friends, turned their backs on her when she passed by and then began to chit-chat and honk as they waddled off.

Each lonely tear that streamed down her face seemed to take an age before it splashed on the cold cobbled pavement. Almost in slow motion and quite like something from a dream, time began to slow. The insults being screamed seemed to tone down to a muffled hum. The familiar faces of the townspeople seemed to blur until they were altogether faceless strangers and it was at this moment, as she was about to faint, that Griffin's face appeared before hers.

He caught her. The pain of the world simply drifted away and for a moment they were alone. Her auburn, unkempt hair danced freely in the evening breeze. Her cornflower-blue eyes stared lovingly into his that were wide and watery. His bottom lip quivered with sadness. He could feel her pain and worry. She softly offered a hand up to his pale cheek, smiled behind the tears and whispered.

'It'll be alright.' She paused, gazing deeper into his fiery brown eyes. She tilted her head ever so slightly, ever so gently and concluded, 'We'll be alright.'

The noise returned.

'We don't want your kind here, nothing but trouble!' said a portly man dressed in ridiculously colourful clothes.

'He put a curse on me the other day. My nose bled all day long, ooh I felt so strange,' competed an old lady with a grimy blue lace bonnet so big all you could see of her face was her beak-like nose protruding from under it.

'Huh, that's nothing!' interrupted another. 'The curse he put on me was much worserer. I was blowing bubbles from my ears for hours and when it finally stopped I hiccupped all night at double speed.'

Forward crept Madam Croaker, the old hag that had once already thrust a verbal knife into Griffin's back. The crowd parted, knowing only too well that what she had to say would be something exceptionally cruel. Her reputation preceded her (as did the vile odour that clung to her). Ugly as she was, she had a wicked tongue and would literally spend a whole day spitting insults at passersby as she perched like a featherless vulture on her favourite barrel outside the Tipsy Toad Inn.

She limped forward, lifting her withered old hand, the ratty nail of her index finger pointed directly at Griffin.

'YOU!' she barked. The crowd were left open-mouthed and silent with anticipation. 'You put a curse on me oafbreaker!'

The crowd gasped almost in unison and started rabbiting among themselves about what it could be.

'I bet he gave her some horrible disease,' guessed one finely dressed gentleman with a monocle as he stepped aside, giving her a wider berth.

'I bet he turned her mead to suede,' added another.

'I reckon he's twisted 'er bones all funny,' suggested a young and quite scruffy looking sewer-rat of a boy.

'Shhh!' she hissed to the gossipers. 'It's my curse and I'll be the one to tell ye all about it. We'll 'ave no 'alf-witted guessing games 'ere.' She awkwardly twisted her hunched body back towards Griffin, her face wild and unforgiving. 'Do ye all want to know what he did to me, hmm…well do ya?'

'Ooh yes, yes Croaker I do!' insisted a young boy.

'Well I'll tell ye. There I was t'other day sat aloft me barrel looking beautiful as ever…' at this point half the crowd began to chuckle and laugh uncontrollably. Croaker paused and spied those who dare interrupt her speech until they were silent once more.

'Looking beautiful as ever, when he comes along…' Her long boney finger once again gesturing at Griffin. 'And turns me into a hag!'

The whole crowd burst into a fit of laughter, Griffin included.

'She's drunk!' yelped Mrs Macrocker, proprietor of the famous Pie Potions Shop on Cowslip Lane. The well-rounded lady sported a dusty pink apron and wielded an enormous rolling pin that had moving multicoloured swirls snaking all over its surface.

'The old crone's been sat on her barrel too long,' joked one of the guards.

'Right I've heard enough, c'mon let's get this over with,' ushered the captain of the guards. 'Make way!'

The hag, Croaker, was still doubled over with laughter, cackling through a broken smile. An odd whistling noise crept out every now and then where she had some teeth missing.

It was only as Griffin and his family edged away from the bystanders and turned onto Eastgate with the guards that Croaker stopped laughing and, amid the shrill of howls, turned to Griffin and gave him a heartfelt, if warty, wink and a smile.

Griffin, gazing back in amazement, realised what the old hag had just done. She had interrupted the onslaught of insults and harsh words from the townspeople. She had stopped them in their tracks with her wretched presence and then made an outrageous claim that she knew only too well everyone would find funny. This had the effect of clearing the hazy atmosphere and allowing the banished family to retreat with what was left of their dignity intact.

He simply smiled, mouthed *'thank you'* in her direction and continued to amble along with his family by his side and some fifty-two guards about his person.

They passed Proofgrease's Bacon Grinders, Halfsheckle's Bakers and Mrs Stopclock's Candlestick emporium. Griffin noticed that Mr Proofgrease had an abundance of red meat lining the shelves and hanging in the windows: obscene cuts of Curdlecow beef, roughly-cut pigdog chops and stacks of venison.

Next they turned left onto Rotten Row. First on the left was old Mr Drinkin's Pipe Shop where Griffin had bought his favourite Cherryberry hardwood pipe and smoking box.

Mr Drinkin was remarkably fond of Griffin, who remembered how the old pipe master had once added a pouch of indisputably strong *Thinkers* tobacco to his wicker purchasing basket for no extra charge.

The thoughts and ideas Griffin got from that pouch of tobacco could have been catalogued into twelve, two hundred page volumes and possibly made a small fortune along the way. Unfortunately, the thoughts came that quick and fast that Griffin had no time to write any of them down and, with his memory not being one of his strong points, came away with only two ideas. One being a device for talking to people over long distances (without shouting) which consisted of a long piece of string and a couple of lead tankards. The other being a self-propelled cart that ran on steam. Unfortunately for Griffin these two ideas he deemed to have been the worst of the lot so he kept them to himself to avoid any embarrassment.

Next was Kudoo's Rat-Catchers shop. The smell of the small furry corpses hanging outside was enough to make anyone feel queasy. But the sight of hundreds of cats was even more amazing, all of them scurrying around. Some, with rats in their mouths, were going into the shop, others coming out licking their lips. One in particular caught Griffin's attention that reminded him of Fonzo Fidrib instantly. It was a large moggy with bright orange fur, a patch over its left eye and a tattoo on its right hind leg.

Interestingly enough a new shop was due to open right across the street. The sign leering over the door read: *Bobbin's Cat-Catchers.* Griffin continued onwards, agreeing in his mind that he was going to miss parts of the town including the entrepreneurial magnetism the town had – cat-catchers shop indeed he smiled.

The Black family, along with their heavily-armoured escorts, finally turned onto Bridge Street and ambled past Scrotts Jewellers and Cumber's Cloth Merchants before they reached the drawbridge. The large lanterns swaying gently on either side of the drawbridge tower added a little light to the lonely track that gently sloped down and out of the town's limits. About halfway down Griffin noticed a small huddle of people all dressed in glorious cloaks and pointy hats. As he drew nearer he realised it was the Council Elders.

Noticing Griffin and his family approaching – or prodded more like – down the winding hill towards them the Council Elders quickly stopped their ranting and all lined up. Griffin, noticing this, wondered if this lining up was to make them appear more professional or whether it was meant to make them look more imposing and authoritative.

Either way their words would echo in Griffin's ears until his dying day. His ancestors had helped dig the great well at the very heart of the town. There had always been a member of the Black family living in Brickabrack. *"It's part of your heritage Griffin,"* Master Agar would frequently remind him, *"and the town was very nearly renamed Brickablack because of that heritage, so I would urge you not to forget it."* Being marched through an angry mob of former friends and out of the town's limits undid years of family tradition and the thought made Griffin's heart sink – that it had been during his time, his watch, that he had allowed this to happen.

Council Elder Agar, Lizzi's father stepped forward.

'Evening Griffin, Lizzi, children. We all know why we are here and it is with deep regret my name was pulled for this duty. Never is it a happy occasion when one must banish family and loved ones from their home. A sorrowful heart beats in my dusty old chest tonight. What with Lizzi being my youngest and this being her home,' said Master Agar, turning to his colourful colleagues and giving each of them a stern, disconcerting look before he continued. 'Granted there is speculation over this case and we will be leading a full investigation into these bizarre goings on. There are so many questions. Questions that are in desperate need of answering. But for now you are all…' He paused and drew in an unwanted breath knowing that when it exited his body along with the words he had to say it would cause grief and hurt. 'You are all henceforth banished from the Town of Brickabrack, the Port of Mûr; including the Golden Wharf and of course the City of Tilös for none of these places want you near their borders.'

'Banished on pain of death!!' cried the ever ginger Fonzo Fidrib.

'Yes I'm getting around to that bit Fonzo and may I remind you that this is *my* duty, not yours so step back, keep your slimy tongue behind those teeth of yours and look ill or whatever it is you do. Lizzi, Griffin, I beg you to stay away from these places for you are banished, as stated by my withered colleague here, on pain of death and I fear not even magic will save you from what awaits you should you try and enter their gates. In fact magic will not be able to help you at all,' the old Wizard paused turning on his heel to face Griffin, 'I'm afraid my lad, a condition of your being able to reside in safety whilst we continue with our investigations, is that you surrender your magic and allow us to perform the necessary incantations required to prohibit you from using even the simplest of spells.'

'That was never a condition of my release!' Griffin spat.

'It is now.' Councillor Fidrib said gleefully.

'But how will we stay safe in the forest if Griffin has no magic?' Lizzi said worriedly.

'Provisions shall be put in place, I shall make sure of it,' Master Agar said, 'Lizzi, do you understand what I am saying to you?'

She heard him but was still in a state of shock.

'Lizzi!' he snapped like any concerned parent would.

'Yes Father I understand,' she replied, her mind still stuck on *'pain of death'* and *'surrender your magic.'*

'Good girl,' he finished.

'But Father what are we to do? Where are we to go?' Lizzi now quizzed like any concerned mother would.

'Get back to basics,' smiled the old man. His sparkling silver gown glimmering fiercely in the moonlight. 'Why back in the day when the first Agar settlers moved here they lived in the forests and open plains and marshlands.'

'But we have no shelter! We need a roof!' panicked Lizzi.

'Well I have managed to make some arrangements there and well…the best I could do…and believe me it took a lot of convincing…well not loads of convincing, but a fair deal and bearing in mind the situation…'

'Oh Father do get on with it!' Lizzi snapped. Her curiosity and frustration clearly mounting with every second and extra crease on her forehead.

'Well the Council have kindly granted permission for you to all reside within the old temple on the outskirts of town, outside the walls.

'The temple?' Lizzi pondered openly.

'Not *the* temple? The temple that is crumbling down? The one with no roof, half its walls and all covered in black scorch marks from the fire? That temple?'

'Erm, yes dear that temple and may I suggest you take it. The Council were also kind enough to allow you to – well – patch it up a little if you desire.'

'Patch it up! Patch it up! I'm sorry Father but I would need one very large patch to sort that place out. Ooh I know, maybe we could set Griffin loose on it. Maybe he could destroy it…oh no, hang on, he won't have any magic for that, she jibed sarcastically,

'I've got it – me and the children can build a nice quaint cottage out of the rubble with our bare hands.'

'That's the spirit dear!' enthused Master Agar, not fully appreciating his daughter's sarcasm.

'Father you baffoon! That temple is no place for my children and furthermore…'

'We'll take it,' interrupted Griffin.

'*Take it?* I will not raise our children in a run down, crumbling wreck of a temple.'

'Well it's there or the forest Lizzi. And if half the things said about the forest are true, trust me, we're better off taking the temple.'

Lizzi gave Griffin the *'I'm not very happy with you right now you silly Wizard'* thousand yard stare before continuing.

'The forest might not be so bad. Closer to food, flowers and…'

'And ogres, and trolls, foul beasts, pigdogs, ghouls, marsh rabbits, those sorts of things. Children, would you prefer a charming old temple with a lockable door to sleep in or would you rather have the forest floor with all the monsters?' asked Griffin.

'Temple please Father.' his daughter Pereé replied immediately. Pereé was a pretty four year old girl who looked like her mother. She had captivating eyes, blue eyes that shone bright with intelligence – like two windows that offered a glimpse of her potential brilliance, for those that cared enough to see it. She stood, still wearing her night gown, feet turned in, her mousy-brown hair in as much of a mess as her mothers and still clutching her favourite bogey doll that had one of its six legs missing and a large stitch where one of the button-eyes had been accidentally misplaced by Garad. Her lack of hesitation was solely due to the vivid imagery cast by her father's stories of battles with pigdogs that once again made her skin go all goose-pimply.

'Um, Griffin…' said Master Agar with an air of uneasiness in his tone.

'One moment there Luther. Right Garad – your turn. Where do you fancy? Bed with a troll or bed with a pillow?'

'How about my bed Father, how about the bed I like and love in our house? Our house in our town where I grew up and where all my friends are. How about that Father? Hmm?'

'Sounded like temple to me.' Griffin said, turning to Lizzi while almost ignoring his son's *stereotypical teenager* facetious attitude.

'Griffin!' pleaded Master Agar once more.

'Won't be long now Luther. So Lizzi, what about you? We can make this work. We can rebuild, we can gather firewood and food from the forest and try and get back to normal.'

'Okay! Okay! We'll take the run down temple. I suppose it does have a lockable door so we can at least try and sleep safe and sound at night.'

'BUT THAT'S JUST IT!' growled Master Agar, his eyebrows protruding a tad more than usual which normally meant he was either angry and frustrated or trying to stare at the end of his nose. 'The temple doesn't have a door. It was destroyed during the great battle; Lizzi you'd be too young but Griffin may remember the tales of Spineback and Dithers.'

Griffin stood looking puzzled at the old man. The names sounded familiar and yet he had no clear memory of them.

*'Spineback?'* the old man offered. 'The greatest dragon of all time?' he added trying to allow Griffin time to solve the riddle himself. *'No?* A week long battle with Dithers the famous dwarf explorer and his merry band of warriors. And I say *merry* because most of the time they were more tankered up than old Croaker normally is. Come now, I shall escort you to your new home and show you all about it along the way.' The old man smiled. He gracefully turned to the still, colourful line of Councillors: 'I take it we are all done here. Upon my return we shall perform the necessary incantations, I will sign the papers, and we shall discuss all other relevant and associated matters.'

Master Agar took his two grandchildren by the hand and led them down the path leaving the twinkling lights of the town behind them. The old man, foreseeing this to be an uneasy journey for his daughter, immediately produced a glass orb from one of his glittering silver pockets.

'Ah, here, this should distract us from the dark,' he smiled, hoping it would make the journey less arduous.

'What is it Gwangad?' Pereé squeaked in an excited fashion

while tugging on his shimmering cloak.

'Well Pereé, in the Great Library they call them *Visual Historic Records*. They show you detailed accounts of the past – some are very old. Why, I remember seeing one when I was a boy – thick with dust it was – and can you believe, it was about Merlin, before he disappeared of course. So old was it that Merlin's beard wasn't silver at all, it was brown, and, and not a wrinkle in sight. Yes Pereé, he was young.'

'Merlin had a brown beard?' cried Garad, himself now full of intrigue and disbelief.

'Oh yes, brown indeed with the odd streak of gold here and there, yes very queer, ha, haha, now that I think about it, maybe his beard will be bronze when he returns. Well don't you see now, Gold, Silver and Bronze. Only Merlin could pull that little chestnut out of the bag. Haha.'

'So what will we see with this one Gwangad?' asked Pereé who hadn't understood his attempt at a joke.

'Ah, well this one is very special, oh yes, very special indeed. This one is a *linker* orb. I can see any of the historical events that are held within the Great Library archives, and some, I might say, that are not. I call it my *Visual Historic Shower* or *V.H.S.* for short.'

The trees seemed to be closing in on the small huddle and the moonlight fading.

*'Oculus Luxaurea,'* whispered Master Agar as he tapped his crooked wooden staff on the ground.

A beautifully warm orange light tiptoed out in all directions, almost like golden glittering smoke from a red gem held firmly in place at the top of his staff. It pulsed out like music, catching the trees and their branches as it went, and to the family stood behind him, it appeared as though the forest was being turned to solid gold.

Shadows stirred, and spiny gangly legs along with masses of teeth scurried back to the darkness.

'Yes, they'll be no supper for you tonight!' chuckled Master Agar as he turned to face the rest of the group.

'Ah…' He stopped, realising that neither Lizzi or the children had ever seen anything like that before. 'They're pretty harmless provided there's a good source of light nearby,' he warmly added.

'Well would you mind turning that *Ocleus* thingy of yours up a notch or two please,' insisted Lizzi. The thought of the temple was bad enough, but the thought of not even making it there alive seemed much worse. 'What were those things anyway?' she asked her father.

'Well there's the creepies, they're the skinny ones with all the spikes and the long gangly legs. They're exceptionally fond of hiding behind trees and pouncing when the – oh how should I put it – *opportunity*, arises. Hence their name.' he concluded.

'By *opportunity*, I take it you mean supper.' Lizzi quizzed.

'Erm, yes dear,' said the old man quietly and hurriedly hoping the children wouldn't hear, 'and, and then there's the crawlies, they don't hide. They're the ones that look like big fat caterpillars covered in large black spikes with masses of teeth; one hundred and seventy-six on average I believe. They crawl along quite lethargically, their black beady eyes rest upon tall slimy stalks – like those of a snail – so they can see you coming a way off. The difference with this one is that its name doesn't suite its character. Yes, at first they seem quite docile, squidging their way through the foliage but once they see food they stand up and charge with their gaping, slobbering mouths wide open.'

The old man paused and turned to his clearly frightened daughter.

'They don't ever stop charging until they have a mouthful of something. In fact, the poor scientist – *Movewell,* I think his name was – who discovered them had barely enough time to draw one and name it a *Crawlie* before he realised he should have named it a *Charging Teethie.* All they found was his catalogue of findings along with his broken spectacles. It's a shame he didn't… move – well…on that day,' chuckled the old Wizard unveiling his normally dormant, uncaring nature.

'So, now we all know about creepies and crawlies shall we continue?'

The whole family stood, staring blankly at Master Agar, not wanting to move. That is of course apart from Griffin who had heard the same story at school when he was being taught by the old

Wizard. And also who had had several run-ins with both creepies and crawlies himself.

'Just get us to that temple.' Lizzi insisted, pulling both Pereé and Garad closely to her. Pereé, who feared spiders above all other creatures, buried her face as deep as she could into her mother's robes whilst letting out little muffled whimpers of worry.

'Don't worry pumpkin,' Griffin said stroking Pereé's hair, 'your Grandfather has fended off creatures twenty times worse than a few creepies and crawlies.'

'Can everyone just stop saying their names,' Lizzi said feeling highly uncomfortable.

'Well there was that incident with the flying Ogre Demon of Nazaroth,' Master Agar added.

'Oh yeah. What happened to him?' Griffin asked.

'Well I was on my favourite broom fighting him, ooh he was a devil…'

'Don't you mean demon?' Garad jumped in.

'Well yes a demon – thank you Garad,' said Master Agar. 'It was a bit tit for tat for a while, you know. He'd throw spears wreathed in flame at me, I'd clobber him with lightning bolts and trees and boulders and well, anything I could lay my magic on really.'

'Then what Gwangad? Then what?' asked Pereé frantically, having now removed her face from Lizzi's robes.

'Well…then he got me very angry. Yes very angry indeed.'

'What did he do? Tell us!' Garad insisted like a spoilt brat.

'He summoned a cloud demon. Some friend of his from the elder days. Rumour has it they used to go drinking together, I don't know, but this cloud demon turned up and between them, one using his flame and the other using his cumulonimbus, rained fire down upon me! My poor polished wooden broomstick, that had belonged to my father I might add, ended up all scorched and covered in ash. And, and the tail of it, well, you should've seen it. Ruined, it was, never the same again.' The old man stopped, gazing deeply into his memory. Like a child's favourite toy that broom was like a brother to him. They had spent so many years together.

'So how did you defeat them both?' Lizzi joined in – her face full of intrigue and enthusiasm. She realised she had never really asked her father about what he had got up to in his youth.

In fact it was at this moment that Lizzi realised she didn't really know her father that well at all. What his favourite colour was. What his favourite spell was. It all seemed too vague. All she knew was that he had just always been there. Protecting her, much like he was now.

The old man smiled proudly at his youngest and continued.

'Well, I must admit Merlin did help with the cloud demon. I was fresh out of ideas but thankfully he had a Mini-Maxi pipette with him and he quite simply sucked the cloud demon up. He now keeps it in a Mini-Maxi vial on his mantle at his cottage.'

'How can a pipette suck up a whole cloud?' asked a very puzzled Garad.

'Ah, still so young and unaware,' the old man started.

'What's a pipette?' asked an even more puzzled Pereé.

'Well to answer both of your questions, a pipette is a tiny glass tube with a rubber teat at one end and a Mini-Maxi pipette allows the bearer to collect a huge amount of a substance in one, tiny, glass tube. Just like a Mini-Maxi vial can hold vast quantities of a substance.' Master Agar concluded.

'Wow!' Garad replied while looking rather dim and awestruck at his grandfather.

'There was once a Necromancer, Garad, and the inventor of the Mini-Maxi apparatus range that wanted to prove their powers to potential investors. He claimed that he could suck up the entire sea and store it in one of his remarkable, if tiny, vials. He promised he'd put it all back afterwards but naturally, he wasn't given the opportunity. Yes, he's an accountant now, has to catch the horse and cart to work. Never gave up on the old Mini-Maxi concept though. Now he holds masses of people's financial scrolls in a very small building. Ah a har har!'

'So what about this, erm, fiery demon thing,' Lizzi began, making the old man realise he had meandered off course with the story somewhat.

'Oh yes, I'd almost forgotten about that. Well, once the cloud demon had dispersed, Merlin rather casually went back to his supper and I, well naturally I continued. The beast flew over the town, burning and ravaging as he went. Drinkin's pipe shop ironically went up in smoke and it may actually have been the *Thinkers* tobacco that helped but something hit me.

'Another one of his massive flame spears!' Garad added eagerly.

'No not a spear or an object – an idea! This fabtabulous idea just hit me out of nowhere. I decided to lead the beast over towards the old forest, allowing me time to formulate a more soundproof plan.'

'So how did you defeat it?' Lizzi insisted, now deciding that this story had dragged on for long enough.

'Well I just said it my dear…*soundproof.* If there's one thing an ogre demon despises it's silence. Which I suppose could explain as to why they make so much noise, you know, with the constant roaring and all. I simply fired a few lightning bolts at him, as a distraction of course, then flew up behind him and stuffed my hat in one of his ears and my shoe in the other.'

'THAT'S IT!' exploded Garad shortly followed by Lizzi. 'No magical, amazing dooh-dah. Just a hat and a shoe!' Garad cried.

'That's it me boy,' replied Master Agar. 'Oh but it didn't end there. The beast twisted and squirmed in the air, which allowed me time enough to bind his thrashing wings using an old snare charm of mine. He plummeted down and hit the forest floor with such a thud. From there we had a little bit of a gossip and a chat but, unfortunately for him, his unwillingness to co-operate left me with no choice…'

'You killed it!' said Garad gleefully.

'Oh frogspawn no!' Master Agar tutted. 'We never kill unless there is no other alternative.'

'So what was the alternative?' Lizzi speedily asked.

'I turned him into a golden statue,' the old man whispered.

'And where is he now?' Lizzi added quicker still.

'Well, I suspect he's still in the forest. A little overgrown with ivy but still a seventeen foot solid gold statue.'

'What do you mean you suspect? Do you mean to tell me that this ogre demon of yours is still somewhere in this very forest?'

Lizzi froze, listening intently for his response.

'Well I didn't want him to be a statue forever. That wouldn't have been fair.'

'Fair!' Lizzi cried with a repulsed look on her slender face. 'What about the townspeople? What about their safety Father?'

'I'm sure when he returns he'll be better behaved, you know, learned his lesson and all that,' the old man said calmly and softly, all the while seeming quite naïve to the rest of them, save Griffin who had become quite used to keeping quiet.

'What, so ogre demons are normally quite pleasant creatures are they?' Lizzi uttered sarcastically.

'Well they can be very nice but I happened to upset this one, that's all,' the old man retaliated.

'Oh yeah! And how did you upset him Father hey? How do you upset a fire-breathing, flame-throwing demon?'

'I beat him at a game of poker!' The old man barked. His eyebrows once again, pushing out into the cold autumnal breeze.

Lizzi sat dumbstruck by what the old man had just said. Was he going senile?

*'What?'* the old man began in his defence. 'Poker. He thought he had it in the bag. I bluffed. He lost. That's it. Poker.'

*'Poker?'* I think I need to go to bed now. This is just too bizarre and ridiculous for this hour,' Lizzi finished.

'Why, don't you see though m'dear – in deafening the beast I was able to turn him to gold. So I suppose one could say silence is golden. You know I like the sound of that!' the old man revelled. 'I tell you what Lizzi, there's a clearing up ahead – once we reach it I'll show the children and Griffin the linker orb and you can get some rest. *Oculus Luxaurea Maximo!*' Agar whispered, banging his staff twice harder on the pale, leaf ridden ground. Within the blink of an eye the whole forest appeared illuminated. It was a breathtaking marvel. The forest's trees and leaves and even the very animals within it skipped around as if they were made of pure light. And almost as if it were day the birds began to sing.

# CHAPTER FOUR

# Spineback and Dithers

The family arrived at the clearing and true to his word, Master Agar produced the linker orb once more. They giggled and laughed in the magically-lit void, joking at the plethora of moving images that the orb emitted. Some were from the old man's past, some of when Griffin was a boy and finally they linked to the tale of Spineback and Dithers.

'*Agarictum Orbis, Spineo-Ditherum, Sixeus,* no no, *Sevenus* - well you can't get it right all the time,' the old Wizard proclaimed. He then nestled the orb tightly between two large roots that snaked their way sideways and upwards and round and down.

The orb shone brightly and within seconds revealed a picturesque building, tall and proud, surrounded by trees and lush greenery.

'Is that the temple?' exclaimed Garad with excitement. 'It's massive! Makes our house look a little…well…shabby really doesn't it?'

'Yes m'boy, that's it. Well, as it was,' replied his Grandfather, with a similar tone of excitement.

As the orb continued to explode its truly brilliant images around the clearing Griffin and the children sat and watched the story unfold.

Quite suddenly a small huddle of dwarves sprinted into the shot, stopping just by the impressive building.

One, a robust dwarf with a thick, matted grey beard, who was wearing enough armour to easily satisfy a small army of the vertically-challenged folk, was unmistakably their leader. He raised his arm with a clenched fist at which the rabble stopped abruptly and rather clumsily, with those at the back of the group bumping into those in front. By the time they had all halted, the dwarves looked like they were about to start a piggy-back, three legged race.

Once they had regained their balance he then, again using no words, raised both hands and performed a rotating gesture with both his index fingers.

Forward crept a rather timid looking dwarf with a nose as bent as a troll's elbow. His beard was gravy brown and only down to his waist suggesting that he was quite a young dwarf, probably only in his sixties. He was rosy cheeked and carried a huge keg on his back along with a staff bearing the colourful flags of Dithers, the leader of this small band. Like an overly voluptuous ballerina he spun on the spot and pliéd so the barrel lowered to a specific height.

From here Dithers, along with all his companions, produced large lead and pewter tankards from their outrageously thick belts. Each of them took a turn using the heavy brass spigot to fill their tankards with foamy grog. Moments later nine dwarves stood swaying in front of the temple with foam lining their beards and axes ready in their hands.

The family giggled at the sight when, suddenly, a great shadow swooped over the huddle of drunken dwarves as if a large cloud had just blocked the sun. They ducked and dived behind various solid objects – rocks, boulders, and large tree trunks – before a massive belt of flame erupted from above.

Dithers was the first to stand. Red faced and now sporting a smoking and rather singed beard he commanded his band of tipsy dwarves into the temple.

After heaving the huge front door back into place and systematically turning locks and shunting bolts (well, the ones they could reach) Dithers once more invited the Flag-bearer forward. A few tippy-toed moves later and they were all drinking again.

'Why do they drink so much of that fizzy stuff Gwangad?' asked Pereé, who was much too young to comprehend the bizarre effects a good malt grog could have.

'Well dear, the dwarves think it's actually *courage juice* in the barrel you see and they believe the more they drink the better they will be in battle.'

The family gazed on as Dithers and his men sat about the great temple belching and laughing aloud, appearing quite oblivious to the terror that lurked outside. It was as if they had totally forgotten about the great black shadow as the seemingly irrelevant conversations continued. Of course the family were unable to hear what was being said (which was probably a good thing) as the linker orb was for showing only.

It was only when a blazing shaft of autumnal sunset suddenly pierced the roof of the temple that the dwarves sprang into their well rehearsed, fully-crazed dwarf attack positions. They all snorted and cursed as they rose to their dumpy feet and huddled together, forming an almost solid mass of dwarf, chain mail, axes and beards.

Next came a thundering crash as debris from the roof hailed down upon the tightly packed gang below. Cherryberry rafters and beams, chimney stacks, chimney pots, enormous stone blocks, ogre-scale tiles, joists - it was like a shopping list for a builders merchant.

Unfortunately for the dragon, for dragon it was that had interrupted the band's pause for refreshment, Dither's hadn't ordered these goods. Nor did he have the inclination to build a house or a cottage for that matter and, like any dissatisfied customer, decided it was time to complain - something he had years of practice at and prided himself on greatly. He stood, at the ready to perform yet more hand gestures. His loyal companions remained still as stone waiting for him to make even the slightest of movements.

One could say the *courage juice* was certainly working well. And so they waited with gritted teeth and baited yet smelly breath. Ready. It was not long before their winged guest struck again.

Another large crash sent the great scribed bell along with its solid Cherryberry frame and ogre-scale tiled roof screaming to the temple floor, splitting not only itself but the band of merry dwarves as well.

This was the moment.

With lightning speed all nine of the dwarves' axes deployed ropes from their stubby handles. Dithers signalled to the Flag-bearer who crept behind an enormous pale tablet fashioned from the most beautiful stone and marble. It had a large gold plaque set into its cold smooth surface that read:

Here lieth
Reginald Pendragon
Wielder of the Four-sided Coin

and underneath it went on:

One is for Peace
One is for Anger
One is for Magic
And the fourth a Mirror

The dwarves waited silently, each of them holding firmly to their leather-bound axe handles. Amid the silence a faint clicking and scratching appeared like the annoying next-door neighbour who insists on having trolls for tea at midnight.

Its volume increased, mimicking a thousand dry twigs being snapped as it echoed around the beautiful archways and intricate timberwork high above them. Dithers strained his neck trying to make sense of the noise and, looking high up into the cavernous chamber, watched as the enormous charcoal black, thorny head of Spineback slithered into view.

The Flag-bearer, who was still cowering behind his tablet, now had sight of the beast. The spines that graced his naturally aerodynamic, if bulky head explained the noise. They clicked and scratched against the rafters as Spineback heaved his enormous black body through the vast hole he had just created in the temple roof. Row after row of pearly daggers crept forward as a slender tongue tasted the fear in the air.

Dithers turned to his band of warriors and began wailing various stereotypical dwarven expletives at them. His face turned a more vibrant shade of red with every vowel and consonant.

'What's he saying Gwangad?' asked Pereé.

'I think he's just asking his men why the dragon couldn't have used the front door,' replied the sensitive old Wizard.

'I know Gwangad, I know!' she replied. 'He's much too big!' she continued, to which Griffin and Master Agar exchanged looks as if to say: thank goodness she can't lip read and her vocabulary is limited.

Spineback, being huge and full of self importance (resembling a winged Mrs Macrocker), had underestimated the nine dwarves skipping and darting about on the floor below like panting dots of insignificance.

He opened his monstrosity of a mouth and let out the deepest roar that soon turned to glowing orange flames that licked every stone, beam, bolt and cross member of the roof space, leaving it looking rather dishevelled. He scratched and clawed his way through the progressively growing hole in the ogre-scale tiled roof. Lugging his thorny carcass through proved harder than he had anticipated and he put it down to the aperitif of nine dwarven gruff horses he had squeezed in prior to this, his main course, scrambling about below swinging rope-axes.

Dithers' rope-axe was in a full spin, ready to be deployed. He stood in perfect alignment (for a drunk) to the crooked-nosed Flag-bearer who was also in a full swing-ish. And behind, seven more clad in heavy armour were frantically thrashing their rope-axes ready for the order from Dithers.

"Ready!" cried Master Agar, narrating Dithers' words.

"Aim lads! Oi! Flag-bearer, aim I say! Not at me! At the bloody dragon you fool!"

'There's no blood on the dragon,' Pereé insisted with a confused frown on her forehead.

'Shhh!' Garad hissed, watching intently and not wanting to miss a beat.

"RELEASE!"

The family watched as nine very clumsily thrown rope-axes showered off in all different directions. It looked as though each of

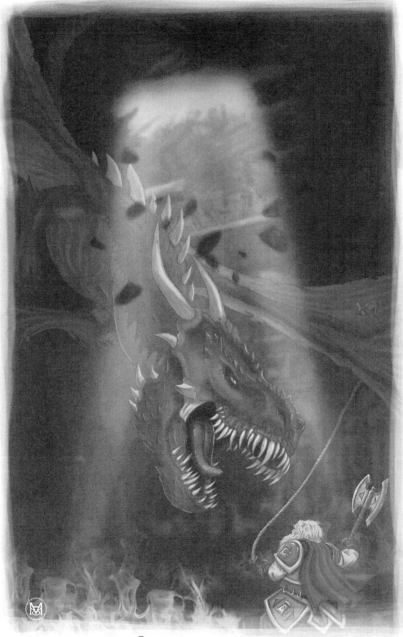

Spineback and Dithers

them had been staring at a different dragon - and after all that grog they may well have been.

Dithers turned with a furious red face to once again quiz his men about the atrocious use of the front door when he was suddenly ripped high into the air. Where his men had failed he had succeeded. His rope-axe had quite miraculously hit its target, which meant two things: one, the dragon was now injured and two, that Dithers was in no way drunk enough.

He hung on as Spineback thrashed around, tumbling here and there with a rather heavy dwarf hanging from his left wing.

Walls were scratched, flames were spat, and as the wooden frame of the roof cracked and fizzed with the increasing heat, Dithers, always in charge but also always concerned for his merry band's wellbeing, ordered them outside.

Not realising the rafters were on fire they all assumed he was in a grump because none of them had hit the beast. So to avoid any further ear-bashing they hastily stumbled back outside but not before another lengthy period of fumbling with locks, turning of keys and shunting of bolts.

As the door finally closed again Dithers returned his attention to the dragon. He smiled and waited, listening to the uneven flapping from Spineback along with the loud cracks that shuddered from high above him. With every crack another beam snapped. The impatient dwarf listened, his frustration growing as row after row of trusses turned black and split.

With an almighty groan the temple roof collapsed, falling directly on Spineback, who fell harder still on Dithers.

*

The eight companions awoke to a splendid morning. The flowers were out, the thrushes and robins were whistling their troubles away and the morning sun tickled all that it touched.

Having been nine for so long it didn't take the still heavily intoxicated remaining eight to realise one, their leader, was missing.

Master Agar began to narrate again but this time putting on eight different voices as he did so often when reading to Pereé.

"Where's Dithers then?" started one who had no name,

or hair for that matter, but who the group had nicknamed *Shiny head.*

"Anyone seen him?" replied another.

"Maybe he's still with the dragon – think they had stuff to talk about," added the Flag-bearer.

"What dragon?" quizzed Old Mgee.

"Y'know that Spineback feller," said another.

"What – the potion dealer?" asked a different one.

"No. That's Binespack. *Spineback's* the dragon," crept in another.

"Eh? Sticklebacks?" the partially deaf Old Mgee retorted.

"Oh go back to sleep Mgee!" said the Flag-bearer.

"Yes! Maybe on Tuesday but only after I've had a sleep," replied the ancient Mgee.

Between the eight of them they began to build a fire and start preparing a hearty breakfast. As the gruel and ox tongue bubbled and sizzled in the stewing pot none of them had actually noticed the monstrous mound of rubble, burnt roof and crispy dragon wings behind them.

One embarrassingly thin dwarf had actually used a dragon leg as a pillow.

An extremely fat dwarf with the largest golden platted beard called Booka stood up.

"Well lads, you continue with the feast, I'm off for a…" he paused. The rest of the group turned to find out why.

The fat dwarf was perfectly silhouetted against a still glowing burnt down temple.

"Shovels lads! Right now!" commanded the Flag-bearer as he reached behind his back for his own.

With spades at the ready, and with the might that only determined dwarves possess, they set about shifting the muck and rubble all the while panting through wiry beards and crying out their heroic leader's name. All except for the Flag-bearer who had a different name for him:

'Father!' the young dwarf cried.

Several hours passed and still they continued. Shifting

tonne after tonne of stone and blackened timber. Unfortunately for him, the Flag-bearer was to uncover that which he least of all desired. Amid the sweat, bloody palms and tears the young dwarf, still with his keg on his back and his flags caught high in the late morning breeze, lay his wooden spade to rest on the dusty forest floor. He knelt down and began to sob, at which the others, who were also covered in blisters and sores, stopped their sobering search. As they, one by one, huddled around the Flag-bearer they realised that he hadn't just given up - as they stood over him it became clear to them why he was so grief-stricken. Laying delicately in the Flag-bearer's lap was the motionless arm of their leader. The short, dumpy fingers lay outstretched and still. The rest of him was still covered in temple and spiny dragon.

"What's going on then?" cried the inconsiderate Mgee, who was still hobbling over a pile of rubble to see what all the fuss was about. "Why's young un kneeling down? He got himself a lady-dwarf, eh? He proposin' a say's he proposin'?"

"Shush you babbling old fool!" barked Booka to which old Mgee looked shocked.

"No respect these days, these bloody young un's. In my day I'd 'av 'acked your head off for such a tone."

"Oh, so you heard me then!" retaliated Booka.

"Yeah, I heard ye, ya little gob of troll spit - and there's one thing ye need to be a rememberin' Booka."

"Oh yeah, and what's that gramps."

"These are still *my* days!" concluded Mgee as he made a move for his ancient looking scimitar that dangled freely by his worn, knock-kneed old legs.

"Enough. Both of you," Shiny head demanded. 'It's Dithers – think we've lost him."

"No. Not Dithers," Old Mgee spluttered. "He's invincible - told me once after we'd defeated an entire army of trolls, orcs and goblins. Ha ha. Took us all afternoon as I recall - but - (sniff) - we were done be teatime."

"Mgee you old fart. Look at him! All we got is an arm.

Can't even see what the rest of 'im looks like," Booka spat.

"He be laughing under that rubble, you mark my words," Mgee chuckled.

"He's dead!! You crazy fool! Look, the Flag-bearer's holding his hand and still it lies without so much as a flinch. Now, don't you think that if he were alive under there he'd want to let us know – ya know, give a little squeeze or something?" continued Booka, who had not been in the gang for very long (some thirty years) in comparison to Old Mgee who had actually taught Dithers all he knew and consequently had known him the longest.

"Look 'ere young un, just cause his arm is still, don't mean he's dead. He could be 'avin a nap under there," Mgee said, turning to the young dwarf with the bent nose who was still holding his father's cold hand and said: "Here, try this instead."

The old dwarf unclipped one of the many lead tankards from his weathered leather belt – that no longer fitted him – and passed it to the Flag-bearer.

"This is no time for grog!" yelled the Flag-bearer who now had two distinct damp patches in his immaculate gravy-brown beard from where he had been crying.

"No young un," Mgee said softly, "try it in his hand." He pointed at the motionless limb surrounded by bricks and mortar.

The Flag-bearer slowly lowered the intricately deco-rated lead tankard down and placed it softly into the palm of Dithers' hand. They waited, all of them with their breath held and no more so than Old Mgee. It seemed the whole forest had fallen silent. The birds had stopped their singing. The trees had stopped dancing in the breeze. The wind gave respite: its howling through the burrows and hollows ceasing momentarily. It felt as though time itself had frozen.

Then, quicker than a lead shot from a blunderbuss, Dithers was gone. The birds started up once more, the trees began to sway and even the wind once more howled its eerie song.

"FATHER!" cried the Flag-bearer.'

'What happened to him Gwangad?' called a very insistent Pereé to Master Agar.

'No one, not even old Merlin has ever solved this riddle. Dithers' body was there one moment and – poof – gone the next.'

When they eventually excavated the area where Dithers had been laid the sight before them was one of both worry and amazement, from a dwarf's point of view anyway.

It seemed that when the roof had fallen the battle hadn't ended there. Spineback's head lay heavy with a large axe in it, and in his razor-sharp, teeth-laden mouth lay Dithers - well, all of his armour. In fact his leather gauntlet was still holding the axe.

'You see Pereé,' Master Agar began, 'both Spineback and Dithers had such enormous egos that even when they knew they were going to die they were still trying to outdo one another. They truly did fight to the bitter end.'

The image projecting from the linker orb began to dull and flicker before zipping inwards until it was a small ball of white light, glowing in Master Agar's hand.

'Wow!' squealed Pereé with excitement. 'We're going to live in the dragon-house!'

'Ha ha. Yes m'dear, that you are,' said Master Agar while looking exceptionally proud of his granddaughter.

'Father, when it's rebuilt can I live in the bell tower?' joined in the ever-disgruntled Garad, who had a noticeable flicker of excitement in his voice.

'We'll see,' Griffin smiled. He would have said yes but knew he would have to clear it with Lizzi first, she always had the last word when it came to the children.

'Well. Now you know the famous history of your new home shall we go and see it?' asked the old man addressing his banished family.

'Yeah!' cried the children.

'Right then, hop-too, whizz-bang and off we go,' said the jittery old Wizard who now actually found himself rather excited.

They continued their ambling, all the while crunching leaves and trampling wild flowers as they went. The soft majestic glow from Master Agar's twisted wooden staff still lit the way.

Finally the carpet of moss and foliage began to change to lumps of broken stone, bricks and the odd marble pillar here and there. They had reached the temple.

It stood, broken but impressive. The tallest tower had only three of its four walls, exposing the multitude of stairs and scorched, moss-covered beams and rafters leading to the bell tower that jutted out like a sore thumb. The main entrance was no more than an archway. Its door too had been ravaged by Spineback's ferocious breath and all that remained was a pile of rusty hinges, bolts and locks scattered on the ivy-covered ground.

It appeared exactly as the linker orb had shown – perhaps more overgrown but all in the same place.

Griffin, taking in a full panoramic view of his surroundings, asked rhetorically: 'How is it that the plants and trees here have grown so much larger and fuller than in other parts of the forest?' trying to solve the mystery for himself.

'It's the temple,' answered Master Agar boldly. 'Garad, go and touch the walls of the temple.'

Garad, who would normally have retaliated with some form of disgruntled questioning or remark, stepped tentatively towards the nearest temple wall just by the entranceway.

With his arm outstretched, his hereditarily-pale fingers groped at a stone that stood out proud. He pulled back with a startle.

'Tell us what you feel Garad,' probed the old Wizard who already knew the answer to the riddle.

'It's warm. In fact it's really quite hot!' said Garad as he went in for another feel of the rough yet confident stone.

'Dragon breath!' thundered Master Agar dramatically. 'When Spineback breathed his last flame, the very flame that destroyed this building, some of the magic in it transferred in the form of heat to the stone walls. You may not have a front door as of yet, but at least you'll all be toasty warm!'

\*

It was a few hours after Master Agar had left them; venturing back to the town to join the other twelve elders, that Griffin felt it. He had just helped Lizzi settle the children in some make-shift beds and was crossing their new hallway with Lizzi a few steps ahead, when he stopped mid-stride, squirming as a sickening wave of uneasiness welled within him. It began like the fluttering of butterflies in his chest, then quickly turned to a deep pull like some foul phantom had thrust a wispy fist straight through his ribcage and was now attempting to wrench his heart from his body. The feeling grew stronger and stronger, so much so that Griffin began to lean backwards on his heels in a bid to fight it.

He let out a howl as the pain increased, shocking Lizzi who spun around immediately, 'Griffin what's wrong?' she screeched in a fluster.

Griffin clutched his chest in a bid to fight the pain replying, 'It's happening.'

'What?' she snapped with panic, but Griffin could not answer. With a final tug, he was pulled forward sharply, whipping his head back and jarring his neck, he fell to his knees and was left coughing and spluttering for breath.

'Griffin? Griffin what's wrong?' Lizzi said kneeling beside him, placing a gentle hand on his back.

But her words could wait. He focused on his breathing, his hand still pressed firmly to his chest. He felt immediate loss and sadness, like a bird with no wings must feel, or a flower with no petals, useless and without purpose. The elders had just taken his magic.

# CHAPTER FIVE

# The Door with Secrets

The thrushes and robins awoke, as per normal, with a stretch and a song. As they sat in their usual nests and perches gazing, like their ancestors before them, at the ruin below, they noticed something new. A crooked, twisted staff was stuck in the ground outside the main entrance of the temple and stood next to it was an old man dressed in a shimmering silver cloak that had wonderfully large pockets; the kind of pockets that could probably carry a great deal of breadcrumbs or seed. He was talking to another man, dressed in brown who was holding an axe.

'It has to be big enough to fit that archway, and - and solid, yes very solid. Double the thickness of any normal door. In fact better make it double the thickness of any *non*-normal door, just to be on the safe side. They must be safe,' finished Master Agar.

'S'only one tree big enough s'I can think of but none'r us wood-cutters go near it.'

'Why ever not?' enquired the old Wizard.

'S'cursed. Or so folks reckon,' insisted Mr Eavsalot, a stocky well-built man with a short fuzzy beard, rosy red cheeks and a smile as wide as his head. 'Some say this tree has a hollow in it 'n' if you's ever look inside…you'd be pulled in and lost forever!'

'Intriguing,' replied the puzzled looking Wizard as he played with his remarkably long beard. 'Ah Griffin! Morning m'dear boy, morning.'

'Morning Luther,' replied Griffin addressing his Wizard elder-in-law.

'Griffin, this is Mr Eavsalot. So recognised as the best wood-cutter this side of Tilös. In fact the last job he did was for the dark lord Gruntsmead - fitting some planters outside his black tower's windows.'

'Got a tip an'all,' Mr Eavsalot said proudly.

'Anyway, I've commissioned him to build you a door, a very large, very thick and heavy door.'

'Why Luther, you don't have to do that,' said Griffin.

'Oh yes I do!' he chortled. 'If Lizzi is anything like her mother was I do - if not to make her feel more at ease then to save your ears from all her ranting. Ha ha!'

'Well that's very kind of you Luther. Oh, and thanks for leaving your staff last night, that protection charm worked a…well – charm. It's amazing you know. All my life I've had magic running through my veins and it's only when it's gone that you realise how important and useful it truly is.'

'This is true for all things Griffin, not just magic. We never quite realise what we have until some troll eats it or some flying dwarves take it for their own,' the old man philosophised.

'When do you think I'll have my magic reinstated Luther?' Griffin asked.

'When the elders are all satisfied that you are no longer a threat my boy.' the old man said honestly. 'You see the Witch who took your magic; she had power beyond measure. The power she instilled in you as Blackmouth was not of this world. We don't know how she did it, but we desperately need to find out. In my mind boy, you are no threat to anyone, she is.

It took all thirteen councillors, myself included, a great deal of effort to revoke your magic and it will take no less than thirteen to grant you your magic back again. Thirteen satisfied council elders…that's what we need – so far, you have one, me.'

'Ahem…' interrupted Mr Eavsalot.

'Oh sorry Mr Eavsalot, yes, quite right, enough of this jibber-jabber,' said Master Agar, noticing the woodcutter's blatant attempt at diverting the conversation back to the task at hand.

'Griffin, I want you to go along. Familiarise yourself with the forest and gather your own thoughts about which tree would best suit your new front door. I'll stay here and look after Lizzi and the children.'

After a few short handshakes and goodbye's Griffin and

Mr Eavsalot headed for the nearest break in the dense thicket, allowing them to enter the older parts of the Cherryberry forest. They pushed and heaved their way through the thorns and snare-like creepers until they were surrounded by tall, elegant trees for as far as they could see.

Willows, oaks, Cherryberries, ash, thornsnickets, pantrees, gobblestops - all of them sporting different barks, leaves and colours.

'What we need's a good Cherryberry, an old un,' Mr Eavsalot said openly as if talking to himself.

'Why a Cherryberry?' asked Griffin who although knowledge-able about plants assumed the rosy-cheeked woodcutter must have a greater knowledge.

'Simple really Mr Blackmouth Sir...'

'It's *Black*,' Griffin corrected.

'Sorry, I's always getting confused with names. Master Agar's paying me te find ya the strongest tree and everyone knows there ain't no tree as stronger than a Cherryberry.'

'Oh, strong, yes of course,' squirmed Griffin, who felt rather silly that he hadn't seen that as being the reason.

'Let's split up and try and find us a nice one,' said Mr Eavsalot as he pushed past Griffin.

Griffin paced a few steps here and a few there, spying all the trees. Nothing really seemed to jump out at him, which when he recalled the creepies and crawlies decided that this was actually a good thing. He had been walking for hours. He skipped across a babbling brook and turned past a large mossy stump before he saw it. In the distance, through an almost impenetrable wall of ivy and gobblestops he made out a clearing with one lonely tree at its heart.

He raced forward, fending off a willow's fringe before he stopped at the edge of the clearing to take in the spectacle in front of him. It was beautiful and massive – the largest Cherryberry tree he had ever seen. Its bark was rich and its roots ran deep like thick silvery rivers meandering through the forest floor. Its trunk was a solid wall of shimmering white timber, which tapered off and twisted at the top before the endless canopies of cherry-red leaves blurred as they rose higher and higher into the unknown. He reached out and touched it, caressing every crease, bump and groove. He began walking around the full uneven circumference of the tree, all the while feeling both intoxicated and flabbergasted by its overwhelming size and power. At the halfway mark, which took an unusually long time, he noticed it. A hollow, about the size of a large pumpkin now faced Griffin.

'Blackm…I mean Mr Black, please step back quickly.'

Griffin jumped out of his skin and turned to see Mr Eavsalot charging towards him.

'What's wrong?'

'Oh, sorry t'startle ya Sir but this tree aint no good t'no-one. S'not safe Sir. S'cursed y'see.'

'Cursed? In what way?' grimaced Griffin, knowing he now wanted this tree.

'That hollow Sir! Something terrible lives in there, something foul. A beast!' declared a rather flamboyant Mr Eavsalot.

'Beast?' came a voice suddenly that appeared to echo out from the tree.

'Beast?' came the voice again. It was gentle yet grunty, like that of a young boy with a chesty cough.

'Beast they say Orbulous. Beast! Ha!'

Griffin and the woodcutter froze and gawked at one another, listening and not daring to speak.

'Oh, and now they'se quiet! All nasty words and no perpologising,' came the voice again.

'Say something,' ushered Griffin to Mr Eavsalot.

'Err, sorry Mr tree-dwellin' creature Sir, please don't eat my soul,' attempted the axe-wielding yokel.

'S'a pretty shiny sharpy you's got there,' replied the voice from the tree.

'Your axe,' Griffin hastened, 'It's talking about your axe. How is it creature that you are able to see us and yet we cannot see you?' Griffin asked using his most authoritative tone, trying to almost mimic Fonzo Fidrib.

'Why you's need to see me? After all I's just a foul Beasty is I not?'

'I don't like talking to things I cannot see,' Griffin replied, while firmly trying his best to avoid any unwanted flashbacks from his recent past.

'Well here I am!' came the voice suddenly from behind them. Both Griffin and Mr Eavsalot turned to see a small creature with pale-green skin standing before them. It had a small purple pointed floppy hat resting snuggly on its round lemon-shaped head with a large flat nose and a smiling mouth that had a tooth protruding from each corner; one blunt, the other sharp. The creature appeared old as it had a long (for its size) white beard. Also a small pair of dirty purple trousers and a tiny leather belt which had various oddities dangling from it – two crystal shards, an impressive feather, a rusty key, a small skull and a little leather pouch.

'I's Orbulous Gnomei-I and I's a forest gnome,' said the little pale-green man as he bowed with one arm behind his back and the other out in front of him, which had two glowing orbs resting in his palm. One was purple with a spiky glow about it whereas the other was golden-orange with a soft swirly glow.

'A *forest gnome?*' Griffin said, looking confused. 'Never heard of a forest gnome before and believe me I know my creatures.'

'S'probly 'cause I only ever spoked to one 'o'your kind afore. You's ever heard 'o' Merlin?' asked the little creature.

'Merlin, why yes. He's the greatest Wizard that's ever lived. Why?' Griffin replied.

'Well, Merlin named me, that's why. He couldn't speaks my name as I told it so he gave me a new one: Orbulous Gnomei-I and he teached me ta speaks like you's.'

'Merlin named you? He has been missing for years. When did he name you?'

'Ooks, now let's us think. Orbulous when was it? Ah, bout six thousand and twenty seven years ago,' came the little grunty voice.

'But Merlin's not that old! Is he?' said Griffin.

'He was just a youngsy when he named us,' the creature added turning to Griffin with his orbs still in his little pale-green palm. 'So you's be wantin' my tree. Well I'll tell you's Blacky, you's can have it but, you's gotta take me with you.'

Griffin stood amazed and utterly speechless. Mr Eavsalot dribbled a little before dropping his axe.

'How did you know?' Griffin insisted.

The little creature smiled. 'Tell me Blacky, who do you's think taught old Merlin his tricksies eh? You's thinks they's just in his heads from birth? Merlin is one of the greatsies but, there are some who are greatsier,' explained the funny little creature.

*

'Tell me Father, tell me!' pleaded Pereé.

'It's a surprise and you'll see soon enough,' said Griffin.

The whole family, Master Agar included, were stood outside the temple staring at a curtain of glowing blue mist that spanned the whole length of the building. It was concealing whatever secret Griffin was hiding from them.

'Ok Luther, ready,' Griffin said to Master Agar.

'*Caligum Cadere.*' said the old Wizard, and with a swish and a swoosh of his staff the curtain dropped to the floor and disappeared to reveal a huge and quite beautiful door made from Cherryberry hardwood. It was hand-carved with glorious detail; pictures of dwarves and dragons and the whole Black family had been carefully carved from its polished surface and at its centre was a massive brass knocker. The support cladding was fixed with glimmering brass bolts and matching hinges that were so huge you could've hung a giant from them.

'Best door in the whole of Brickabrack!' Griffin enthused proudly, 'and not just because of its size either; it's made from one solid cut of wood, not planks like most.' He finished.

Lizzi stared lovingly at her husband. Even in these difficult times he still managed to bring the unlucky family some joy. Both Garad and Pereé stood admiring the door with smiles cast over both their faces and it was for this reason that she loved her husband – his almost effortless affect upon their children. Without meaning to, and without even noticing, he had the whole family smiling proudly.

'Wait children, wait. There's more. Right, stand back. Luther, if you wouldn't mind.'

'Oh yes, right.' The old Wizard raised his staff and aimed it at the massive door and chanted: *'Draco Dormum'* to which the door clicked and clunked before prising itself open. It swung inwards effortlessly and they all entered one after the other.

Once in the grand entrance hall that the children had nicknamed the Dithers lounge, it became apparent to them all that the other side of the door looked nothing like the outside. It looked like an old tree, it was barky and covered in moss with the odd collection of fungus and mushrooms dotted here and there, and in the very middle of the door was a large hollow. Oddly, the hollow didn't show the forest outside as they expected just darkness.

'Oh Griffin, we couldn't afford to have both sides of the door carved,' Lizzi offered sympathetically.

'Actually we could,' Griffin replied with a rather arrogant smile. He walked up to the newly installed door and pushed it shut. The huge ornate handle clunked loudly.

'Is it safesies?' came a grunty little voice which could have been mistaken for the door creaking except of course the door was firmly shut. To all the onlooking family, save Griffin, it seemed as though the door had just spoken.

'Yes I think they're ready,' said Griffin mysteriously to the door.

Lizzi stood bewildered, staring at her husband with a disconcerted expression on her delicate face. Was he going mad? Was she going mad? He was talking to a door and she was hearing voices.

As the group of family members gazed on they noticed two small pale-green hands emerge from the hollow.

'This is Orbulous Gnomei-I,' Griffin said loudly so as to provide a sufficient and impressive introduction. There was an awkward silence as everyone was trying to make sense of what it was they were looking at. They watched as a purple floppy hat rose from within the door followed by a pale-green lemon shaped head.

'He's so cute!' screamed Pereé as she rushed over to investigate further. 'Can we keep him Father?' she wailed as if she were choosing a puppy.

'Orbulous is here to stay. He is now a part of our family,' Griffin explained to his grateful daughter, 'He's an old friend of Merlin's. In fact, Merlin named him.'

'Oh but Father, Orbulous is such an oldy person's name. Can

I choose him a new name?' said an over-zealous Pereé as she hoisted the poor little forest gnome into the air like a doll.

'Ask Orbulous. He may like his name just the way it is sweetheart. And don't throw him about like that darling – he has feelings too you know, just like me or you or your Mother.' Griffin glanced over to Lizzi to try and get that look of approval from her but she still seemed in a state of shock at the sight of the little green man that had just hopped out of her new front door and that was now being tossed around by her youngest child. She herself had seen some sights in her time but this topped the lot.

'We can be best friends!' Pereé said excitedly. The thought of having someone else to talk to apart from her less than kind older brother sent little flutters of joy racing in her heart.

'So, what name d'yous think me should be having youngsy one?' Orbulous asked with a slightly scared look cast across his face and an apprehensive lump in his throat that was ready for gulping.

'Hmm,' Pereé pondered loudly. She placed the little creature back upon his mushroom covered perch and stepped back to admire her new pet. 'Orbs. I think you should be called Orbs.'

# CHAPTER SIX

# The Butcher's Son

Meanwhile back in the Town of Brickabrack as the Night Watchmen doused the last of the tall street lamps on Rotten Row the bone-chilling scream of a child stabbed at every brick in the town. It echoed around every grimy archway, every slop-filled gutter and stairwell of the desolate grey streets – all subject to its tell-tale sound.

Mr Proofgrease the local bacon grinder woke with a startle. As he attempted to focus on the flickering ceiling above him his mind cleared and his body suddenly fell heavy. All too afraid to move, the painful scream that would unnerve even the ugliest of trolls had erupted from downstairs.

He offered a partly chewed finger nail up to his mouth and began to gnaw at it, which eased his anxiety a little. With his eyes wide open, he listened intently under the covers as it came again.

'AAAAAAARRRGH!'

The scream, with deadly tone and deafening pitch made the large butcher jolt with fear. Mr Proofgrease had never had any dealings with ghouls or mystical creatures. He even sub-contracted a huntsman to do all his dirty work in the forest for him as he was secretly too afraid to enter the woods, not that he'd admit that to you. 'I'm just too busy here in the shop,' he'd tell the folks of the town. Five guilder groats he'd pay, just to avoid any unwanted introductions in the old forest.

A banshee, he thought to himself. They have a wail like that. Although equally he thought it did sound like a small child.

A thought then entered his head that made his heart race and his face drain until its colour matched that of the pale sheet he was hiding under. The hairs on the back of his neck stood tall as if they themselves were trying to escape this new frightful thought.

Suddenly the flickering candle on his bed stand went out. He pulled back the unwashed sheet from over his head and scanned the darkened room. A dim light was now creeping through a crack in his dusty oak bedroom door.

'Jered!' he whispered loudly to the darkness. 'Jered, are you there?' he inquired again, raising his voice a little in the hope that he would catch his son's attention but not that of whatever it was that fumbled and crept downstairs.

Another scream came, followed by a loud crash that sounded like an empty wooden crate being smashed. Then, silence. Mr Proofgrease listened intently. He identified no clear sound except a muffled gargling noise and the uneven pitter-patter of footsteps.

Had the beast gone? Had it taken Jered? The guilt that now began to swell within him made his heart feel like it was trying to jump out of his chest. He had done nothing, just laid there. A coward. With a sudden disregard for his well-being Mr Proofgrease tossed back the covers and sprang to his feet. The love for his son he could feel surging through his veins pushed him on. The rough floorboards splintered his bare soles as he slid slowly forward to the door with the crack of light beaming through it.

He held his breath so as not to break the silence that lay before him. He reached for the ordinary brass handle and pulled it firmly with his large, coarse hands. The door glided open beautifully without so much as a whimper or a creak to reveal the pale landing before him.

The eerie yet now familiar gargling noise came again from downstairs, this time a little louder. Was the beast now coming for him too? Was it at that very moment ascending the stairs with all its spikes and teeth bared ready? Mr Proofgrease sucked in another huge breath, and with his chest now full and stuck out like that of a plump pigeon, he began to edge forward again.

With the balustrade on his left and a kaleidoscope of once colourful paintings and intricately stained glass windows along the wall to his right he passed a large mirror that was hung crooked. He gazed in astonishment at his reflection to slowly watch his rosy cheeks fade until he himself was a ghostly shade of white.

Once he reached the top of the stairs he gripped the lip to the top step with his bloody toes and, hanging onto the banister for dear life, leaned as far forward as he could until his body was almost horizontal. All the while he was trying to catch a glimpse of whatever it was that had breached his home and was now, Mr Proofgrease had decided, presumably stalking him. If nothing else, one thing he was sure of – it hadn't left yet. It was still downstairs – lurking in the darkness, monstrous and hungry.

All he could see from his perch, as he gazed over the banister once more, was the dimly lit tiled floor that lay three and a half flights of rickety stairs below him.

With a newly found and rather disconcerting courage, Mr Proofgrease began his descent. Each step, unlike the cracked bedroom door, creaked, and what made matters worse was that none of the creaks sounded the same and so before long Mr Proofgrease was performing a creaking concerto.

'I must get these infernal stairs sorted!' he whispered to himself angrily.

Another step. Creak!

'Frogspawn and confound it!' he replied.

But it was no good, the further he descended the louder the creaking seemed to get. Mr Proofgrease scanned his limited surroundings for another route down and preferably one that drew less attention to himself.

Another step. CREEAK!

'Oh please, for pity sake – shhh!'

He checked over the banister again for any huge beast or ogre sat ready below with a bed sheet for a napkin and a meat cleaver and pitchfork for cutlery. Thankfully, just the same cold tiled floor stared back at him.

Pulling his body back into the rigid position it had previously been in he noticed his pale hand against the dark oak banister and then, it was obvious. Hitching his bed robe up he swung his right leg over and reverse mounted the wooden banister.

'Ha. Not so bloody clever now are we,' he muttered to the inanimate stairs that had caused him such grief and that surprisingly didn't creak back with laughter. On his slow slide down Mr

Proofgrease gave thanks to the fact that the banister was in a much better condition than his splintering floorboards.

He landed on the hallway's tiled floor with a thud and immediately spun on the spot, obsessively scanning to make sure that, for now, he was alone. He listened. The gurgling noise had evolved somewhat and now seemed to have a slobbering element to it. The odd noise continued to acoustically flutter past him and fill the cavernous void that was the stairwell.

The dim light he had noticed earlier he now realised was coming from an open door leading to the narrow corridor which Mr Proofgrease used as his butchery store room that continued down into his shop front.

Placing one foot carefully in front of the other he tottered forward, passing through the open door into the store. The half-festering carcass of a deer lay on his well-battered butcher's table. This one had only been half carved up – only the best cuts taken for now - the offal he had intended to deal with in the morning. He wasn't keen on leaving meat out on the table too long, didn't like the blood lingering and then there was always the smell to contend with. Gazing over the half-finished carcass Mr Proofgrease noticed his large cleaver complete with matted fur and dark scabs lying next to it. He grabbed it quickly and pulled it close to his chest.

'Jered!' he croaked down the long corridor, hoping with all his cowardly might for any form of response. The gargling noise had stopped and in place of it came a more frightful sound.

Some form of chewing, crazed and frantic now filled the air, like that of a boar chewing through gristle. Grinding and slobbering.

Mr Proofgrease could stand the uncertainty no more and in an emotional concoction of frustration and worry his fear lifted.

'Jered!' he wailed lifting the cleaver high above his head, 'Jered! Are you there?'

The incessant chewing stopped. Mr Proofgrease listened as the beast scrambled in a rather clumsy manner around his shop. Enough was enough and the large butcher heaved himself forward and through the door.

The dank room was well-lit but empty. Droplets of condensation picked out the cobwebs as a lonely candle cast sharp shadows over meat and brick.

None of the butcher's stock appeared to be missing. All the curdlecow beef, pigdog pork and venison were stacked on their shelves as the butcher had placed them there, looking dry and ill as ever.

He scanned the shop once more and it was only then, as he gazed down behind the shop counter, he noticed what appeared to be the remains of a well polished small wooden box glistening on the floor. He now crept as the beast had and fumbled at the ground for the tattered remains. The strong smell of tobacco burnt his nostrils as he picked up a piece of the broken box and placed it upon the counter, offering it up to the candle to allow for a better inspection. Mr Proofgrease turned the splintered piece of wood over to reveal a beautifully intricate box lid that bore the initials: *G.M.L.B.*

'Blackmouth!' Mr Proofgrease scowled furiously. With his teeth gritted and his grip tightened he raised the rusty weapon so high he ended up on tip toes before thrashing it down upon the box lid, sending it broken and flying in all directions.

A sudden heavy breathing entered the room. Looking down to his left where the noise was coming from Mr Proofgrease noticed a pair of legs poking out proud of the counter.

'JERED!' he gasped as he frantically clambered over but it wasn't Jered he saw. It was little Eloise Elmwood, the Mayor's daughter lying in a heap on the cold floor. A dark crimson halo lay fresh about her pretty head, like jam spread thick between a sandwich of cold shop-floor tiles and pretty golden ringlets.

'Ferret's Freckles! What's happened sugar plum?' Mr Proofgrease said full of concern.

The young girl offered a frail hand towards the butcher and whimpered:

'Please, help me, please, he's taken it…'

'What's he taken sugar plum?' the large butcher gently asked, his lip quivering as he took in the sight before him.

'Please, don't leave me, he's taken it, oh please…' little Eloise replied, her eyes wide with fear.

'I'm not going to leave you, now I need to know sugar plum, what has he taken?' the startled butcher said again.

Eloise began to cry.

'My ear! He's taken my ear!' she screamed.

The crunching of the gristle returned, no remorse, chewing like a care-free scavenger.

Eloise turned her head to one side, her cheek flat on the floor as she gazed to the darkened far corner of the room.

She turned her head back to Mr Proofgrease to reveal a beautiful complexion cast against dark red.

The butcher's rage began to swell, 'BLACKMOUTH YOU WILL DIE FOR THIS TREACHERY!' he screamed to the darkened corner of the room where the persistent chewing remained ever present.

'Don't worry little darlin' you're safe now,' the butcher said reassuringly.

He grabbed for his cleaver that he had temporarily placed on the floor by Eloise. Thick red treacle dripped lazily from the rusty blade. It was her blood, warm and fresh. He rose to his feet and calmly made his way to the other side of his shop. The rage had taken him. His reassurance to Eloise had clouded his mind but in his heart he felt they may well both die in his shop tonight. How could he, with only his rusty weapon, contend against such a powerful Sorcerer? For now though, he didn't care.

Three loud thuds erupted from behind him.

'Mr Proofgrease are you in there?' came an official voice. 'Are you alright Sir?'

Mr Proofgrease spun round to see several glowing orange torches swaying to-and-fro outside his leaded windows, although he was unable to make out any faces.

'I say again Sir, is all well?' came the voice again. 'Speak man.'

Ignoring the rather anxious crowd of orange gathering outside his window Mr Proofgrease turned back to face the darkness once more. He crept forward, edging past the counter, picking up the lonely candle as he went. Oddly there were two mugs of half-drunk cocoa sat in a solidified mass of wax. Unbeknownst to Mr Proofgrease a regular pastime of Jered and Eloise, was to secretly sneak into his shop and drink late-night cocoa without the prying ears of grown-ups. He reaffirmed his grip with the cleaver and once more with his arm raised shuffled forward, the flickering of the candle gradually revealing more of the room.

A candle is such a simple object and yet in the wrong circumstances can be something no-one would want to possess. Unfortunately for Mr Proofgrease this was to be one of those occasions for, as he took the last few steps forward, that little candle finally revealed a horror he could have never expected.

There, sat on the floor and facing the wall away from him, was his son Jered. The small boy was rocking frantically back and forth, almost defying the laws of speed and time. He was moving so quickly he was almost a blur. The bloodied cleaver rang out loud as it hit the floor. The sight was too much for Mr Proofgrease as he offered a shaking hand up to his mouth in utter shock and disbelief. He had thought his son was missing or dead and the sight of his boy raised both joy and concern within the large butcher, but for Mr Proofgrease the revelation was far from over. As he hauled in another one of his almighty breaths and the room fell silent again the grinding, biting and slobbering returned…and it was coming from Jered.

'Jered, what are you doing?' Mr Proofgrease asked his son.

No response came save for the same relentless chewing.

'Jered. Are you ok son?' he pleaded.

Nothing. Mr Proofgrease stepped forward and seized his son by the scruff of his neck and spun him round.

'Answer me when I…' His mouth continued to move and yet no sound escape his lips. The very breath within him had been stolen by the hideous image that now befell his eyes.

His son turned to the light, his eyes wide with rage, bloodshot and glassy. The candle flickered dark shadows on the wall behind him. His face was pale and wormy purple-blue veins writhed proud at his temples. Blood drooled from his gaping mouth and in his left hand sat the remains of a once pretty human ear.

'WHAT HAVE YOU DONE BOY!' Mr Proofgrease exploded, his voice roaring with confusion.

Thud. Thud. Thud.

'Mr Proofgrease please open the door,' came the Brickabrack Night Guards once more from outside.

'What have you done!' Mr Proofgrease waited. Again ignoring the guards, his mind could not fathom the sight before him. The butcher was altogether lost.

'HELP ME!' screamed Eloise, realising herself that the guards had arrived.

'Right lads, step aside. I've heard enough.' Came a gruff voice. Stern and confident.

A silence fell, shortly followed by an almighty explosion of blue sparks and splintered wood. Eloise mustered what strength she had and gazed up in one last effort to see the shop door had been completely obliterated. In its place stood an athletic man, sporting a well trimmed beard and a bald head. About him was a cloud of black smoke that spiralled and turned and fizzed blue, like lightning. It was Cedric Crunkhorn, the newly appointed Sheriff of Brickabrack. His famous pewter sceptre was outstretched in front of him.

They burst through in droves; row after row of Brickabrack's finest marched in sweet succession until the seemingly small butcher's shop was crammed full and the floorboards groaned like an empty belly under the immense weight.

The guards, Sheriff Crunkhorn included, assumed the worst and bearing in mind Mr Proofgrease's unwillingness to co-operate grabbed him firmly and threw him to his knees before clamping him in enchanted irons - the sort that turn you into an inanimate object should you try and escape them as Mr Proofgrease was to find out. As he sat on the stone floor of his beloved shop his son's monstrous image still plagued his mind and so in one last effort to ascertain the truth from the boy the large butcher rose to his feet and ran forward, almost ignoring the several guards he bowled over as he did so.

'*Morphidius Throni!*' belted Sheriff Crunkhorn.

When the smoke cleared Sheriff Crunkhorn sat victoriously upon a large sturdy chair and Mr Proofgrease had altogether disappeared. A score of younger guards looked blankly at the Sheriff, not fully understanding what had just happened. He smiled back like some greedy king of old sat upon a throne. The Sheriff revelled at the thought of others knowing less than him. He enjoyed gazing back at their puzzled expressions knowing too well that none of them would question his methods for fear of looking like a moron.

It was as the Sheriff bent down to retrieve the bloodied cleaver he noticed him, sat quietly in the darkness.

'Nobody move,' Crunkhorn ordered as the room fell silent.

A rather ill looking child gazed back at Crunkhorn. There was a pause before the boy's body began to writhe and contort in ways that it shouldn't. An evil gargling noise emanated from the small child as he raised something to his mouth and began to chew on it while sat, sporadically thrashing around before them.

'Bring me that boy,' Crunkhorn ordered to one of his guards from his throne. The guard edged towards the eerie looking child, his leather-clad gauntlet outstretched before him.

The child stopped nibbling at his snack and raised his head. He stared at the guard with wonderment but this soon changed to an expression of confusion. The boy tilted his head to one side as a puzzled puppy would.

'Don't make this difficult boy,' requested the guard as he edged a little nearer.

Jered continued to assess the creature before him. It was as if he had never seen a human before.

'RAAARRRGH!' Jered shrieked as he leapt forward. His gaping mouth encompassing one of the guard's outstretched fingers. With the force of a heavy blade Jered bit down hard, severing straight through the leather gauntlet and the guard's finger with surgical precision.

'AAAAARRRGH!' wailed the injured guard as he fell to his knees. 'Bit me…the little freak bit meee,' he yelped, holding his newly acquired four-fingered hand.

Two more night guards rushed to where Jered was, who had now turned to face them.

'ENOUGH!' Crunkhorn shouted. 'Men, stand aside,' he continued, lifting his pewter sceptre and aiming it straight at the boy. 'It's your call boy, but there will be no more appetisers for you tonight I can promise you that.'

The butcher's son looked blankly as ever back at the Sheriff, his eyes still blazing with fury. Another silence befell the room, then, like a savage, Jered ran screaming at a huddle of dazed guards.

*'Capticlaudis,'* Crunkhorn uttered, his voice low like thunder in the distance. A beautiful blue net of light rocketed out from the end of his sceptre and wrapped itself around Jered, slowly weaving itself tighter and tighter, engulfing him like a cocoon.

The boy fell, hitting the shop floor hard.

'Feisty little one isn't he,' Crunkhorn said, watching intrigued as Jered squirmed about on the tiles like a giant glowing blue caterpillar. 'Lads! Get this little demon to a cell where we can have a better look at him. And where no one is likely to lose any appendages. Oh that reminds me, Dunhill!'

'Yes sir,' replied the guard with the missing finger.

'Hold up that hand,' Crunkhorn said sympathetically.

'Oh thank you Sir, you are kind and...'

'Save your thanks Dunhill, I won't replace the lost finger, but I will heal it,' Crunkhorn interrupted.

He reached for a small glass vial from many on his belt and pulled the cork from it. The red liquid inside began to fizz and bubble as the air hit it.

The fumes, along with a pungent, rotten smell, filled the room. The Sheriff then pulled a slender glass rod from his pocket and dipped it in the vial. A droplet of the crimson red elixir clung to the end of the rod like rain on the end of your nose in a storm.

'Here Dunhill, glove off and hold that hand steady. Well hurry lad, this stuff doesn't wait for you ya know. Needs to be administered quickly.'

The guard pulled himself to his feet and hurried past the shop counter to Crunkhorn's side.

'Sorry for letting you down Sir, I have failed you, it won't happen again,' Dunhill ensured.

'You failed yourself Dunhill and now you pay the price. Brace yourself lad, this is *really* going to hurt.' With that Crunkhorn tapped the glass rod and the blood red droplet fell to the fleshy stump of Dunhill's hand.

The skin began to burn and hiss, the torn edges and messy flaps began to tighten and pull together, almost weaving themselves until Dunhill had a nice tidy stump where his finger had not moments before been wriggling.

'Thank you Captain and sorry, feeling a little faint.' Dunhill finished.

'Apology accepted Dunhill,' the Sheriff said as he turned to the rest of his troop, 'and may this be a permanent reminder to all of you to never underestimate children or any small creatures – particularly those chewing on ears. Just because a creature may be small it does not mean they aren't powerful. I have had dealings with remarkably small creatures that could crush you in one go, all at the same time.' Crunkhorn finished with a grimace as if a repressed memory had just resurfaced. 'And besides, Dunhill, even if I had wanted to replace the finger it would be half digested by now and mixed in with half an ear. Wouldn't want to get that one wrong now would I,' he finished. 'Ah Mr Proofgrease – had almost forgotten about you,' the Sheriff chortled as he gazed back at the lonely plump chair sat in the middle of the shop.

*'Expoverum,'* and with a flick of his sceptre Mr Proofgrease appeared once more, looking a little ill and unsteady.

'What's gonna happen' ta my lad?' Mr Proofgrease spluttered.

The Sheriff turned to the worried butcher and grinned wildly.

'Tell me Mr Proofgrease, have you ever visited a dungeon before?'

*

Knock! Knock! Knock! The noise came from Griffin's bespoke and quite charming new front door.

'Who's that at this hour?' Lizzi mumbled into her pillow using some form of half groaning, half drooling slumber language that only Griffin could understand.

'Or what is it,' Griffin added as he slipped on his stripy blue and white night gown complete with matching night cap. 'If it's another one of those blasted creepies I'll go mad.' He fumbled through the sleepy temple and descended the open-air stairwell to see a small knot of people leering outside the entrance. Seeing this he placed the badly burnt dwarf battle axe he had grabbed from under his pillow, into the umbrella stand at the base of the stairs.

He made his way across the great hall which was now full of all the family's possessions. There were scorched Faery-woven rugs on the floor that looked a little lost in such a vast space. Paintings and tapestries adorned the walls. His favourite red leather chair sat cosily by the enormous fireplace and by its side, a table stand with a pipe lying neatly upon it.

'Odd...' Griffin pondered. 'I could've sworn I'd left my *Thinkers* tobacco box by my pipe last night – Lizzi and her confounded cleaning,' he muttered as he reached Orbs' side of the large door.

'Strangers Blacky,' came the now familiar, squeaky voice from the mushroom-encrusted hollow.

'Yes Orbs, that they are, and at such an odd hour as well,' Griffin said to the little green man as he began to orchestrate the multitude of locks and bolts.

Knock. Knock. Knock.

'Yes, yes, hang on a moment!' Griffin snarled.

The door slid open as if it had been hung on a bed of ice to reveal a bald, athletic looking man with a neatly trimmed beard – it was Sheriff Crunkhorn.

'Morning Sir. Are you a mister...' the Sheriff gazed down to a piece of parchment 'Blackmouth?'

'It's Black. Yes I am and who are you? What's all this?'

'My name is Cedric Crunkhorn. I'm the newly appointed Sheriff of Brickabrack and these are my men. Oh, and to answer your second question sir...' continued Crunkhorn as he pulled his pewter sceptre from his side and thrust it through the large door at Griffin 'we are here to arrest you – again – for the use of the dark powers – again – under section seven hundred and sixty three thousand of the *Where and When to use Magic Act*. And might I suggest that you come quietly Sir. The last person that tested me ended up totally – well, let's just say she never made the trial.' grinned Crunkhorn.

# CHAPTER SEVEN

# A Ghost in the Night

The rusty lock rang out as Crunkhorn stood one side of an uneven mass of iron bars and Griffin sat coldly, still wearing his blue and white stripy night gown, on the other.

'Time will tell Blackmouth. Oh yes my friend, time will tell. And please, for your sake, don't try any games with me. I know exactly what to do with *your* sort.' Crunkhorn snarled. He turned with a glimmer of craziness in his eyes and whistled to one of his guards that Griffin could hear scuffling his way along the stone, dungeon-like corridor.

'Bring him over!' Crunkhorn ordered impatiently.

'I'm trying Sheriff,' replied the guard, 'this one's a particularly bad un Sir. It don't respond to any commands and well…it's bloody vicious Sir.'

'And that is exactly why he was chosen,' added the Sheriff.
Griffin gazed on through the discoloured metal bars and watched as a young Brickabrack guard (who's helmet was too big and subsequently kept sliding down over his face) struggled and tugged on a large and heavy looking chain that disappeared into the darkness.

It rattled left and right as he heaved and pulled. Griffin wondered if the other end was attached to a wall but before long the darkness gave way and a creature emerged. It was enormous. Its sunken head thudded along the curved stone ceiling of the dungeon. It was covered in matted green hair that resembled wet seaweed and instead of skin it had scales, shiny green scales.

Its arms were monstrous, each one jutting out wide at the shoulder, like tree trunks that dangled heavily.

The knuckles of each hand bumped and scraped along the cobbled floor.

The young and now rather insignificant-looking guard was pulling what looked like a living and rather ugly partition wall through the corridor.

'By the power of Merlin, he is a brute!' gasped Crunkhorn in admiration. 'What's his name then?'

'This one, erm, Polly Sir,' replied the guard.

*'Polly?* Yes well, probably the name of a warrior in some, very far off distant land eh Polly.' Crunkhorn backtracked to avoid having to use his pewter sceptre again.

'Right then Polly, now you listen. This Wizard, or Warlock of sorts is my prisoner, all mine, and I want you to guard him. Is that clear?' The bald Sheriff explained as if trying to train the local dunce. 'If he tries to escape I want you to eat him, do you understand?'

'Ugh yeth both,' the lumbering green wall replied. Its lisping tongue fanned the air while it scratched its flat head with one of its enormous, grubby hands.

'Eat me!' Griffin exclaimed. 'That's a little much isn't it? I mean, even if I did get past the bars I couldn't physically get past that thing anyway.'

Crunkhorn smiled wickedly as if he had just won a round of cards.

'And just *what* would you mean by that?' he boomed. 'Are you implying that Polly here is fat?' to which the beast turned its head (and attempted to turn its body but failed due to its size) and spied Griffin like a crow would a morsel of food.

The beast lowered itself towards Griffin and with lots of blunt, cracked teeth exposed, bellowed out the loudest of roars. The whole dungeon shook. The grimy chandelier looming over Griffin's head began to sway violently and Griffin was left drenched from head to toe in spit, gloop and slug-like seaweed.

'No. That is not what I meant at all Polly,' Griffin said, realising the game Sheriff Crunkhorn was playing. 'I was simply implying that your impressive size would scare even the largest of giants. Tell me Polly, how do you get your seaweed hair so slimy?' Griffin finished as he pulled another piece of it from his cheek while grimacing behind a forced smile.

As Griffin's compliments serenaded the swamp ogre's small warty ears his menacing expression changed to that of a toddler grinning contently.

'Just you make sure this prisoner remains in that cell Polly or you'll never see your precious swamp or your wretched family again,' the bemused Sheriff barked. Crunkhorn turned on his heel with military precision and stormed up the gloomy stairwell with the young guard skipping along behind him, trying to keep up.

Polly took hold of his chain and stared at it with hatred. He missed home, he missed the mud and moss-covered trees with their wide buttress roots. He missed his wife and the little ones.

'Why do you allow him to treat you like this Polly?' asked Griffin.

'It'th whath me to do if I want-th go home, I do mith it thow much,' the ogre sobbed.

'But surely a brute like you could break those chains,' Griffin added warmly. He couldn't help but sympathise upon seeing the pain and grief in the beast's eyes. Scary or not, Griffin knew exactly what it was like to be held captive and more to the point what it was like to truly miss home and all those whom you hold dear.

'It-th no good. They-th all magic-th. Every time I rip-th them apart they-th juth mendth again.'

'Well Polly my dear monstrosity, I think I may be able to help you there. I think old Crunkhorn's using an *Invictacorum* spell on those chains. So no wonder you couldn't break them. But don't worry, even without magic there is a way to free yourself of them...' Griffin took Polly's gigantic hands and pulled them closer to him, turning them over to inspect the chains. 'You see Polly, if you manage to find the weakest link and tickle it in just the right spot...' Clink. Polly's little warty ears wagged with joy as the chains fell loosely to the ground and his blunt-toothed smile spread across his simple face once more.

'Right Polly, we haven't much time,' Griffin said hurriedly, 'do you think you could get us through there?' he finished, pointing to the dungeon wall. Polly's smile spread wider.

'Oh and Polly,' Griffin added, 'if it helps, just imagine Crunk-horn is stood in front of it.'

\*

Cecil Blomquist, one of Brickabrack's more experienced night watchman pulled back the hood of his muddied cloak allowing the light drizzle to pitter-patter on his face. The moon hung, evil and yellow, in the dim night sky. Halfway down Upgate and halfway up his rickety ladder he lifted aloft his lantern-douser that comprised of a long wooden stick with a metal cup fastened upside down to one end. As the shiny cup neared the top of the lantern a loud rumble echoed towards him from the other side of the town. Moments later, something caught his eye. He stared long and hard, past the market place and the great well, looking down Cannon Street and then he noticed it – the lantern at the very end that swung off the prison walls had gone out.

'Hmm, that's odd.' He thought. 'Old Pete's already up his ladder and dousing his flames.'

Just as he was about to extinguish his own lantern he saw another one go out.

'Bless my soul, he is quick tonight – must be two for one on grog at the Tipsy Toad,' he garbled in his head.

Still up his rickety ladder the lantern-douser watched as another lantern was snuffed out, this time quicker than the last. A faint rumble echoed down the street towards him, bouncing off shop fronts and darting in and out of archways. The noise was getting louder. Phum! went another lantern, leaving only seventeen between him and this oddity that he had now decided probably wasn't old Pete in a hurry.

Phum! Phum! Phum! went another three, all the while the noise getting louder and Cannon Street getting darker. Quicker.

'Pete?' the watchman shouted. 'Hey there Old Pete? You there?'

Phum! Phum! Phum! Phum! Went another four of the lofty, crooked lanterns.

'Blimey! Never in all my days…' uttered the watchmen as he stuck to staring down Upgate, watching the lights disappearing.

He couldn't see a thing, which at a time like that was no good thing. When faced with uncertain danger it is always a comfort to have all of your senses about you. And to this the night watchmen had to agree. You see for him, the whiff of the gutters was as foul as ever. The noise, still in attendance, thundered towards him like a stampede of crawlies. And yet he made out no hint of a shape down the street, just shadow and mystery, rushing towards him.

The last of Cannon Street's lanterns went out. It had reached the marketplace.

The night watchman, still halfway up his rickety ladder, now began to panic.

'What do I do? What do I do?' he whimpered to himself. 'I'm not a Wizard!' he shouted at the noise hurrying towards him. 'Or a Warlock for that matter,' he added. 'In fact may I take this opportunity to say I don't really know that Blackmouth feller at all.' He paused. 'Ok, well we did go to school together but he went down the magical route and I stuck to lantern dousing. Pete? Are you there?' he repeated as he began to climb. One wobbly rung was followed by another and before long the petrified night watchman was clinging to the very top of the lantern.

For his own piece of mind, and with arms and legs wrapped around the large glass housing, he kicked his own ladder away. It fell hard, hitting its mark – that being a dark side alley which hid the ladder from sight. He had decided that whatever was dousing the lanterns, and rushing towards him, would not be able to reach him without a ladder. And so he waited. With the rumbling getting louder, the lanterns on Upgate now began to go out. The noise became deafening, like an obese giant charging towards him. The houses began to shake. Tiles cascaded down like rain as his lantern swayed back and forth. The night watchman, who was now clinging on for dear life with his eyes firmly shut, peeped one last time to try and see what was about to eat him. There was still no sign of the giant, only a few lanterns left alight.

Phum! Phum! Phum! It was upon him.

'Evening Cecil!' Griffin wailed as he flew past.

The night watchman's jaw fell open as he looked up to see a colossal creature as tall as a house run past with Blackmouth sat on its shoulders, wearing a blue and white stripy night gown and smiling like a mad man.

Griffin and Polly escape the dungeon

A few moments after, an almighty gust of wind whistled after the beast rocking the lantern. As Cecil swayed once more from side to side, the little candle inside the glass housing to which he was still clinging with white knuckles, flickered wildly and went out.

\*

'Everyone, this is Polly and he's a swamp ogre,' Griffin said after getting back to the temple in the old forest.

'Ah, evenings Polly,' came a voice from by the door.

'Orbuluth! Ith that you, you wittle wrathscal.'

'Been's a very long times since we see's you last,' Orbs squeaked with excitement. 'How's the swamp being these daysies?' And your wife, Bruce, is she as ugly as evers?'

'She geth uglier by the day Orbuluth. I thill wonder why she mawied me thumtimes,' Polly answered.

'Ah that's lovely Polly, I'm sorry to have to interrupt this little soiree of ugliness but after freeing you, escaping the dungeon and demolishing half the prison I do have, ooh, probably half the townspeople out searching for me with wands and staffs and pitch forks and various other blunt objects,' Griffin despaired.

'And nathy Crunkhorn man!' Polly added.

'Ah yes, Crunkhorn – he is going to be a problem.' Griffin agreed. 'Right, Orbs – you are part of this family now, correct?' Griffin retorted.

'Yes Blacky, I's never be having a proper family before,' Orbs replied gleefully.

'Well you have one now and we need your help,' Griffin insisted, feeling more and more nervous at the prospect of Crunkhorn and several regiments of Brickabrack's finest storming his quiet home, again.

'What's me to be doing Blacky?' Orbs queried.

'I need you to help me get to the bottom of this. I need you, my little green friend, to help me solve this confounded riddle. What's going on in the town and who or what is causing this chaos?'

\*

Lizzi and the children waved as Griffin and Polly fought their way through the dense thicket, into the old Cherryberry forest.

Orbs however, skulked in the opposite direction towards Brick-abrack. The same evil moon loitered in the sky, bathing the ground in a sinister shade of yellow.

The little green forest gnome scurried and skipped through the familiar undergrowth and over fallen tree stumps. For what seemed like quite a trek – for a creature of Orbs' size – he arrived at the dusty track that led into town. Although Orbs followed this for a short while he would not be entering the town in the conventional manner.

'Once the path runs parallel to the river, at its widest point, look for the pebbled bank,' Griffin had explained earlier. 'At that point swim across and look for a small grate that is little more than a drain. From there, a pinch of magic should grant you access, if you know what I mean. Oh, and you'll need this…' Griffin had given Orbs one of Lizzi's small, dainty mirrors, 'remember, you're not the only creature who has the power of invisibility on their side.'

Sure enough Orbs reached the pebbled bank. He gazed over to the far side, bewildered by the colossal walls that stretched tall into the night sky.

He waited patiently, spying several guards on night patrol. They paced up and down the great walls, spears firm and armour clinking almost rhythmically. When one more had past, Orbs ran down to the shoreline – the river didn't appear to be too deep although the current was very strong.

Orbs, in his haste and desire to remain unseen, plopped into the cold torrent and began a rather shameful doggy paddle. You see forest gnomes are incredibly clever and magical beings but are not well-famed for their swimming.

After some time, he reached the far bank. The rusty grate was coarse on his small hands. Its intricate design wouldn't allow him to squeeze through and, due to his impish size, there was no way he could physically shift it.

'A pinch of magic boss Blacky says to us. I don't think he's be underperstanding our magic,' he murmured to himself.

To make matters worse he noticed an old but very large lock on the grate. The small forest gnome took a step back and once more gazed up at the wall in front of him.

'Okay Orbs, it is time,' he said tucking his soggy white beard into his soggier little trousers.

He put his hand into a small satchel and produced two gleaming balls of light. One was golden yellow with what looked like swirling fire trickling over its surface. The other had a more sinister appearance. It was midnight purple and had small spikes of darkness protruding from its surface, like teeth and claws.

He opened his palm at which point the two orbs began to float and rotate around one another. The light they were emitting seemed to intensify and flare more brightly.

Orbs himself began to rise from the ground and was soon hovering above the river with both orbs swirling above his little lemon-shaped head. He held his hand out. His short, dumpy fingers were spread wide. He opened his buck-toothed little mouth and grunted.

*'Flesruoy kcolnu esaelp os ni tnaw I'* his voice was an unnaturally low shuddering rumble that sent a tremor around the whole town.

The whole place fell silent. Orbs, still dangling in mid air over the fast-flowing river looked up into the sky and waited, as the orbs, which were now a swirling vortex of gold and purple, began to slow. As they ground to a halt above him the golden orb sat above the purple one. Orbs smiled and once more focussed his gaze to the grate and the lock.

With a sudden rush of power, like a gale-force wind, the golden orb pulsed energy and the vast wall in front of Orbs split and creaked and crumbled. The gigantic stones began to slide out of place, flying past Orbs, twirling and skipping as they went.

'AAAAARRRGH! AAAAARRRGH! Help me!' shrieked a guard as he whizzed past Orbs, clinging onto a giant block of stone that he had not a few moments earlier been patrolling.

'Oops,' Orbs chuckled. He spun around and watched as the whole South Eastern wall began rebuilding itself, brick-for-brick on the other side of the river. Even the lanterns, arched windows and wooden struts scurried around in the air trying to find their place.

After the dust settled back in place and the cobwebs had re-spun themselves, half a glorious wall stood proud on the other side of the river. It looked like the last piece of a giant jigsaw puzzle, waiting to be pushed into place.

Despite it being just past midnight, a crowd of confused and flabbergasted faces began to appear, marvelling at the spectacle through the newly formed, and quite tidy, hole in the wall. The two balls of light floated down to Orbs' palm and rested neatly side by side like a couple of well trained pets. He smiled and placed them lovingly back into his satchel.

Splash! Orbs gasped as he resurfaced. He was once again in the river. After another frantic and nearly pointless swimming session he was now back on the bank where the grate with the old lock had been.

As more and more faces appeared, with mixed expressions of fear and wonderment spread across them, Orbs decided the last thing they would want to see now was a little green man peering back at them. Like the flame of a freshly blown out candle, Orbs disappeared. He pushed past the onlookers, completely invisible. He skipped away, leaving the crowd behind him, who were already all too eagerly muttering about Blackmouth and Warlocks and curses.

The little forest gnome ambled down a thin road. The cramped houses leering over him, he felt, would topple at any moment. Before long he came to a junction. A signpost, ugly and tatty, posed him with three options. He could go left, past the Imperial Guards quarters that led to Cannon Street. He could go right which would take him along Broadbank past the bakers onto Eastgate or he could go straight over and into the aptly named *Archway to Nowhere.*

'We's not liking cannons Orbs do we, means big noises to us eh. And nowhere archwaysies are normally being dull. Hmm, we's go East, yes Eastgatesies is being the ways for us.'

He trotted rather carefully past the bakers that neighboured the candlestick emporium and opposite poor Mr Proofgrease's butchers.

Feeling somewhat confident due to being invisible Orbs rushed straight over Eastgate and was now on Rotten Row. The air was rank and a putrid mist clung to the gutters like mud on a stick. In an instant Orbs felt unnerved. This was a world away from his comfy, mushroom covered hollow. A chilly silence settled to which even the invisible gnome was afraid to break.

He sneaked here and there, tip-toeing slowly to avoid making a sound. He crossed over the cobbled road aiming to venture down Bridge Street past the side of the Rat Catchers. As he did so something stirred in the darkness behind him. He froze before remembering that he was both very small and very much invisible.

He quickly jumped forward and pressed himself flat against the side wall of the Rat Catchers shop.

'S'probably a cat we thinks,' he whispered to himself.

Still pressed firmly to the wall he edged left, back towards Rotten Row. He could now see the Cat Catchers shop on the opposite side of the grotty street. A sudden heavy breathing meandered towards him; it was coming from further down the road. The little forest gnome gripped the wall tightly and in an effort to get a better look, poked his rounded invisible head out into the open.

Much to his surprise the street was empty and yet the breathing went on. Then he remembered the mirror. He reached into his small satchel and pulled Lizzi's dainty mirror out. With a fearful hesitance the little forest gnome angled the looking glass so he could see along the road but remain hidden himself.

What Orbs saw next made tiny invisible goose-pimples flutter all over his body. In place of a mangy moggy as he had expected to see stood a tall creature, cloaked in black. It was hunched, bending down, slipping something under a door to one of the houses. It breathed heavy and cackled insanely. Orbs watched, not quite understanding the creature's intentions, as it went to another door and again, appeared to push something underneath it.

Then another door. Then another.

It continued down the rest of Rotten Row all the while relishing its evil deed until it disappeared out of sight. Swallowed by the rank mist that hung, thick and heavy in the cool night air.

# CHAPTER EIGHT

# Which Witch is Which?

Griffin had decided that while Orbs was running his little errand in the town the best thing for both himself and Polly to do was to simply hide. He made no excuses – 'That pewter sceptre of Crunkhorn's gives me the judders'. And so they were to spend the night in the old forest.

After a small supper of giant crispy batwings and fizzy mushrooms that Griffin had cooked in one of Lizzi's self-bubbling hot pots, the disgraced Wizard and the short-tongued swamp ogre sought refuge high in one of the older Cherryberry trees.

Thankfully Polly's well adapted claws helped with the climb as Griffin once again sat aloft the beast. After a long climb, the two nestled in for the night and began to story tell and reminisce from various excerpts of each other's lives.

'Bruce, oh yeth, as soon ath I thaw her wallowing in the thwamp I knew she was the ogre for me. I err, propothed to her there and then,' said Polly.

'How did you do it eh, you devil, down on one knee, eh?' Griffin quizzed intriguingly. For all his teachings at school about ogres he had never really spent a long period of time with one. In meeting Polly he had come to realise that for all the bad tales of ogres he was used to hearing, Polly's affectionate nature and respectful demeanour undid years of stereotyping.

'No, I clubbed her a big juithy fith, biggesth one I could find, and then I chewed ith head off and squeezed out ith guts and prethented her with it,' Polly answered.

'And she went for that then did she?'

'She wath so imprethed she clubbed me over the head and dwagged me to her cave – the west ith hithtory,' the simple ogre grinned.

'Ah Polly you are a character. For years I've studied, trying to fully understand and appreciate this world and all the wealth of knowledge it has to offer and yet here I sit – up a massive tree, hiding, talking to a swamp ogre who is teaching me new things. Things I didn't know. You remind me of my youngest, Pereé. She is so small, and yet incredibly gifted and she doesn't even know it yet.'

Griffin gazed up through the trees and over to the orange ambient light that flared brightly into the night sky from the town's enormous street lanterns.

'Speaking of small, I wonder how our little green friend is doing.' He turned to Polly who was wedged tightly between two giant branches, eyes shut tightly, dribbling. 'Rest easy my friend, for tomorrow we face the truth.'

Griffin opened his eyes after what seemed to have been a comfortable sleep. The forest floor beneath him was stirring with activity as all manner of ground-dwelling creatures skipped and meandered through the trees below.

Polly too, had woken but for different reasons – a large scowler pheasant was trying to build a nest on his head.

'Geth off thtupid bird!' he moaned.

'Polly the time has come, we must be off,' Griffin insisted.

A long climb down and a short walk later the duo arrived back at the temple. As they reached the grand door Griffin glanced over towards the town to see a red sun rising.

'Something terrible has happened this night Polly my friend,' Griffin mused, a look of sadness cast over his face that even Polly couldn't miss.

They pushed the door ajar and stepped inside the lavishly deco-rated entrance hall to the sound of pots and pans clanging and bashing through in the kitchen. The Wizard and the ogre rushed through with panic but couldn't help but grin and chuckle at the scene unfolding before them.

The cupboards were throwing things out left, right and centre. One cupboard door opened by the sink and a rather dirty bar of soap was spat out. Then another near the stove hauled a large bag of kindling out plus potatoes, one grey sock with a hole in it and some bottles of pickled newt livers.

'Okay! Okay!' Lizzi wailed, throwing her hands high into the air with frustration.

'Cupboards, when I said "throw me everything" I meant everything I can cook and then eat. I can't very well throw old socks and soap into a stew can I?' she explained.

'Why'th not?' Polly grilled with a slightly disconcerted expression about his green scaly head.

'Trust me Polly, even your rough tongue would squirm,' Lizzi added. 'Soap indeed – cooking a good stew is a delicate process, much like making a perfect potion, eh Griffin, although there was that incident with the dragon poodle. Tell me Polly, have you ever seen a bright pink woolly dragon?'

'Ugh, no.'

'Yes, most unfortunate. Anyway, suffice to say you just need the right ingredients in the correct proportions,' she finished as she added another dash of blue Firebolt salt to the bubbling broth.

All the cupboard doors started banging in protest.

'Yes, yes my dears, I know I wasn't very specific but…'

BANG! A tatty-looking cupboard door by the sink made itself heard.

'Well that's not very polite.'

BANG! The cupboard door slammed again, joined in by another.

'You are doing a fine job but please, just edible ingredients for now,' Lizzi pleaded.

Another loud bang came but this time it wasn't from the kitchen cupboards – the noise was coming from the front door.

Griffin, Lizzi and Polly stood silently, listening. Even the misbehaving cupboards had stopped their ranting.

BANG! BANG! The front door rattled under somebody's fist.

The three edged forward slowly, creeping across the void between the kitchen and the entrance.

'Who's there?' Griffin apprehensively questioned.

'I have an important message for a Mr Blackmouth, is he present?' came a strange voice from the outside.

'It's Black!' Griffin spat as he hauled back the door. In front of him stood an imposing but magnificent creature. Half man, half bird, with dazzling multicoloured feathers and plumage that swathed his entire body. Crests of vivid blue and gold crowned his elegant head.

'By the powers of the elders, you're a…a…'

'A thunderclapper Mr Black, a guardian of the sky, what of it?' replied the feathered creature.

'But no one has seen any of your kind since the great battle. I thought your kind were extinct.'

'Not extinct Mr Black, just out of sight. My name is Kestrell and I am a courier, well…more a slave to the new Sheriff.'

He extended one of his beautiful wings to reveal a satchel strapped to the underside. From this he pulled out a large scroll with brass tips and black parchment.

'Blackmail?' Griffin wailed.

'I'm afraid so Mr Black,' said the birdman who, with his feathery fingers broke the blood-red wax seal and began to read. 'Ahem, Griffin Black you are hereby accused of the following crimes:

> *Setting free a vicious captive by the name of Polly;*
> *Corrupting said captive and destroying the west wall of Brickabrack Prison;*
> *Relocating a large section of Brickabrack's defensive wall across a river – without a permit;*
> *Scaring a candle-douser half to death (and might I add Mr Black that he is actually still clinging to his lantern);*
> *AND, killing three citizens of Brickabrack.'*

'Hold on! I did none of those things! Well…yes, I did set Polly free and we did destroy the prison wall. Frightening poor Mr Blomquist was regrettable – such a pleasant man. I definitely didn't move a wall across a river…although I…I may have had a hand in that. But I certainly didn't kill anyone.'

'You are requested,' the creature went on, 'to visit the Sheriff's quarters in the Town of Brickabrack no later than midday.'

'And if I were to refuse?' Griffin remonstrated.

'The scroll will destroy your house, and your family will slowly perish from the illness known as Jittery-boils.'

'Jittery-boils! Curse all wretched Blackmail!' Griffin griped. 'And what makes matters worse is that my dear great-great-grand-mother Prudknott Black invented it.'

'Why would someone invent such a horror?' Lizzi questioned.

'Well let's just say my great-great-grandfather Lovias was exceptionally handsome and he had many female friends. And so one day, when her envy had amassed to the point of no return, great-great-grandmother Prudknott presented him with a black scroll with brass tips and a crimson wax seal. It insisted that he never see any of those ladies ever again or his good looks and charm would diminish leaving him deformed and dim-witted.'

'So what happened darling, was he grotesque?' Lizzi presumed.

'No, quite the opposite in fact. He never saw his friends again and until his dying day his life was a tale of loneliness and misery. A strong Wizard held at the mercy of his wife. The one person that was meant to care and love him the most.'

'That's awful,' Lizzi said.

'Indeed,' Griffin said solemnly. 'Stand aside my feathered friend I have business in the town to attend to.'

\*

'Ah, Mr Black! So glad you could make it,' said Crunkhorn with his back to Griffin as he gazed out of an impressive arched window. His keen eyes meticulously scanned the streets below taking in everything all at once: the shops, the stalls selling anything and everything you could ever wish for, market traders whistling and chanting their sales patter at passersby.

'You know full well I had no choice but to come,' Griffin said furiously, 'and was the Blackmail scroll really necessary?' he added. 'A simple friendly invitation would have sufficed.'

'Ah yes, a stroke of genius in my mind,' Crunkhorn said arrogantly as the corners of his normally stiff upper lip twitched towards becoming a smile. 'But I'm afraid Mr Black that it was absolutely necessary. You see, if you had merely pinched a potato from Madam Thumbclunk's market stall, a pretty embossed invitation with frilly ribbons and shiny hearts would have been hand-delivered to your residence with a full regalia of silver trumpets and colourful dancers,' he enthused pedantically while turning to face Griffin. 'Unfortunately for you Mr Black your desires are not of ill-gotten vegetables – you simply murder people,' the Sheriff finished.

Griffin stood silently with a vacant expression cast over his face much like he had in the Council Chamber some months back while being interrogated by the very ginger Councillor Fidrib.

'I haven't killed anyone!' Griffin boomed in protest.

'And where might I ask were you last night?' asked Crunkhorn, continuing his inquisition.

'In the old forest. I spent the night up a tree, squashed among the branches with Polly.'

'The swamp ogre?' Crunkhorn said rather confoundedly. 'Come Mr Black, do you really expect me to believe that Polly, the witless, bumbling swamp beast not only managed to successfully haul his lumbering mass to the top of a tree but at the same time, and somewhat more incredibly, befriend you – a mere morsel in his eyes?' The Sheriff leered forward, looking Griffin up and down with suspicion and doubt. 'Why would you even spend the night in the old forest?' he continued.

'Because if you hadn't forgotten, both Polly and I had just demolished half your prison and fled the town's limits without so much as a peep from your guards,' Griffin said sharply, while offering the Sheriff a smug smile that wrinkled his eyes.

'ENOUGH!' Crunkhorn thundered. 'I put it to you Mr Black that you are both a liar and a murderer and I will prove your guilt.'

'Prove away Sheriff, prove away. I have nothing to hide,' Griffin said gleefully, rubbing his hands together.

For a moment there was a somewhat haunting silence in the Sheriff's office and Griffin watched as the normally rosy-cheeked Sheriff turned a paler shade of puce. For Crunkhorn had not expected Griffin's compliance at all. In fact his heavily-jewelled sceptre was tucked neatly in his belt, ready.

\*

Nearly five hours had passed since Griffin had entered Sheriff Crunkhorn's quarters. The highly illegal truth serum was finally wearing off and Griffin's slurred speech was now returning to normal. Though truth orbs have the same effect it is the person's story or account to tell and all an audience may do is listen.

With a potent truth serum the audience may ask questions and for this reason it is illegal within the magical community.

'Mr Black, Mr Black are you with us?' asked the Sheriff.

'Yes, I'm here Sir, right here, in Sheriff Crunkhorn's office. Sat on a well-worn chair, not the type of chair I'd buy or own – it's not really to my taste you see, and hard, huh! – well, let's just say between you, me and the gatepost a cushion wouldn't go amiss. My rear is numb, yes, an odd sensation – feels quite like I've sat in a large patch of numbing nettles and…'

'Yes, thank you for that Mr Black,' Sheriff Crunkhorn interrupted. 'So, following our little chat I'm now assured that you aren't the murderer we are hunting and I thank you for your willingness to cooperate with my investigation, although I really didn't need to know about Polly's flatulence following the fizzy mushrooms.'

'Ooo! Did you know that fizzy mushrooms…'

'Mr Black, another hour of fizzy mushroom facts and I'll go mad. We have a killer on the loose. A killer that I intend to catch!'

Griffin's eyes uncrossed and slowly focussed on the shine coming from the Sheriff's bald head.

'I have one final question Mr Black,' Crunkhorn asked, his face a bewilderment of odd expressions, frowns and deep thoughts.

'Go on,' Griffin encouraged.

'If you were in the old forest last night, eating fizzy mushrooms and climbing up trees with Polly, who destroyed half the Eastern Wall and rebuilt it on the other bank of the river?' the Sheriff finished.

Griffin smiled, almost thankful that the Sheriff had finally asked a sensible question rather than the verbal finger-pointing he had just spent the last five hours having to endure.

'Time to come out Orbulous,' Griffin said, standing up to stretch his legs and relieve his aching bottom from the hard, unfashionable, cushionless chair.

'Orbulous?' said Crunkhorn quizzically. 'Who's Orbulous?'

The Sheriff gazed on in sheer amazement as a small green creature flickered from thin air into a solid form in the space between
himself and Griffin.

'What is this…this witchcraft?' Sheriff Crunkhorn insisted, his
tone changing in an instant. 'Not up to your usual tricks again are
we Mr Black?' he said firmly, his sparkly sceptre outstretched in
front of him.

'No, no, fear not, this is Orbulous Sheriff, Orbulous Gnomei-
I,' said Griffin speedily, stepping forward so as to protect his little
green friend. 'He's a forest gnome, a tree-dweller from the elder
days,' Griffin boasted in admiration.

'Yes, I know of his kind,' the Sheriff said sternly, 'not to be
trusted according to the dusty scrolls.'

'Why ever not?' asked Griffin.

He stepped forward and placed a gentle hand on the forest
gnome's shoulder.

'*Why ever not?* I take it you don't do much reading Mr Black.'

'Quite the contrary actually Sheriff – I have several books on
the go at home at the moment, all of them are floating quite nicely
now.'

'Then perhaps I might recommend an afternoon pouring
through the dusty archives in the City of Tilös. You see, story
tells of these tree folk. First they befriend you, acting all innocent,
luring you in with their pretence and false displays of affection.
Next they conjure up ill-conceived sob stories to win your heart
– like pretending that they are the last of their kind and that they
are all alone.'

Griffin gazed deeply into the Sheriff's eyes which were serious
and did not move nor falter. He took his gently-placed hand from
Orb's shoulder and stepped away from the little green creature as
a sudden wave of anxiety barrelled over him.

'Then, when they have you right where they want you…'
Crunkhorn stopped and swallowed hard, all the while starring at
Orbs with a hatred like Griffin had not seen before.

'What?' Griffin pleaded. 'What do they do?'

'Just mark my words Mr Black, you let this creature into your
life or near your family and you will regret it forever.'

'B-But he's living with us!' stuttered Griffin as the wave of anxiety now turned to panic and his pale face drained to bright white, like bleached bone.

He turned to address Orbs but the forest gnome had once again disappeared.

'Orbs?' he asked into the blank space before him. 'Orbulous you come out right now and explain yourself!' ordered Griffin, much like a father would to a naughty child.

'Why Blacky?' Orbs muttered solemnly. 'It's clearsies that you's not be trusting Orbulous anymore.'

'No Orbs, that's not true. We just need to talk to you about all this, that's all,' Griffin said softly, trying to entice the forest gnome back into solid form.

'The only onesie who's be trusting me now is Pereé, she's my only friendsy now,' Orbs finished.

'No Orbs, I'm your friend, please show yourself and we'll talk.'

Silence filled the office. Griffin turned to Sheriff Crunkhorn who had his dazzling pewter sceptre stretched at arm's length, waving it around like a feather duster.

'Any suggestions?' Griffin whispered to the Sheriff who was now dancing around his office, frantically jabbing his sceptre left and right and up and down as if he were trying to pop invisible bubbles.

'We need to recap what we know Mr Black,' said Crunkhorn authoritatively.

'Recap what we know! – Is now really the time? You have just told me my wife and children may be in danger,' Griffin protested wildly.

'I find it clears the mind and hones the senses Mr Black,' the Sheriff explained. 'It's an old technique that the thunderclappers would use prior to battle. They would revisit what they knew about their enemy to ensure that they were best prepared for all eventualities.'

'Okay,' Griffin gasped. 'Recap,' he added as he began to pant. 'What we have learnt, following my trial, suggests we are hunting a Witch.'

'Agreed,' said Crunkhorn.

'And yet still you were convinced that all the evil deeds were my doing – you thought I was your Witch.'

'Yes but I stand corrected Mr Black, for the truth serum I used was the most potent I have come across so I know that you are not the Witch.'

'And now you tell me you believe Orbs is not to be trusted.'

'It is not a question of belief Mr Black – belief suggests an opinion without the need for rigorous proof. I *know* that these forest folk cannot be trusted. I know.'

'So, now you believe that Orbs is your Witch.'

'Hard to tell – having studied these creatures in detail myself, there are no accounts of them being able to alter their appearance but that is not to say the little blighter hasn't unlocked a new-found power. For they are extremely powerful, in fact their powers have not yet been measured for they are so elusive not to mention secretive that no one has ever had the opportunity to get close enough to…well…test them.'

'It's odd,' Griffin pondered, 'that I hadn't even heard of them until I first met Orbulous.'

'There are few of us who have,' replied the Sheriff.

'You've met one of these creatures before?' Griffin asked with an obvious level of intrigue.

'Yes, a long time ago deep within the ancient forests of the West.'

'Well, do tell Sheriff, what happened?'

'I do not speak of it, not anymore,' the Sheriff snapped.

'Why ever not?' Griffin naively questioned.

'I will not!' Sheriff Crunkhorn thundered. 'Like I said Mr Black, you let this creature near your family and…and…'

The Sheriff turned from Griffin to face the beautiful stone archway once more, unable to finish his sentence and for a moment Griffin could've sworn he heard the Sheriff whimpering.

'Sheriff?' Griffin said softly. 'Sheriff are you alright?'

'I had a son once,' he said gruffly with his back still turned. 'Yes, a son. He was strong and brave, kind and respectful. A far greater man than I.'

'What happened to him?' Griffin asked delicately, at which the

Sheriff's bottom lip wobbled.

'He was my finest Captain,' the Sheriff smiled with pride. 'In a city far from here I was tasked with hunting down an invisible murderer. The pursuit cost me many men. After a number of days and countless deaths we tracked the one responsible to an ancient forest – forest so dense and dark we could not tell when it was day-time or night. We were lost and things stirred there as have never been seen before or will ever be seen again.'

'Then what?' Griffin hastened, dying to know the end of the tale.

'My whole regiment was killed, all of them, all at once, all crushed.'

'And what of your son?' Griffin said, his eyes now wide with fear for the safety of his own family.

'It took him,' sobbed the Sheriff. 'Dragged him into the dark-ness, and as my son disappeared from me all I remember seeing was a purple orb drifting off into the distance.'

Griffin's mouth gaped open upon hearing this and it would've probably remained this way had it not been for the dribble that trickled down his chin and onto his robes.

'My family!' he said finally. 'I need to get to them, I need to make sure they're alright.'

'Mr Black I'm afraid your family can wait,' Crunkhorn said.

'What? I have to get to them. They are in danger and…'

'Mr Black! Calm yourself man!' the Sheriff insisted. 'The fact remains that this Orbulous, as you call him, has been dwelling with you for some time now and so I can only assume that his evil little eyes are fixed on other things, and other people for that matter. He has had ample time to slaughter both you and your family should he have wished to.'

The Sheriff had a point and Griffin felt that arguing was not the best way forward, not to mention the fact that it would waste more valuable time.

'What's your plan then Sheriff?' asked Griffin.

'We have a killer on the loose Mr Black. Three people have already died and I will be pickled like a prune before I let there be a fourth. We must stop this criminal now.'

'And how, might I ask, do you propose we do that?'

'We have our methods,' replied Crunkhorn boldly.

'Who were they Sheriff? The ones who died in the night?'

'Last night…well, there was Tofias Sniffin…'

'The Floral Wizard?' Griffin quizzed.

'Yes, and joint owner of 'Sniffin-n-Hard' the best florist this side of Tilös in my mind. Second was Drimbob Thornsnackle, our local goblin taxidermist who was found looking not too dissimilar to one of his stuffed goblins. And saddest of all was young Jered Proofgrease, the bacon grinder's son who was tucked into bed last night by his grief-stricken father.' The Sheriff stopped for a moment, closing his eyes to remember his own son's demise. He reopened them to look hard at Griffin. 'He did not make the night.'

# CHAPTER NINE

# The Tale of the Fallow Deer

Werewolves didn't always exist. In a bygone age, in the old Langrick marshlands, a Wizard by the name of Grimhole was delving in a magical bog that was said to make you live forever. He was obsessed with the notion and craved the prize of eternal life. After some hours he dug up some very queer-looking bones. He hurried them back to his home under cover of nightfall and, once in the kitchen, scrubbed them to see what he had found. It was not long before the Wizard was faced with a horror beyond comprehension. For the skeleton was similar to that of a person but the skull was that of a hound.

Following the initial shock the Wizard poured a glugger of something strong and pondered. After several long minutes he decided it must be a hoax and that the faery folk of the hills in the east must have been up to no good again and left the bones to put the jitters up the locals of the surrounding hamlets.

As he arranged the bones on the floor and supped the dregs of his grog something began to scratch and fumble at the latch of the kitchen door that led to a path outside.

As powerful a Wizard as he was this scared him immensely and so he carefully edged towards the window to see what was trying to get in. As he squinted through the grimy leaded glass pane there in the glow of the moonlight he caught a glimpse of a creature all black and crooked. At first he thought it may be an old beggar because of its hunched state but then it rushed forward and a hideous face appeared at the window – the face of something that Grimhole decided was not natural to the world and must have escaped from a much darker place. He ran to the door and bolted it as the snarling and clawing continued. It was only as dawn arrived that the creature left.

Grimhole wasted no time in gathering the bones back up and taking them back to the magical bog.

At first no one believed the Wizard's tales of the creature but with each passing year more and more sightings confirmed their worst fears and, as a result, the nearest hamlet to the magical bog was renamed Dogdyke. News travelled far and wide about the curse of Dogdyke and the werewolves that crept there.

Their numbers grew and before long they had entered the borders of the Cherryberry forest, biting and gnawing as they went. None stood in their way. That is of course, until they slaughtered the King of the deer. His grief-stricken son, the young deer Prince mustered an army of birds and beasts greater than any in the history of the world. The deer Prince eventually drove them back to the bog where it is said most of the werewolves returned to their graves. Decades passed with no evil daring to challenge the deer Prince's mighty army. He had restored peace to the forest and his name was Cervitor.

\*

As the sun set on another day and the last remaining warmth trickled through the trees of the old forest, Cervitor, King of the deer stood high upon his rocky throne.

His stance, tall and proud, was a mere facade to save his followers from discovering the ever-growing worry that wormed inside him.

For some time now Cervitor had noticed the numbers of his herd declining and yet there were no reports of any new huntsmen leering through the forest. However, possibly of greater concern was the odd behaviour of some of his kin who would return from a day of heavy grazing seeming possessed and not entirely themselves.

It was as this thought lay heavy on his mind and the evening sky grew more crimson he heard it. The most beautiful sound, like a thousand songbirds all harmonising together but manifested in one voice. Oh how it tantalised his senses. He closed his eyes and floated off to a distant place; a place far more serene and tranquil. The fur shuddered tall along his spine with excitement as the sound wrapped itself around his entire being like warm silk caressing him gently.

He opened his eyes again with the deepest curiosity. As much as he desired to just stand and relish each moment of being drenched in such beautiful tones, his curiosity outweighed all other thoughts and before long he was seeking to discover the source of the melody.

Some miles from Cervitor's throne evil deeds were taking place.

A mysterious cauldron bubbled and hissed its own tune. A rank odour withered flowers and trees alike while claw-like hands rummaged for more ingredients to throw in the pot.

There was a loud crack and the Witch span around, her eyes burning green with fury. Her face was hideous; wrinkles, warts and decay was all she had to offer.

'Ah a doe – well aren't you a pretty one then,' she squawked as the elegant Queen of the deer paced forward in a trance-like fashion. 'And what brings you to my humble forest clearing m'dear hmm?' the Witch asked, while already knowing the answer.

The Queen giddily bucked and stomped the dry earth.

'Oh, I see, you want t'dance then do yer. Tell me dear, did you like my little song earlier?' The Queen replied with another stomp of her hoof. 'Well, I'll let you into a little secret, you know, between us girls,' she said, gazing around as if others were likely to hear. 'It wasn't actually me, oh no. You see someone very dear to my heart gave me this some years back.' The Witch then pulled a wooden flute from her long, draping sleeves. It was elegant, polished like glass and had an ancient scripture carved into its surface.

'The scripture tells of a world like no other, an underwater world where music and songs are so beautiful it is said they could kill a person. The underwater realm of the sirens. Stunning creatures but deadly just as sure, like me!' the Witch cackled wildly. 'I'm only joking my dear, I'm not deadly. Anywho, it is said that this magical flute contains the voice of a siren and that is exactly why you are here m'dear, you see. I summoned you with it!' the Witch admitted honestly.

The Queen stood ever still like stone – entranced, enthralled and ever hopeful to drown in the beautiful tune once more.

'Don't feel sad m'dear, you see, there are very few who can resist it.' The cauldron suddenly puffed and wheezed. 'Ah, I think the next batch is ready.' The fiery-eyed hag mumbled as she hurried over to the bubbling pot. Pulling back her sleeve revealing frail skin like tracing paper, the Witch quickly, and without hesitation, dipped her arm into the pot up to her boney elbow without so much as a yelp.

'I don't feel much these days m'dear,' she explained to the Queen who was looking rather shocked. 'Ah, here we go. Here's a nice one.' The Witch drew her withered arm from the boiling broth and stepped towards the Queen. Slime lazily dripped from her pale mottled forearm.

'Trust me, these are best served hot,' she enthused, her arm now outstretched in front of the Queen's nose.

The once pungent smell seemed to disappear and was replaced by a sweet, pure smell like honey.

As each long claw of the Witch's hand cracked open the Queen watched in amazement as the most sumptuous and beautiful flower parcel lay neatly in the old crone's palm. It was golden-yellow, a delicacy for sure, smelling of warmth and sweetness. A striking rare flower, its petals folded delicately and were pinned immaculately with whipplesnap sugar roots.

The Queen had never seen anything more captivating and offered a fleeting look to the old hag in admiration.

'Go on m'dear. Have a taste,' the Witch smiled, 'you are Queen after all.'

A moment later the parcel was gone.

*

Cervitor glanced up as the first twinkle of the inky night sky caught his eye. He had been charging through the forest for hours, headed solely in the direction of the beautiful sound. That was his focus, it was the only thing he cared for, even with his great knowledge of the dangers that lie in the forest after sundown.

Without warning, a horrendous cackle screeched from the forest floor up leaving Cervitor instantly frozen to the spot. Tentatively he edged forward, every now and then checking behind him for signs of danger. It was at this point the King realised that in all his years of living in the old forest he had never been to this part before. The trees smelt damp with age as if rotting from the roots up. The vines, like huge ropes, draped down from the massive Cherryberries like he had never seen before, and all of them looking grey, brittle and dead.

As the King queried his surroundings the beautiful sound returned. His knees trembled with joy and the warm silk wrapped itself around him once more.

'So, you're the one they call Cervitor. Well aren't you a handsome stag then,' the Witch squeaked with excitement as the proud King ambled into the clearing. The soft moonlight picked out his crown of antlers which now appeared as if they were made of pure silver.

'The tales of you are legendary,' the Witch began. 'They say you fended off thousands of werewolves before your army even had to move. And I can see why m'dear, you truly are the purest creature I have ever seen.'

The King's expression did not falter. He was still transfixed by the beautiful sound. He had not even considered the whereabouts of his Queen.

The Witch smirked, knowing that she had him.

'It's an odd coincidence,' she began, 'as I had dinner with your Queen earlier. No need to worry though Cervitor, I've been watching over her, see, she's over there, sleeping,' beamed the Witch.

Cervitor scanned the clearing and sure enough there was his Queen, lying down peacefully, dreaming on a bed of soft moss and flower petals. His gaze returned to the Witch with the burning green eyes who presented a clenched fist before his nose that dripped and oozed. She cackled uncontrollably like an insolent child before saying delicately:

'Tell me Cervitor, are you hungry?'

# CHAPTER TEN

# Master Blundell

Pipers practiced, fiddlers fiddled and all manner of preparations were taking place throughout Brickabrack. Flags were hoisted high and buildings were magically decorated with all the colours of one of Merlin's rainbows.

The Council elders mingled quite happily with the hustle and bustle of the townsfolk. Master Agar joked and laughed with several burly men who were fastening pretty coloured ribbons across the normally dank streets. Reds, greens, blues, oranges and purples zigzagged back and forth from house to house until a multicoloured web loomed above the cobbles.

All the elders seemed to be enjoying themselves. That is of course with the exception of Fonzo Fidrib. He felt uneasy as he aided a hobgoblin roll a keg of the Tipsy Toad's finest grog down Westgate towards the marketplace. This was mainly due to him not being overly familiar with manual labour.

'We have wands and staffs for this sort of thing!' he grunted to the hobgoblin.

'Sometimes it is wise to remind our limbs what they are here for,' she replied.

'You're a female!' the inconsiderate elder bellowed. 'I thought you were a male!' he spluttered with embarrassment, after realising he had been letting her do all of the work.

'What gave you that idea?' she questioned. 'Is it because I'm not in a dress?'

'Quite!' he replied, without so much as a glimmer of remorse or compassion. 'In fact, I think it's the beard. Yes – most confusing!'

'You are indeed wise Councillor Fidrib,' the hobgoblin wife began, 'and yet I fear your mind is somewhat lacking.'

'How so, you repulsive creature?' the ginger elder spat.

'Well, it is undeniable that when it comes to magic you are regarded among the greats and yet you have no knowledge nor desire to learn of non-magical beings or their ways.'

'And tell me beast, what am I to gain from learning such things?'

'Well there's compassion, and respect. What about laughter or even love?'

'B'ah love! And what would you know of love creature? What in all this great land could possibly love you?' said Councillor Fidrib sharply while sneering.

'Why my family of course. My husband and my little hoblings,' she finished anxiously – she could tell that the elder was growing more foul-tempered with each sentence.

'Poppycock!' Councillor Fidrib yelled. 'Love is a fool's errand. Magic is the true path to enlightenment and those who do not accept this will simply pale into insignificance.'

'And while I respectfully acknowledge your opinion you show no willingness to accept mine,' the bearded hobgoblin wife said hotly.

The elder stopped pretending to push the barrel and stood up straight to address the impertinent creature that dared to backchat him.

'And just what would that be creature – eh? What opinion of yours could possibly contest the power of magic?' the withered Councillor proclaimed loudly as if suddenly in an argument so those around him could hear. A crowd soon materialized, much to the delight of the Councillor. He quickly drew his staff from beneath his rusty-coloured robes and aimed it straight at the barrel.

His eyes widened before turning from old grey to electric blue.

*'Morphidius Avemaquila!'* the ginger Wizard thundered. His voice rumbled through him into the ground leaving a few of the less well built houses swaying.

The barrel rose from the street. It groaned and creaked, and the rivets popped and twanged off in all different directions. The wood began to twist and contort as grog spewed down towards the crowd below; some squealed and yelped while running away, others cheered, pushing forward with their mouths wide. Although not one of them would get a sip, nor would any get wet as the grog too stopped mid-air, floating like a shiny blanket filled with froth and bubbles.

As the crowd watched on, two spindly legs sprouted from the bottom of the barrel, the wood continued to twist, forming two wings, then a beak, then a tail and finally a head. Next the most beautiful feathers ruffled and pinged from all the cracks in the wood. Within moments a shimmering bird as no one had ever seen before began squawking and circling overhead.

The Councillor hoisted his staff high into the air to which the bird began an almighty shrill of further squawks. Every twist and turn of his staff the bird would mimic. Round and round went Councillor Fidrib's staff as the bird circled overhead squawking furiously.

'Rostrolata!' the ginger elder screamed as he thrust his staff directly at the hobgoblin.

Fear now spread across her gargoyle-like face. The bird barrelled mid-air and then plummeted down towards the crowd below.

'What are you doing?' screamed the hobgoblin as she turned to run, panic-stricken, back down Westgate towards Griffin's old house and Council Chamber two.

'Why, trying to enlighten you my dear,' Fidrib said as a broad smile of grim satisfaction spread across his gaunt face. The magical bird gave chase, skimming the heads of the onlookers, as they gasped. The blanket of grog followed. The tips of the bird's wooden wings clipped and scratched their way along the houses that lined both sides of the street. It let out an almighty squawk that carried like the throttling roar of a dragon. Its mouth getting wider and wider still as it gained on the poor hobgoblin.

With no time to scream the bird widened its beak and swallowed the hobgoblin whole and as it neared the end of the street it squawked a last time before exploding into a million tiny orange sparks.

Jaws were left agape as the crowd looked on. As the sparks settled and a thick plume of smoke rose high above the rooftops a single barrel was left standing proud at the end of the street. The magnificent bird had gone, as had the grog and the hobgoblin.

'ENOUGH!' Master Agar exploded, which didn't happen often. 'Everybody, stand aside, quickly now.' His voice thundered with anger. A clear path soon formed between the elder and the barrel as the crowd parted left and right. He raised his crooked wooden staff and aimed it directly at the barrel before bellowing,

*'Barelius Oblitundo!'*

A ray of golden light shot straight to the barrel, smashing it to smithereens. Grog and damp wood showered off in all directions revealing the hobgoblin who coughed and spluttered as she sprawled out onto the cobbles.

'As I recall, drowning hobgoblins was not on the agenda for today Fonzo,' the ever-wise Master Agar said calmly. He offered his ginger counterpart a poisonous glare topped with protruding bushy eyebrows.

'You dare to counter my magic!' Councillor Fidrib belted, his eyes now glowing wildly like two burning balls of blue flame.

'Of course I do,' Master Agar chuckled, 'I have been doing this since before you were born Fonzo my lad. You should be ashamed of yourself and particularly today of all days,' the wily old Wizard lectured, at which the ginger Wizard scuttled off, mumbling and cursing under his breath.

'What's happening today Master Agar?' questioned one of the burly men he had moments earlier been laughing and joking with.

'Yeah! What's happening?' joined in the rest of the crowd.

'Well, it was meant to be a grand surprise for you all but I suppose I could tell you,' said Master Agar.

'Oh please tell us sir!' whined a young boy.

'Well,' Master Agar began excitedly, 'he won't be here for a little while yet, mind you he's always one for being fashionably late, ha-ha, the rotter. Oh, and his favourite colour as you will learn is purple, yes purple don't you know, and I suppose this is mainly due to the fact that he took up residence within the great purple crystal mountains in the north some years back. Great shards of crystal as wide as this very town and as tall as the mountains themselves jut out all over that range – it is truly something to behold and he…'

'Who?' questioned the crowd again who were growing impatient with the old Wizard's overly descriptive revelations.

'Why, a very powerful Wizard of course,' Master Agar revealed. 'He's coming to Brickabrack on special business to aid us with the terror that lurks through our streets come nightfall. He is a very dear friend of mine. We were at school together don't you know, yes, although things were very different back then and...'

'Who?' the whole crowd demanded in unison with red, angry faces. Mrs Macrocker looked like she was about to pop with sheer frustration.

'Ah yes, well, he is the Controller of the Seasons, the recently appointed Master of the Seas and, the Tilös Welly-wangin' champion four hundred and sixty-two years running. His name is Master Blundell,' the old Wizard finally revealed, much to the delight of the flummoxed crowd who let out deep sighs and hoots as if they had all been holding their breaths for a very long time.

'You be meanin' he's comin' t'rid us of this 'ere killer then, hmm?' slithered forward Madam Croaker, who had left her barrel (which didn't happen often) to see what all the fuss was about.

'Yes, my dear old hag!' Master Agar responded charmingly. 'And that's not all my good people, for tonight we feast! Tonight, we hold the largest street festival as has ever been seen in this town to welcome our honoured guest,' Master Agar finished, his arms held high in the air. He waited for some outrageous, thundering round of applause and cheering but it did not come. He lowered his head to stare at a sea of blank expressions and heads being scratched.

'Grog, ale and wine will flow like the very river that lies outside our walls.' Again silence.

'Salted and roasted meats of every kind will melt in your mouths while fruits and desserts of every colour, flavour and texture shall tantalise your tongues until they hang, worn out - in fact I should like to think that a good lot of you shall resemble a pack of panting dogs before this night is through.'

'Ow?' Madam Croaker belched. 'Ow do ye s'pose we 'old a fine street festival wiv no food? Hmm? And, and wiv only as much grog as could fill me belly, hmm?'

The old Wizard now understood why his enthralling words had fallen on deaf ears.

'Magic!' the happy old Wizard beamed. 'Tonight my good people the elders, along with other members of the magical community have granted a special treat. Tonight, everybody drinks. Tonight, no one goes hungry. Tonight, each and every last one of you shall receive a magical goblet and a bewitched plate. Whatever you desire to drink shall fill your goblet to the brim, and whatever you want to eat shall appear on your plate, before your very eyes.'

There was a slight pause before the entire town burst into cheers and merriment.

'And if you feel hungry or thirsty at anytime just imagine what you fancy and you shall receive it, the more creative the better,' Master Agar chuckled. 'There will be a prize for the best meal and another for the most creative drink so have fun.'

\*

As the evening drew near and the final preparations were being made for the festival the elders' work continued. All the rickety lanterns that ran along every street and hung from many buildings, shops and archways were now radiating a purple glow rather than the traditional orange haze of fire. After all, as Master Agar had described, purple was the colour of Master Blundell who lived in the north by the lake of the Crystal Mountains. A huge tower hewn from a single shard of purple crystal was where he lived and so the elders had concluded that a little purple here and there would make the great master feel more at home during his stay.

Master Agar was still on Westgate, orchestrating a floating mass of furniture, chairs, tables and barrels that he sent prancing and dancing down the street towards the marketplace. All of a sudden two familiar faces came rushing towards the old Wizard.

'Master Agar I'm afraid we may have to postpone Master Blundell's visit,' Sheriff Crunkhorn said urgently.

'You must be joking my lad. Do you know the last time Wilbur Blundell was in this town? Well put it this way m'boy, I was wearing shorts and carrying school books.'

'And believe me Councillor I am as excited about his arrival as the next person, but we have a murderer on the loose and myself and Mr Black here have our suspicions as to who it may be.'

'Really, well do tell,' the Wizard said curiously. 'Griffin, who do you think it might be?'

'Well – Luther, we think it might be…Orbulous,' replied Griffin.

'What? That little green friend of yours? Poppycock! He's harmless and quite the friendly little character.'

'It's true, I thought the same as you but Sheriff Crunkhorn has more sinister tales of these tree-folk,' Griffin said slightly nervously.

'Never! I don't believe it! True enough they are ancient beings, even claiming to pre-date Merlin. But tell me, how could it be that, if indeed these tree-folk are sinister and evil as our dear Sheriff here claims, that in all my long years of reading and researching, not to mention my many travels and adventures across this world, that I have never heard of any accounts or old tales of ill deeds by them? Hmm?'

'One of those beasts killed my son – dragged him from me into the darkness of the ancient forest. I need not parchment nor tales of old to convince me – I have seen it with my own two eyes!' the Sheriff blubbered, trying hard to fight the lump in his throat. His head was full of emotions and his heart raced.

'Then allow me,' the old Wizard asked stepping forward and placing a gentle hand softly on the Sheriff's forehead.

'You can perform memory traces?' gulped the Sheriff. 'Safely?'

'Fear not m'boy I've done more of these than you have eaten hot dinners,' Master Agar said confidently. 'How do you think I became so knowledgeable. Still, there was that one time I left the dwarf King thinking he was a goat,' he chortled.

'He's fibbing I take it,' the Sheriff posed to Griffin, his nostrils flaring with anxiety.

'Of course I am m'boy. Ah, here we are, hold still.' In a flash, time stopped and Master Agar was thrust into the Sheriff's memory. He stood, as the Sheriff had, in the ancient forest. It was dark and the branches and boughs clanged against his regiments' armour, sounding like pots and pans being bashed together.

The trees craned over the men, each of them appearing to

threaten the brave group.

'Father, there, up ahead, do you see it?' a voice whispered to Master Agar. It was the Sheriff's son. A young man, full of pride and valour, much like the Sheriff - yet younger and with hair.

The old Wizard watched on as the men came to one of the many river crossings that lie in the old forest.

All of a sudden, as the men were waist deep in the middle of the river, Master Agar noticed a monstrous dark shadow appear on the far bank. And yet none of the others saw it. What they did notice however was a purple orb that fluttered out from the thick line of trees lining the edge of the river on the far bank. It skipped to and fro before hovering above them.

'What is it?' cried a brute of a man, clad in heavy armour with a thick beard.

'Not sure,' joined in another.

'Is it a pixie?' another wondered.

'It's beautiful!' said another, wading forward to get a better look. The purple orb's haze began to shine out all the brighter. Even Master Agar found it stunning to behold, but it didn't last long.

The orb pulsed out purple energy and all at once the men disappeared under the water of the river. Just Master Agar and the Sheriff's son had remained on the bank, watching. The waters turned dark and no one resurfaced. Instead, bent armour and crushed helmets started to wash up on the far side of the river.

'Where are they all?' the Sheriff's son cried. But Master Agar could not answer, and neither could the Sheriff.

'NOOO!' shrieked the Sheriff's son. 'No more!' he wailed as he dived into the now murky waters.

Master Agar soon found himself charging down the bank after the young Captain and before long they were both thrashing and kicking frantically to get to the other side.

Robias, the Sheriff's son, reached the far side first to find himself surrounded by shattered swords and broken shields. He stared with both fear and sorrow at the crushed helmets of his kinsmen while his heart began to fill with hatred. Master Agar was soon standing next to him.

'AAAAARRRGH!' the young Captain growled at the dark forest in front of him. His heart was pounding with a rage so pure that Master Agar could hear every thump and every beat.

'Why not me? Hey, you coward?' he called to the darkness. 'Why don't you take me?'

Master Agar placed his hand gently on Robias' shoulder (as the Sheriff must have done) and as he did so the darkness replied.

'Happy to oblige,' came a thunderously deep voice that turned into a growl.

The memory began to slow. The Sheriff's son turned to face Master Agar who threw his arms around the boy. Darkness surrounded them so neither one could see. Master Agar held on as tightly as he could.

'Something's got me father!' the young Captain shrieked.

'Hold on son!' Master Agar wailed, 'Hold onto me, and don't let go!'

The young Captain mustered his strength and heaved Master Agar close to him, so they were in a tight embrace. Robias then whispered softly into the old Wizard's ear:

'I love you father.' and as Master Agar stared into the boy's watery eyes the young Captain let go and was dragged off screaming and full of fear by darkness and shadow into the deep of the forest, shortly followed by the purple orb.

'Nooooo!!' screamed Master Agar. He dropped to his knees on the river bank and began to sob, and with his face buried in his trembling hands, he heard one last almighty roar that sent great flocks of birds high into the night sky as it echoed off into the distance. Then silence.

Master Agar took his hand that was still trembling, from the Sheriff's forehead and stepped back to swallow the lump in his throat.

'Most puzzling,' the old Wizard choked.

'You see,' Sheriff Crunkhorn said in somewhat of a fluster, 'I told you the tree-folk are not to be trusted.'

'Orbulous didn't take your son,' Master Agar said with resounding confidence, 'this was something else.'

'What makes you so sure?' the Sheriff contested immediately.

'Neither you, nor any of your men saw it.'

'Saw what?' the Sheriff ordered.

'A monstrous shadow on the far bank of the river,' the old Wizard said, as the hairs on the back of his neck tingled and jumped up.

'I saw the darkness. My son was ripped out of my arms by it.'

'No, it wasn't just darkness. This had a shape to it, a blackness so thick and evil that it took a solid form and it most definitely wasn't Orbulous.'

'So what was it then?' the Sheriff begged, 'I must know.'

'Difficult to say,' the Council elder mumbled, 'and for now we need say no more about it.'

'It took my son!' the Sheriff barked at the Council elder, almost forgetting his place.

'And a sad tale it is Sheriff, yes very sad indeed, but the last thing our people need right now are more rumours. You will just have to trust me. One thing I can promise you is that I will not rest until I have answered this riddle and solved the mystery behind your son's disappearance.'

The old Wizard looked at both Griffin and the Sheriff with a sternness as like neither of them had seen before.

'Keep this between us. Yes very hush-hush – do not even mention this to Master Blundell, not until I have done more research,' the Wizard explained. 'Now, we have other tasks to attend to. Master Blundell will arrive shortly at which point the great festival will begin. Sheriff, I want people smiling and merry-making, yourself included,' he said, winking at the seemingly broken bald-headed man.

'Griffin, a word…' the Wizard requested, at which point the Sheriff realised he was no longer required.

'Yes Luther,' Griffin said stepping forward after what seemed like hours of listening.

'We must find Orbulous. That creature is innocent – of that I'm sure – in fact I'd bet my broomstick on it!'

'Okay, but he's invisible and no doubt disgruntled at being accused of being a murderer – where would you suggest I start?'

'He will be feeling abandoned at the moment and without

friends.'

'Yes, and how does that help?' Griffin asked the old man.

'Tell me, where did you first go when you escaped the dungeons with Polly?'

'Home,' Griffin said, as he now realised his Wizard-in-law's plan.

'Exactly m'boy,' grinned the old Wizard like a proud teacher, 'start there – we must get the forest-gnome back on side.'

'Why?' Griffin asked his old master.

'The Sheriff's memory – it stirs a fear that has been lying dormant for an age beyond you or I and I feel we will need his help – oh and Griffin...keep Lizzi and the children close, for dangerous times lay ahead of us.'

'Okay Luther, leave it to me,' Griffin said.

'Good boy, now hurry along.'

Griffin turned and scurried down Westgate towards the marketplace leaving a ponderous Master Agar behind him. For the first time since he was a boy the streets looked clean and colour blotted the houses, reminding him of the once popular summer fetes the town used to host.

He passed through the marketplace which was a vision to behold. The great well at its centre was gleaming; its tall pillars and domed roof had never looked better. Tables and chairs lined the whole area ready for the bountiful banquet to begin. He then moved onto Eastgate before turning left onto Rotten Row, which smelt sweeter than normal but still like a sewer. Lastly came Bridge Street between the rat-catcher's and the impressive Council Chamber Three. As he tottered past the Gatehouse and through the enormous arched entrance to the town the wind picked up. It twirled and swirled, leaving the great lanterns swaying back and forth like two enormous, yet silent cow bells.

Not long after this a beautiful purple comet rocketed overhead leaving a trail of purple mist behind it that danced and swayed and made pretty shapes.

All of the townspeople gazed up into the cool night sky and watched as the fierce purple comet spiralled and corkscrewed through the air, drawing pictures of trees and horses and dragons among the stars. It began to fashion a great circle above them, quicker and quicker it went, plummeting down further and further towards them, creating a whirlwind of purples that twisted down into the centre of the marketplace.

Light pulsed all over it like a storm brewing behind clouds. The vortex then exploded into an almighty puff of smoke and a sea of multicoloured sparks whizzed and whirred around all the streets. As the smoke thinned a glorious man appeared, standing tall on top of the domed roof of the well, with his arms outstretched so wide, it was as if he was preparing to cuddle the whole crowd in the marketplace before him.

'Greetings my dear people of Brickabrack,' came the cheery voice of Master Blundell.

The whole townspeople cheered as one.

'Word has reached my ear that an evil lingers here and does not rest,' began the impressive Wizard from afar. 'Well, let me assure you good people that *I* will not rest until this evil has been vanquished!' he finished with a thunderous roar.

Another tremendous cheer erupted from the townspeople.

'Starting tomorrow, myself along with your Council Elders will set about finding the identity of this evil character that dwells in the shadows. The murderer will be wormed out and dealt with in accordance with the magical laws of these lands – so, sleep well tonight and dream pretty dreams. Now to more pressing matters, my good people, let's feast!'

The whole town went berserk, cheering and singing songs. The town's band struck up and began to play merry tunes of old. The magical goblets and bewitched plates were handed out in the hundreds and everyone began filling them with whatever they could think of.

Mystical drinks flowed like an upside-down fountain – you had to stand over them while the goblet emptied itself into the drinker's mouth. At the same time, the drink turned different colours to indicate how empty the goblet was.

One woman, clearly a lover of fruit, had a plate full of oranges and every one she peeled had a different colour, flavour and texture inside.

Master Blundell visits Brickabrack

Another man had a giant, succulent Curdlecow steak on his plate that was slowly being charred to perfection by a tiny dragon. At the same time a miniscule, armour-clad warrior chopped his vegetables for him with a sword the man would later use as a toothpick. Then, as he began to eat his meal, the dragon and the warrior began to battle all over his plate. The man decided to call it: Dinner and a show.

'Luther my dear friend, it's been far too long,' Master Blundell said as he embraced Master Agar with wide purple sleeves.

'Yes indeed. And how are you, you old ratbag – still throwing those wellies of yours I hear,' the old Wizard teased.

'You know me,' Master Blundell replied with a chuckle.

'Yes I do, I do indeed. Listen, about this dark business…'

'Luther, my dear Luther, that is tomorrow's chore. We will out your murderer, and we shall do it together,' interrupted Master Blundell.

'It's not the murderer I'm worried about,' replied Master Agar.

'Oh, do tell,' requested Master Blundell, who fancied himself a bit of a know-it-all.

'Probably best we talk tomorrow,' Master Agar said unwillingly.

'Very well,' Master Blundell jibed, 'you keep your riddles, for tonight let us enjoy ourselves like we used to in that bygone age when we did not carry such burdens of responsibility and duty. My old friend, tonight let's have some fun!' The purple Wizard enthusiastically picked up a plate and goblet. 'Prize for the best entry was it?' he said turning to Master Agar while offering him a childish smile.

'Yep,' Master Agar replied, pulling his own goblet and plate from his shimmering robes.

'S'been a while,' said Master Blundell loudly as he rolled his wide purple sleeves up. 'Okay Luther, let's see what you've got!'

# CHAPTER ELEVEN

# The Taken

Master Agar woke early next morning. He could tell it was early as the low sun soothed his thumping head a little with its warmth. From being slumped over a table, he sat up and wiped the dribble from his cheek, all the while keeping his eyes shut tight.

'Well rattle my bones!' he said loudly to himself. 'It's been a number of years since I didn't make it to my bed following a festival, and beaten again by Blundell,' he chuckled.

'Ah! Percival Fishwickle,' Master Agar said raucously to one of the market traders, 'a very good morning to you. Tell me lad, when are you next going to have some of those scrummy three-tailed rat fish that I love so much?'

'Mornin' Master Agar. S'pose I'll be getting some early next week although…erm…' Mr Fishwickle looked up to see that Master Agar was smiling at him but his eyes were closed and he swayed oddly from side to side with dribble on his chin. 'Are… are you awake Master?'

'Yes, quite my lad,' he said, still swaying as he began to clear up some of the mess from Master Blundell's gluttonous banquet.

'But your eyes are closed?'

'Yes, well I'm not fond of sunlight on a heavy head you see.'

'Oh, I understand Councillor, had a few o' the Tipsy's finest last night did we? Huh huh!'

'Of course not man!' Master Agar said sternly. 'I'm a Councillor, not some drunken lout, but let's just say Master Blundell and I had quite the competition with our goblets last night, that's all.' The old Wizard braved a little wink at the market trader who was now hanging the ugliest fish from his stall that smelt of wild roses and apple blossom.

Master Agar bid the fishmonger farewell before drawing his staff from the side of the grog-stained table. It had been propped there for most of the night – that is apart from the odd occasion where he had entertained the town's children with wondrous party games. 'Floating upside-down Hopscotch' and 'Catch the Sweets' resulted in a great deal of children flying and floating around the town, hell-bent on catching humbugs and other equally scrumptious confectionery. And for the older, more boisterous children: 'Best the Dragon' seemed to be a favourite, in which each child had to attempt to fend off a dragon guarding a mighty chest of edible jewels and gold coins.

He began to amble through the market-place, knee-deep in food, goblets, slurring and snoring drunken bodies, plates, furniture and various other festival paraphernalia. He skipped and hopped for the gaps in the mess so as not to dirty his shimmering silver-pointed shoes. For a moment he considered making arrangements to tidy the town up but the mess could wait, as could any other Council-associated duties he may have had. For now he only had one desire and one destination in mind – Mrs Macrocker's Pie Potions shop (just off Eastgate as you turn onto Broadbank).

*

'Morning Mrs Macrocker, and how are we this fine day?' Master Agar asked, entering her shop, his eyes still firmly shut.

'Morning Master Agar, and what'll it be for you then this morning my loverly? No, no, let me guess,' the rotund woman said, wielding her magical rolling-pin complete with rainbow swirls that slithered and snaked all over it. She looked the old Wizard up and down, pondering as she went.

'Hair o' the dog crust,' she said, nodding to the corner of her shop where a mangy-looking, half-bald dog was shivering. 'You know, for your head.'

'Indeed,' Master Agar agreed.

'Wouldn't be the first today Master,' Mrs Macrocker went on. 'As you can see from poor Tiddles in the corner there, we've already made twelve batches of hair o' the dog crust pies just this morning!'

'My goodness, that is a lot!' Master Agar said speedily, his stomach rumbling more ferociously by the minute.

A little whimper jumped forward from the corner of the shop.

'Now don't be worrying yerself Tiddles m'dear,' Mrs Macrocker said to the half-bald dog. 'There ain't to be another festival for some years now.'

'So, what comes next?' Master Agar inquired so as to hurry the plump Witch along.

'Ah, yes, so, full Brickabrack breakfast filling to re-line your belly and I think we'll go with a dragon-egg glaze to finish – you know, to put that fire back in your ticker.'

'Sounds simply perfect,' said Master Agar as he shuffled over to the counter and, for the first time that morning, opened his eyes to watch the fat Witch at work, which he always found intriguing.

She piled all the ingredients high on the floury counter. There were eggs of all different shapes, sizes and colours, bacon, sausages, porridge, beans, broccoli, three small fish and one big one. It all looked not too dissimilar to the streets Master Agar had just hop-scotched along to get to her shop.

'Oh, almost forgot…' she added before whistling loudly. In a flash, Tiddles the mangy, slobbering mutt bounded over with a bald tail wagging furiously. She licked her magical rolling-pin left to right and up and down and then rolled it along what was left of Tiddles' fur. Master Agar grinned in awe as the large Witch returned to the counter with her magical rainbow rolling-pin now covered in a thick layer of hair.

'Marvellous!' the old Wizard beamed like a child in a sweet shop. Mrs Macrocker without hesitation rolled her magical hairy rolling-pin over the heaped up mess of ingredients just once and as she finished, there on the counter, lay a piping hot, beautifully golden crisp pie.

Master Agar rolled up his shimmering sleeves and reached for Mrs Macrocker's marvellous creation. But before his fingers even touched the pastry a young Brickabrack guard came charging into the shop flailing his arms in the air like a mad man.

'Oh Master Agar thank goodness and praise the elders – I've found you!' said the young guard, while bent over double and panting for breath.

Stern eyebrows came before Master Agar's reply.

'Well? What is it lad? Hop-to now, spit it out – my pie's going cold.'

'You are requested to attend an urgent Council meeting in Council Chamber Three. Everyone else is already there sir,' the guard said timidly, not wanting to upset the already disgruntled Wizard further.

'Meeting? What meeting lad? Who sent you?'

'Why, Master Blundell sir,' the guard replied, with a twitchy nervousness about him. The anxious young guard would have liked to grab the dithering half-drunk old Wizard and frog-march him to the Council Chamber. However, the old man was an elder so the guard bit his tongue and tried to show Master Agar the respect his position demanded.

'Oh, him, the rapscallion – I'll be along in a jiffy just as soon as I've devoured this taste sensation my dear Mrs Macrocker has just lovingly crafted for me – dragon-egg glaze and hair o' the dog crust I might add and –'

'Sir, I'm afraid you're needed straight away. Your pie will have to wait, delicious as it sounds sir.'

'Oh confound him and his bombardment of demands! First, he drinks me under the table, again, and now he deprives me of my breakfast and fizzy-head cure. What should be so important as to come between a Wizard and his pie?'

'I don't know myself sir but we must be away!'

'Very well m'lad – the pie will have to wait,' grumbled Master Agar as they both left the Pie Potions shop and stepped back onto the filthy streets.

'Why didn't you take the pie with you and scoff it on the way sir?'

'And risk staining my robes? Not on your life!'

'You could've always magic'd the stain away sir,' the naive guard suggested.

'What a perfectly good waste of magic my boy – you see, those gifted with the power of magic should not fritter it away on insignificant tasks or duties – magic is meant for greatness. Besides, I quite like washing my robes down by the river, or sometimes –'

the old Wizard paused before scanning the streets for intent ears and lowering his voice to a whisper, 'I let the Faeries do it – shh.'

At that moment Master Agar stepped in some slop that looked like fish guts and smelt fouler than troll dung.

'Ah, yes sir, that reminds me,' the guard began, 'Master Blundell also requested that you tidy up the town of all last night's mess.'

'Oh did he really – well, if I didn't know any better I'd say our guest was taking liberties. All of this mess is here because of his arrival anyway!' The old Wizard lifted his staff high in the air and grumbled, *'Tumulus Tersursum.'*

Before the young guard's very eyes all the mess began to move. Plates, tankards and goblets clanged and clinked as they bounced off one another in mid-air. The mountains of food and leftovers dissolved into a shimmering mist that quickly evaporated. Barrels and kegs rolled back and forth. People still half-asleep floated round corners and down streets before being neatly tucked back into their beds, only to wake several hours later being drunkenly oblivious as to how they got back home in the first place. Even the slop that Master Agar had just stepped in had disappeared leaving his shimmering shoes glistening once more.

'Tidy up the town indeed; what a perfectly good waste of magic,' ranted the old Wizard as he trotted off across Eastgate and onto Rotten Row with the young guard in tow.

\*

'Ah Luther, morning – how is your head my friend?' said Master Blundell warmly.

'It's been better but nothing a good pie wouldn't have remedied.'

'Yes, my apologies about your breakfast, although I fear what I am about to tell you may leave you less concerned about your pie.'

'My dear friend, I feel you greatly underestimate how much I wanted my pie – hair o' the dog crust, and –'

'Luther it's the Mayor,' Master Blundell said looking very grave.

'Oh, Mayor Elmwood, this is his doing is it, and what is it this time? Are we to have another obscene monolith erected in his honour, or perhaps a new law that parts a Wizard from his pie?'

'He is dead,' Master Blundell said solemnly.

'What?' Master Agar spluttered in disbelief as his jaw fell open.

There was a long silence. Then Master Blundell spoke.

'It would seem, my friend, that last night's festival did not deter our killer as we had hoped, instead gave them the perfect opportunity to strike again.'

Master Agar gaped at his old school friend.

'I – I can't believe it. Who would dare commit such a crime and while you are in town?'

Master Blundell recognised the shock and disappointment in his old friend's voice. It had been on Master Agar's invitation that he had agreed to visit the town and assist. Together they had hoped to solve this riddle.

'This foe is cunning,' Master Blundell began. 'This foe is powerful and I fear that all my years of assuming I was up there as one of the most powerful Wizards in this land has actually, on this occasion, been my downfall. I feel that I have simply sat back and let others replace me.'

'That isn't true Wilbur. Why, I can only think of one who is more powerful and that's old Merlin,' Master Agar said reassuringly.

'Ah, maybe my dear Luther,' Master Blundell said, as he paced up and down the large chamber. 'I cannot help but feel that the Mayor's death was a message for us. The killer wants us to know that he does not fear us. He wants us to know that he is powerful. And I fear that unless we find him, he will strike again.'

'Poor Eloise,' Master Agar sighed.

'The Mayor's daughter?' Master Blundell quizzed.

'Yes, it has only been a short while since she lost her best friend.'

'Who?'

'Jared Proofgrease, the butcher's son – he died a most horrific death but not before chewing her ear off. First she loses her friend, as well as a perfectly good ear and now her father has been taken from her.'

'We need answers Luther. We cannot allow further killings to take place,' said Master Blundell determinedly.

'No my old friend, we can't. We need a gathering – Council members, yourself and a select few others.'

'Yes, excellent Luther, we need to gather our thoughts, share our knowledge of this matter but most importantly formulate a plan – guard send for the others.'

'No!' Master Agar interrupted. His voice echoed around the vast chamber at least three times by which time he had begun speaking again. 'I think it wise we keep this gathering a secret, the fewer who know about it the better. For all we know sweet old Nanny Nutton could be our killer. I will summon all those required in person.'

'Summon them to where?' said Master Blundell.

'I know just the place.'

*

'Any sign of Orbs?' Master Agar said hurriedly.

'None,' Griffin said with a sigh, 'even if I could find him I doubt he'd talk to me.'

It was late, the children were in their beds and Griffin was just putting the ancient and rather charred dwarf battle axe back into the umbrella stand. He had just finished greeting his Wizard-in-law when another loud knock came from the other side of Orbs' mushroom encrusted hollow.

'I told you there would be others,' Master Agar shrugged. He removed his pointy silver hat and proceeded to tuck his shimmering locks back into a presentable state, sometimes licking his palm to help flatten the more stubborn clumps that stuck out here and there.

'That you did Luther, that you did – although a little more notice would've been helpful,' Griffin replied as he tackled the assortment of locks and bolts on the door.

'It had to be left to the last moment to disclose the location of this gathering, you know, to keep it secret. We wouldn't want any prying eyes, or ears, for that matter as, for all we know, our killer could be one of your guests here tonight. Keep a keen eye on everyone Griffin,' Master Agar said shakily, winking as he did so.

Lizzi was frantically dashing about in the kitchen, trying to rustle up some secret food for their secret guests. As per usual the enchanted cupboards were trying to help – spitting out various objects that under normal circumstances Lizzi would've rejected, but not this time.

'Keep it all coming my marvellous cupboards!' she wailed as she stuffed another one of Mrs Macrocker's "self-baking" pastry dishes with bars of soap and matches and flannels. She seemed less concerned about the quality and more concerned about the quantity as she saw another two cloaked figures amble past the kitchen doorway.

'More! More!' she demanded as she crammed another pumpkin with fish pâté, washing pegs, lemons, eggs and a dirty pair of Griffin's old slippers.

'Lizzi darling?' Griffin said, entering the kitchen with a well rehearsed smile cast over his obviously worried face. 'Just wondering how things were going?'

Lizzi shot Griffin a look that made him feel dead inside as she wiped flour, slime and mess from her face.

'Someone very kind has brought this for the feast,' he said as he unwrapped several prime cuts of meat that had been pre-stuffed with herbs and flowers and sausage meat.

'Thank goodness!' Lizzi said, letting out a low whistle as she slumped, exhausted onto the kitchen counter. 'I was beginning to worry our guests wouldn't have enough to eat.'

BANG! CRASH! THUD! SLAM! The cupboard doors protested, after realising their glorious few moments of usefulness had now come to an end.

'Right, I'll leave you to it then darling,' Griffin said, promptly leaving the kitchen to tend to his guests in the dining chamber.

He entered the enormous stone hall that had archway after archway dotted along what was left of the walls. And in between the archways were great roaring fireplaces, some at floor level with others halfway up the walls. There was even a magical upside down one floating in the void where the ceiling used to be, that showered the guests below with embers that hissed and crackled.

A monstrous table ran from one end of the great hall to the other. The chairs around it floated; twenty six in all and at each place there was a large brass horn resembling a trumpet that stuck out in front of whoever was to sit there. Each trumpet passed through the table and split into a twisted and tangled mess of brass pipes. This was no ordinary table, this was a Tongue-tie table, so named because when someone spoke into their brass horn only those who were meant to hear it would do so, allowing many conversations to be held and heard all at once.

As well as the fires and the Tongue-tie table the room was peppered with the usual Black family oddities: family portraits and historic tapestries that depicted great battles from long ago between evil-looking creatures and magic folk. There were strange plants that burped and moved as well as all manner of odd-looking devices and contraptions, some of which looked like good fun while others looked like they would be more befitting a torture chamber.

'Ah, evening Griffin,' Master Blundell hailed as the somewhat flummoxed Wizard entered the great hall.

In an instant all the guests rose to greet their host, which left Griffin feeling rather peculiar as he was more recently accustomed to insults, shouting and even the odd rotten cabbage being thrown when he entered a room. He was certainly not used to courtesy and smiling faces. He gazed around to see all the Councillors as well as other important people of the town.

'Firstly Griffin,' Master Blundell began, 'on behalf of all those present I wish to say thank you. It is a rare thing to be offered food and shelter for a secret gathering in the dead of night – and at such short notice I might add. And so to business – we all know why we are here but before we begin I am not familiar with all those present so please stand, state your name and purpose here tonight, nothing too fancy – erm – Luther, let's start with you and go anticlockwise.'

The old Wizard, who was at one end of the table, hopped off his floating chair and bellowed his name.

'Luther Agar, Leader of the Council and Headmaster of Pendragon's school of Magic.'

'Captain Shiverrs,' came another voice suddenly.

'Who said that?' Master Blundell said, scouring the length of the table. 'I can't see you man, are you invisible?'

'No! I'M A DWARF!' the Captain barked angrily.

'Well stand up man, we can't see you.'

'I am stood up!' Captain Shiverrs thundered, while turning a deep shade of purple, not that anyone could see his face.

'Oh, sorry old chap, didn't see you down there, do go on.'

'I'm an adventurer and famous dwarf explorer. I've seen it all and done it all – well nearly,' he said, twiddling with his long brown beard.

Next there was Kestrell the thunderclapper messenger, Mr Eavesalot the carpenter, then two empty seats, then Master Blundell followed by three empty seats. Next came Mr Drinkin the pipe master, then Madam Croaker the town drunk, who was presumably only there for the free grog and nibbles but who merited an invitation based purely on her extensive knowledge of the 'gossip on the street'.

'Griffin Black…' next echoed around the chamber, 'Warlock, button-thief and host to you all tonight.'

All that remained were the other twelve Councillors (Master Agar being the thirteenth) who filled one whole side of the Tongue-tie table and they went as follows:

Litimus Letouche, Candle and Lightning Mistress;
Meragamus Flay, Food, Grog and Supplies Master;
Terrence Twelvetrees, Forest Defence Master;
Fagan Farrowbottom, Creature Control Master;
Dillious Draper, Building Control Master;
Fonzo Fidrib, Crime and Dungeons Master;
Patty Pigswill, Sewer and Waterways Mistress;
Wendomina Wiggs, Trade and Visitor Mistress;
Gregoria Gorygreen, Healing Mistress;
Selwyn Shufflebum, Transport Mistress;
Sooth Scribblesby, Historical Archives Mistress and finally,
Lysa Leggitt, Town Defence and Spell Control Mistress.

'Dear friends,' Master Blundell began, now speaking into his brass horn so only all those present at the table would hear, 'we know why we are here. Something terrible is lurking within your town. Something that is beyond any of you, and, I'm afraid to say, is also beyond my skills. But together, with our collective strengths and magical capabilities, there should be no reason why we cannot solve this.'

'Are you quite sure we have the powers for this task?' interrupted Lysa Leggitt, a stern woman, tall and gangly with piercing eyes. 'I have been working tirelessly with the Sheriff to find the murderer without so much as a whisper as to his whereabouts. He even defied you, the great Master Blundell last night when he murdered the Mayor,' she finished with a huff.

'My dear Witch that is precisely why we are here,' Master Blundell said boldly, addressing the table. 'Tonight, we must answer all the questions and solve all the riddles. What does the killer want? Is there a pattern? Are we missing something? Something that I fear could be right under our noses. So, discuss, plot and ponder. If you need space to think or require no uncertain amount of privacy take your chairs to the fires halfway up the walls and for those of you that work best in utter silence there is the fire in the ceiling. Think long and hard my dear colleagues but remember two things: one, we need answers tonight and two, the killer could be anywhere, even in this very chamber.' Master Blundell's words shocked everyone. Was he implying that one of them could be the killer?

A loud chattering noise erupted almost instantly, as various discussions began. Some people floated straight up to the halfway fires and began to whisper and point at those further below. Others shouted and spat down their brass horns in protest.

Some found Master Blundell's words inspiring whereas others took offence and so different tones of conversation were taking place and echoing all around the chamber.

Some smoked pipes and pondered, others drank and slurred but as Master Blundell had wished, discussions were taking place. There were wild accusations being tossed around that were later quashed. Inflammatory remarks and comments such as Captain Shiverrs blaming the whole thing on trolls without a scrap of evidence, but stating that it must be them due to the fact that they all look ugly and smell suspicious.

Others were trying more methodical approaches, looking at all the events, but drawing no conclusions. They continued for what seemed to be several hours when Master Blundell hushed them all down.

'Someone is coming.'

There was a gentle knock on the door.

'Enter,' Master Blundell said, his voice blasting out of all the brass horns.

Lizzi pushed her way inside with an entourage of floating dishes, plates, trays and cutlery all bobbing along behind her, they then proceeded to set themselves on the table.

'S'about time!' Captain Shiverrs barked, as a bubbling hotpot landed on the table in front of him and began to stir itself. 'A dwarf could quite easily die in such an inhospitable place!'

'Yeah, truth be told I only come for the free grog and grub,' belched Madam Croaker as she sidled up to Griffin with a buck-toothed smile.

'And for that you shall wait until last to eat,' Master Blundell laughed as both of them froze to their seats, bobbing up and down with a purple glow about them and disappointed expressions on their grubby faces.

'So dear Lizzi, youngest of my good friend Luther, what do we have tonight then?'

'Well to be honest Master it's somewhat of a creation. I should say each dish will test your taste buds but under the circumstances…'

'We left you with no time to prepare,' the purple Wizard said warmly. 'Fear not my dear, it all looks marvellous,' he finished as he took a slice of the soapy match-flannel pie.

'The only thing that might taste half-decent are those lovely cuts of meat that were brought. Anyway I best let you get on, wouldn't want to come between you and your killer.' Lizzi said.

'Most kind dear,' Master Blundell said with a soapy mouthful of his pie. 'Your part in this mystery will be noted. As the leader of the Legless Knuckleclunkers once said to me: "an army marches on its stomach"!' he finished enthusiastically.

'Erm, but in that instance Wilbur,' Master Agar began, 'his army literally did march on their stomachs you see, because they were legless,' he finished with a chuckle.

'Well I'll be! Do you know it hadn't occurred to me until now. Ha ha. Well how funny!' Master Blundell said, grinning and blushing at the same time.

Lizzi left the chamber and before long everyone was back at the table eating and drinking. That is, of course, apart from old Madam Croaker and Captain Shiverrs who still looked disappointed as their stomachs rumbled loudly down their brass horns so everyone could hear.

'And let that be a lesson to you!' Master Blundell laughed and several others joined in as they all tucked into what was a sumptuous if bizarre feast.

'Truly Griffin, your wife has a gift,' Master Blundell said, as he burped bubbles across the table again. 'Granted she possesses no magical powers but this meat is cooked to perfection,' the purple Wizard proclaimed as he chewed down another succulent mouthful.

'Yes she's quite the cook,' Griffin said with a drawling tone as he prodded and poked one of his old slippers around his plate. It was steaming hot, soggy, covered in fish pâté and smelled like lemons and eggs. It appeared quite obvious that he, along with the politer guests around the table, had had the decency to wait for their food, allowing the ruder ones (Master Blundell included) to pick exactly what they wanted first, which in most cases was the cuts of meat.

'Agreed!' said Master Agar avidly, 'I didn't know my little Lizzi had such skills in the kitchen. My tongue is dancing in my mouth and my teeth have never felt cleaner!'

'That'll be the soap and lemons,' said Griffin pushing his plate away from him.

'Soap you say? Ingenious!' the old Wizard raved as he went back for seconds.

'Ooh I should like to try some of that and –' Master Blundell paused and appeared unable to finish his sentence. Instead he swayed and stared blankly ahead, his eyes widening by the second.

Griffin and Master Agar shot each other looks of concern and bewilderment and were soon joined by the rest of the table.

'Wilbur?' asked Master Agar softly. 'Are you alright?'

'Yes I'm fine – erp! – ha ha,' he replied in a forceful manner as a little dribble oozed from the corner his mouth.

'Are you sure?' the befuddled old Wizard went on, his eyebrows jutting out with the increasing uncertainty. Suddenly, Master Blundell let out a horrifically unnatural high-pitched screech which was then followed by a voice that was not Blundell's, even though it came from his mouth.

'I have him, he's mine now, ha ha all mine.'

'Master Blundell – who are you talking to?' Griffin asked anxiously.

'Me,' he replied instantly.

'And me,' hissed Fonzo Fidrib.

'And me, me, and me, me, me, me, me too.' Seven of the other guests all suddenly screeched in unison. Griffin took his gaze from the purple Wizard and spied all those present around the table. Madam Croaker and Captain Shiverrs were still locked to the spot although their expressions seemed more like shock now than disappointment. The others around the table, however, were acting very oddly. Their eyes were bloodshot and wide with a glazed look of rage. They twitched and drooled as if possessed. Selwyn Shufflebum, the Transport Mistress was rocking back and forth as if she was sitting on a horse, not a chair.

Terrence Twelvetrees hooted like an owl, then quacked like a duck before finally growling like a dog.

'Erm – Luther?' said Griffin in a low whisper.

'I see it m'boy,' Griffin's Wizard-in-law replied.

'How are you feeling?' asked Griffin.

'Fine,' replied the old Master.

'Good.'

Moments later the odd behaviour stopped. The jerking and shaking and rocking, the odd noises and dribbling all ceased and everyone around the table sat in an awkward silence.

'How do you feel Wilbur my old friend?' said Master Agar sternly as he reached for his staff.

'Fine. I'm fine, lovely food – how are you?' the purple Wizard replied in a somewhat monotone voice while still sporting the same vacant expression with wide eyes.

'Oh – having a lovely evening thank you,' Master Agar replied. 'Say, now that the feast is over shall we continue our discussions?'

Master Blundell did not answer but instead just twitched before drooling down his brass horn which resulted in all the guests being drenched in his dribble. Each of their horns seemed to almost sneeze in their faces.

'I'll take that as a yes then shall I?' Master Agar said, using the sleeve of his cloak to wipe the spit from his cheek. His heart sank as the noise returned and all the guests began talking once more. Although this time the conversations all seemed very forced as they hissed and whispered with the same monotone fashion as Master Blundell had moments earlier.

'Griffin, shall we retreat to the ceiling fire?' Master Agar insisted.

'Why yes Luther let's go and have a chat,' Griffin replied with false enthusiasm in an attempt to appear unruffled by what had just happened. In an instant their chairs floated high into the void above them. Tapestries, weapons and portraits whizzed by as they approached the blazing fire that dangled above their heads.

'What in all of Brickabrack is going on down there?' Griffin demanded in a hastened whisper.

'I have no idea m'boy but trust me, it's not good – I fear they are – taken!'

'Taken? What do you mean taken?'

'Taken – no longer themselves. Bewitched, cursed, damned – take your pick,' the old Wizard finished, gazing down to the Tongue-tie table below and its occupants. 'You need to get out of here fast,' Master Agar whispered sincerely. 'Take Lizzi and the children quickly before it's too late.'

'Where – it's pitch black out there and nothing but forest?'

'You must sneak away quickly, somewhere secret, somewhere only you know about.'

'I know a place it's –'

'Don't tell me,' Master Agar interrupted. 'I dare not know the location in case I suffer the same fate as our friends down there.'

'Then come with us!' Griffin insisted.

'Not this time m'boy,' the old Wizard smiled. 'If our friends are lost to us I am now the only one who can try and solve this riddle before the whole town is consumed by madness.'

'Then let me help you,' Griffin pleaded, 'restore my magic and let's solve this together.' he finished with a hopeful smile.

'No Griffin, you must take care of my Lizzi and the children. Let me worry about the town. I'll do what I can to restore your magic but for now you must stay safe. I will keep an eye on our unsavoury friends down there and see you again when the time is right.'

'How will I know when that is?' asked Griffin, who was now more concerned about explaining to Lizzi why he had left her father to a town full of mad people.

'Trust me, you'll know – you'll have your magic back!' the old Wizard chortled. 'It took thirteen of us to take your magic Griffin, and if the other twelve are taken, I am not sure if I can restore it on my own – I must get to the school library and find the answer. If I succeed, your magic will be returned…only then will it be safe to return to Brickabrack.'

The two chairs soon floated back down to the Tongue-tie table where the taken guests were still shuddering and having conversations that made no sense. Without warning and much to Griffin's surprise, Master Agar began quacking like a duck, then barking like a dog. Then his eyes widened.

'Luther? Not you too?' Griffin snivelled.

'Yes I'm taken too!' the old Wizard said in a dulcet tone but, to Griffin's relief, he winked and smiled moments later.

Griffin smiled back before leaving his floating chair to find Lizzi and the children.

# CHAPTER TWELVE

# Five Friends Forever

The children were both sleepy and grumpy as they trudged the sodden path away from the dragon temple led by their parents. Lizzi and Griffin had literally dragged the reluctant children from their beds leaving only enough time to wrap a dressing gown around each of them.

Pereé clung to her beloved bogey doll and so she seemed content with the unusual circumstances. Garad however was not so jovial. His hair was sprouting off in all directions as he hadn't had time to brush it. Lizzi was as equally displeased, and was making a great deal of fuss about not having time to sort her hair or do her face. Though she had insisted on lugging her large floral travel bag with her, despite her family shaking their heads at her insistence.

'Father why was Gwangad woofing like a doggy?' Pereé asked innocently - she had been quite happily woofing and barking back at the old Master.

'Yeah Father, and what was with all the odd looks we were getting? Most of them back there looked as though their eyeballs were about to pop out of their heads,' Garad added, as they crept silently away from the temple.

'Your Grandfather is fine, he's just pretending,' Griffin said reassuringly. 'It's all the others I'm worried about,' he finished, as he led his family further into the darkness of the forest.

They spent a good while darting from tree to tree, listening carefully for any odd noises – the type you would only hear in a magical forest.

'Are we there yet?' Pereé whimpered, as she felt her legs growing more and more tired.

'We've been out here for ages, how much further is this place of yours Griffin?' Lizzi asked sharply while reaffirming her grip on Pereé's small hand. She had not let go of her daughter since they left the temple.

'Not too much further darling – it's just up here – I think.'

'What place? Where are we going?' asked Garad.

'And what do you mean "you think"?' Lizzi added with a trembling voice. 'Are we lost?'

'Right, everybody calm down. We are going to a very special and very secret place, a place that only five people in the whole world know about – myself being one of them,' Griffin said, hoping to build some excitement about this sudden journey that had torn his family from their cosy beds. 'And no dearest we are not lost, it's just the last time I was here I was at school and both I and the forest have changed somewhat since then.'

'So why don't we use that *Octopus* spell thingy to light the way then?' Lizzi questioned.

'Because darling we are not on the path and lighting up the forest will draw a lot of attention to us – and not the kind of attention we need nor desire if you see what I mean. Besides, it's: Oc-*u*-lus…Oc-*u*-lus Lux-au-rea, not Octopus. The last thing we need is more tentacles after us.'

For what seemed like hours the family trudged through the undergrowth, slipping on moss, tripping on roots and taking the occasional slap round the face from any low-hanging branches. Garad had lost one of his slippers. Pereé, being closer to the ground, kept getting her dressing gown belt snagged in the undergrowth so Griffin had resorted to carrying her on his shoulders.

'I'm hungry Father,' Pereé whimpered with soggy eyes. 'Father I'm hungry.'

'Yes ok darling, it's not much further now.' Griffin scanned in every direction, hoping to see something remotely familiar. 'Okay we're lost,' Griffin finally admitted, as they all slumped in a heap on the soggy, leaf-strewn ground.

'I don't like it Father,' Pereé whined.

'I know precious but once your Father finds his special place we'll all be safe.'

'And how do you propose we do that in the dark?' Lizzi said

frantically. Her faith in her husband was shrinking rapidly.

'We're not going to find it in the dark,' said Griffin, coming to a sudden conclusion.

'What do you mean?'

'We're going to have to draw some attention to ourselves,' he finished, looking around into the darkness.

*'Really?'* Lizzi grumbled, 'Hours creeping around in the dark only to then show all the foul things in here just where we are?'

'Well unless you have any better ideas it's our only option.'

'What about the children?' Lizzi barked. Her concern fluttered through her whole body until her knees began to knock, as every conceivable outcome of what they were about to do flashed through her head like some parental curse. Maybe Pereé would be snatched from her, never to be seen again. Perhaps Garad would fall into one of the many bottomless pits that lie in the old forest or accidentally set fire to all the trees.

'Garad…' Griffin whispered as he rummaged around in the pockets of his robe.

'Yeah?'

'It's time for you to be the Wizard I know you are son – here.' Griffin took an ornate and beautifully crafted wand from his robes and passed it to his eldest. 'This was my wand, from my school days and granted it's not the greatest it started me off on the right path – and now, it is yours.'

Garad took the wand and held it up close to his face. Squinting in the darkness he focused to see its beauty; pale wood with elegant markings delicately carved into its surface.

It was a special moment for the family, despite their surroundings.

'Thanks Father!' Garad gasped with excitement and pride as he turned the wand over to inspect the rest of it.

'Listen carefully my lad. I have spoken to your teachers and they insist that your attitude needs some attention and on this I have to say I agree, but, your magic, they say, for your age is second to none – your Grandfather actually told me that and you know how good he is at magic.'

Both Lizzi and Griffin took a brief moment to be proud of their son. And as they sat, huddled together in the darkness, his face beamed with happiness, as did theirs.

'Father I want a pretty stick,' said Pereé.

'Well you will one day poppet – you can have this one when your older brother is finished with it,' he said, now smiling widely at his youngest.

'Garad, I need you to help me protect your mother and sister until we find the secret place,' Griffin said putting his arm around his son, which Garad was not really used to. 'The Councillors have still not granted me my magic back and so I need you to focus and listen to my instructions.'

'Okay. What spells should we use? Killing ones?' Garad said a little too eagerly.

'No, we'll stick to the spells you have covered at school shall we. Let's have some fun and use *Ludemortis, Insanistultus* and *Morphidius.*'

'Oh okay,' Garad said looking a tad disappointed.

'Everyone ready?' Griffin said as he looked from Garad to Lizzi and then Lizzi to Pereé – they all gulped and then nodded.

'Garad a little light please.'

*'Oculus Luxauria!'* he roared, trying his best to mimic Professor Gruntsquish, his Fire and Illuminations teacher.

The whole forest woke up as it was drenched in an unnatural light – birds scattered into the sky to be later confused as they were confronted with the moon. Gentle animals like deer and rabbits began to graze on the dew-covered ground.

The less savoury creatures, however, retreated back into the darkness; growling and grunting as they did so. Clicks and scratches stayed hidden as the family began to move between the huge trees once more.

Gribblies scurried, while creatures leapt overhead, all the while avoiding being seen, like some very real and very scary game of hide and seek – but this was not to last.

The family had just finished rounding another enormous Cherryberry, clambering over its monstrous roots when Lizzi was snagged on the shoulder by another low-hanging branch – she reached up to ease its grip from her cloak, but this time it didn't let go.

She screamed and turned to see a creepy twitching and clicking, tall, black and menacing before her.

'*LUDEMORTIS!*' Garad shrieked, his new wand aimed at the eight foot creature that looked like a muddle of man, crab and praying mantis.

In a flash of green the creepy was still as a statue; staring blankly ahead through bulbous black eyes knowing it had just been bested out of a meal. Safe as they were the creepy continued with its eerie clicking and scratching noises that made Lizzi judder with fear. Moments later Lizzi's shoulder was free from its grip and they walked onward.

'Excellent use of that spell Garad – well done,' Griffin said eagerly, giving him a firm pat on the back. 'You've just defeated your first enemy.' Garad beamed from ear to ear, standing proud with his wand as if waiting for a trophy.

They had only been walking for a little while when a crawly reared its slimy eyes and was now charging towards them like a huge fleshy caterpillar with enough teeth to fill the mouths of ten dragons.

'*Insanistultus* this time,' said Griffin.

Garad took aim with his wand as his proud father looked on.

'*Insanistultus!*' he wailed as a soft yellowy-green light trickled towards the charging beast, straight into its gaping mouth.

Seconds later the crawly was running round in circles like a dog chasing its tail.

'Excellent!' Griffin applauded. 'Well it's nice to know that you've been paying attention in your classes.'

'If I didn't know any better I'd say you two were enjoying yourselves!' Lizzi said, staring on in disbelief with folded arms.

'Oh c'mon darling. His first two defeats!' Griffin bellowed with a cheer. 'He'll remember this for the rest of his life – taking on dark creatures in the old forest with his father by his side, eh son?'

Garad had never been happier. He craved attention from his father who only ever seemed to have time for Pereé. He would spend hours at night, secretly practicing his magic in the hope that one day he would be regarded in the same league as Merlin, although the real reason he did this was so his father would be proud of him. A fierce level of competition burned inside him. He wanted to outdo his father in every way, the sole person he had put on a pedestal from a young age.

'And that's wonderful,' Lizzi began, 'but for us non-magical people this is not my idea of fun.'

'Nonsense,' Griffin insisted, 'we are protecting you.'

'Let's just please get to the secret place as soon as magically possible,' Lizzi pleaded and they were off once more.

As their journey through the forest continued, flashes of green and yellow fended off all manner of beast, creature and foe: winged ones, horned ones, some with tentacles, some with long slimy tongues that wagged frantically in desperation for a taste of the Black family.

It was as the family stepped into a mossy clearing that things took a turn for the worse. It wasn't that the creatures got larger or even more aggressive, but rather that the number became greater and greater. Swarms and herds and posses and packs of evil things flooded into the clearing and, despite their best efforts, Griffin and Garad found that they were closing in and fast.

Griffin even had Garad using some spells that he definitely hadn't been taught at school in an attempt to slow the advancing sea of teeth, claws and tentacles. They came from the trees, they crawled out of burrows and wormed through the very ground beneath their feet. It was as the creatures were within touching distance that they heard it – a frightful howl came from behind Griffin and Garad.

They turned to see Lizzi, wide-eyed with brutal abandon, wielding a rusty old frying pan in one hand and a somewhat battered rolling pin in the other.

What came next shocked the whole forest, but none more so than the creepies and crawlies, the barrage of other night terrors, all who met their ends by the hands of the dishevelled looking, over-protective mother. She simply went berserk – charging down anything and everything that didn't look like her family.

By the time she was finished she was on her knees surrounded by dark spiky and slimy corpses, unable to raise her arms, covered

Lizzi — the wide-eyed warrior

in entrails and slime with bug juice dripping from her pale face. She didn't know it at the time, but from that day forward Lizzi would be free to walk through the forest without being hunted or stalked. Dark whispers fluttered through the trees of the wide-eyed warrior with the crazy hair that should never again be angered.

Griffin, Garad and Pereé stood for some time, gob-smacked at what Lizzi had just done. Lizzi herself was just as shocked; she had never been brave or vicious or anything. Just a wife and a mother, but as Griffin explained to her later – being a caring wife and a loving mother took more courage than an army beyond count.

'Where did they come from?' Griffin spluttered.

'What?' Lizzi replied.

'The frying pan and rolling pin?'

Lizzi gestured to the large floral travel bag she had insisted on bringing.

'So that's what's in the bag.'

Once Griffin had finally prised the frying pan and rolling pin from Lizzi's hands, tossed them back in the travel bag and got her to her feet once more the remainder of their rambling through the forest went undisturbed and without incident.

Finally they reached a section of the forest that became familiar to Griffin.

'We're here!' he said full of enthusiasm mixed with more than a sprinkling of relief.

As the family continued forward, among the trees there were huge rocks and boulders scattered everywhere, they looked very much out of place – jutting out here and there, forcing the trees to begrudgingly grow elsewhere.

They came to what appeared to be a path that sloped downwards. Tall rocks flanked either side resembling the high walls of the town.

At the end of the path an enormous round boulder blocked their way. Growing disobediently on top of it was a gigantic pantree – it wasn't as tall or as vast as the Cherryberries of the forest but was just as impressive. Its roots hugged the boulder on either side, like two giant hands clasping a ball.

'What type of tree is that Father?' Pereé asked, having never seen one like it before.

'Well darling, it's a pantree. They are very useful if you are ever lost in the forest because of the shape of their leaves.

'They look like saucepans Father, look!' Pereé said excitedly.

'That's right poppet – that's why it's called a pantree. And it's useful because anyone can put things in the leaves for safe-keeping.'

'Things like what?' Garad quizzed.

'Well, anything really,' Griffin said scratching his head, trying hard to think of a good example.

'Well your Grandfather came across one once that was full of treasure,' Lizzi added.

'Treasure!' both children gasped.

'Yes – rubies, diamonds and precious stones, gold – all sorts.'

'I found one once that had a really nice tea set split between all the leaves. A cup in one, a saucer in another – it took me forever to find the whole set,' Griffin mumbled quietly, feeling somewhat bested by Lizzi's tale of Master Agar's treasure.

The family, led by Griffin, hurried down the slope towards the boulder. As they drew nearer they could see markings engraved into it. A circle with a five-pointed star sat inside – it was a penta-gram and on each point of the star a hole had been bored into the rock. Next to each hole there was a letter: two 'B's, an 'R' fol-lowed by an 'F', and finally a 'K.'

Without hesitation Griffin took his old wand from Garad and shoved it hard into the hole at the top of the star that had a 'B' above it. He then uttered the words, *'Five Friends Forever, Black.'*

'But Father, you can't use your magic,' Garad wailed.

'Here I can,' Griffin said boldly, 'but only two spells.'

Instantly the ground trembled and the pantree groaned as a hefty crack appeared in the boulder, splitting the pentagram straight down the middle. Lizzi and the children watched in disbelief as the giant boulder then split itself in two and each half began to move further and further apart dragging the roots of the tree with them. A sudden and strange light bathed their faces with warmth and as their eyes adjusted they realised that a magical entranceway lay before them, passing through the boulder and under the tree.

They were speedily ushered inside by Griffin and moments later the shattered boulder reformed, sealing the family safely inside.

Once inside and much to their surprise, apart from Griffin of course, they were not met with bark or cold stone but warmth and comfort. They trotted down a long, winding stair and emerged into a grand circular hall with many levels.

They entered on the lowest level where there were comfy seats in front of roaring fires that magically lit themselves as soon as someone entered from outside, and desks that were scattered with old maps and dusty parchment.

The upper levels were stacked floor to ceiling with books and odd objects all of which looked useful. In fact Garad believed it to resemble the school library, and soon went skipping off to investigate further.

Griffin was now relaxed – he knew his family was safe. Lizzi and Pereé had found some snuggle-blankets and both settled down into one of the large comfy seats in front of the fire.

Garad had now reached the next level using a different stairway that spiralled on the inside of the chamber but in the opposite direction to the one they had originally come down. He leaned over the balustrade to notice the room below actually mimicked the engraving on the boulder outside. The same pentagram was detailed in the intricate flooring of the lower chamber, albeit disguised in places where desks and rugs covered it.

He soon realised that the room seemed divided into five clear sections and each section had its own theme as if personalised. In the centre of the chamber a large circular desk with five chairs was sat boldly, with all manner of objects on it.

As his keen young eyes scanned the room again but this time in more detail he noticed a similarity among the five sections: each one had a stone plinth within it. So, following a short stint of pulling old books off shelves (some of which had *Pendragon's School of Magic* stamped within them) and poking old suits of armour, half-expecting a reaction, he made his way back downstairs where his mother and sister had now fallen asleep.

'Think it was all a bit too much for them,' Griffin said, stepping forward from behind a mountain of scrolls.

'Father, what is this place?' Garad asked as he continued to gawp and stare at all the amazing things in the secret chamber. He removed his muddied dressing gown and paced over to where his father was sat.

'It's a place from my youth,' Griffin began. 'Five of us found it while we were at school – well, at least we should've been at school. Anyway we believe it used to be a pit used for darker deeds, abandoned and long forgotten, but we found it and changed it to suit our own needs at the time. And, made it – well, more homely.'

'What needs?' said Garad looking at his father with intrigue and a certain level of doubt.

'Mainly academic – well, to start with it was a place we could all escape to study or forget about the troubles of the world. But over the years it has proved a most useful venue for all five who know of its location, for we also came here in times of desperation when there was nowhere left to go.'

'Who are the other four? Old school friends of yours?'

'That's right m'boy. And I expect they will all be here soon enough – well, once I have let them know we are here anyhow.' Griffin rummaged through some of the ancient scrolls that were nearly falling apart in his hands.

'Won't it be dangerous out there for them in the forest?' Garad said caringly. 'Wouldn't want them to go through what we just did, especially without Mother and her kitchen utensils.'

'They won't have to travel through any forest my lad,' Griffin chuckled.

'So how will they get here then?' Garad asked

'Henge Stones!' his father replied gleefully.

'What's a Henge Stone?'

'Well, there are always a pair, see,' Griffin said pointing at the five stone plinths that Garad had noticed from the upper levels. 'Each one of those stone plinths has an identical twin somewhere else in this world of ours and provided the owner of the stones stands on them and recites the correct words they will instantly travel to the twin stone.'

Garad stared blankly at his father, relishing the thought of being able to zip instantly from one part of the world to another without the use of a broom or worse – walking.

'So you're telling me the other four are dotted in different parts of the world and in a flash they could be here?' he said excitedly.

'Exactly m'boy' said Griffin who was himself rather excited about seeing his old school friends.

'Hang on!' Garad said suddenly. 'If one of these Henge Stones is yours, where's the other one? Where's the twin stone?'

Griffin let out a deep sigh.

'Always so many questions Garad. You remind me of me when I was younger, always keen to learn. Each of us always keeps the twin stone in our home – mine was at our house in town opposite the Tipsy Toad but it was destroyed when I disappeared.'

'That's why we had to risk coming here on foot through the forest then,' Garad finished.

Griffin paced over to one of the stones and carefully stepped onto it.

'How do I look?' Griffin asked Garad, as he patted his hair flat and practiced his smile a few times.

'Erm, okay for an old Warlock,' Garad replied feeling it was an odd question. 'It's only an old bunch of friends, I'm sure they'll have aged too.'

'Aged!' Griffin howled. 'One of them is dead – well, half-dead at least.' He finished rolling back the black muddied sleeves of his cloak. He raised both hands up towards the ceiling and performed his second spell.

*'Amicis Retrivo.'*

Much to Garad's disappointment nothing spectacular happened for a good while but before long a glaring light filled the room and once it died out two people were standing on their plinths. Garad recognised one of them instantly as Thomas Fineart, the tall, good-looking Wizard from the trial who was wearing his top hat, fine clothes and held a cane.

The second person Garad had never seen before in his life but was instantly captivated – for on the other plinth stood a Witch, stunning and confident. She had dark ringlets, and looked incredibly fashionable with an intricately designed gown and crimson lips.

'Thomas! Robella! It's so good to see you!' Griffin said whole-heartedly, rushing forward to give them a hug. 'Thank you for coming so quickly and coincidentally at the same time – I don't think that's ever happened before,' he chuckled. 'Garad, step forward m'boy – don't be shy now. Garad you know Thomas, and this my boy, is Lady Robella Riveaux. She is an incredibly powerful Witch so I want you on your best behaviour.'

'Griffin, please,' Lady Riveaux began with a smooth voice like silk or liquid gold that Garad thought had an interesting accent. 'You make me sound like the type of Witch that would turn him into a slug if he misbehaved.'

'Yes, well I haven't forgotten what that feels like,' Griffin blushed. 'But he is a good lad – defeated his first enemy tonight using an excellently placed *Ludemortis* spell and then went on to do an even better *Insanistultus.'*

'Takes after his father then,' Fineart said stiffly. 'Come, enough about you, how are Lizzi and Pereé?' he finished, looking around the chamber.

'It's been a long day for them, they need their rest,' Griffin said pointing to the comfy chair by the fire. There Lizzi lay sound asleep with Pereé snuggled under a warm blanket. Both of them smiling as they dreamed of sweet, wonderful things.

'Nelson or Blue here yet?' asked Fineart.

'Not yet although I expect they'll be along any minute,' Griffin replied.

Moments later another flash erupted by one of the other plinths, followed by a billowing green smoke that spread throughout the chamber. As the soupy smog thinned Garad stared on in disbelief as a slight man with dark skin and a bald head sat cross-legged in mid air. He had markings all over his body like ancient scripture. His eyes burned bright-white and a slightly decay-like odour offended his nostrils.

Upon closer inspection Garad noticed that this new Wizard's skin was mottled and pitted with open sores as though he was half-rotten.

'Garad, this is Nelson Kroon. He is a half-dead necromancer

from the desert lands far to the east.'

'Hellow maan!' Nelson said floating over to Garad before offering him a half-rotted hand to shake.

'P-P-Pleased to meet y-you,' Garad stuttered with uncertainty. He felt both impressed at the sight of the half-dead necromancer but also at the same time repulsed by him.

Garad had just finished wiping his hand on his robes before he started yet another bombardment of questions - this time all aimed at Nelson.

'How do you float like that? Why do you float? How are you half-dead? And - '

'Woah maan!' Nelson interrupted, 'me need me pipe before answerin' any o yer questions maan. Now it should be round 'ere somewhere,' he finished before floating over to his section of the chamber. Next he began making objects float here and there just by looking at them with his glowing white eyes. Masks with feathers, a staff clad with skulls as well as jars full of eyeballs and pickled things all went scooting through the air.

'Where me damn pipe maan!' Nelson said, his rotting face appearing angrier by the second. Moments later plumes of thick smoke were exhaled out of Nelson's gangrenous nostrils.

'Me love ya pops t'inkers bacco – clears me rotted ed better dan any pie or potion,' he said, heaving in another putrid lung full.

'So you be wantin ta know bout me den do ya lickle maan?'

'Yeah please Nelson,' Garad began, 'and I'm sorry I keep asking all these questions but I've never met any Witches and Wizards like you before and you are all so different and interesting.' He blushed slightly in admiration.

'Ha! Wait until Blue arrives,' Fineart chortled, 'he's the oddest of us all.'

'Well maan, to answer all ya questions: I is able to float cause I is half-dead and so me body is no longer bound to dese lands like de rest of you. Why do I float? – well it makes life, and death for dat matta, dat lickle bit easier – would you walk if you could float maan?' Nelson asked rhetorically. Garad replied by shaking his head.

'An finally, you wanta know how me is half-dead – well I died at de hands of a very powerful Wizard, willingly o'course maan. Ya see for me to become more powerful me had to die and den be brought back.'

'But, what Wizard would kill another Wizard?' Garad asked, looking baffled.

'A Wizard who me could trust, a good friend and one me knew would bring me back,' Nelson finished, smiling through sore lips.

'Who?' Garad pleaded.

'Him be standing right behind you maan,' the necromancer smiled again as his dead eyes scanned over Garad's shoulder.

Garad instantly froze to the spot, too afraid to turn around – who could it be? Seeing Nelson smiling in front of him he drew a large breath, summoned his bravery and slowly turned around.

In place of an evil sorcerer as he had imagined, Griffin his father was staring back at him.

'You?' Garad yelped in utter shock. 'You've killed someone? – I mean I know you've killed before but that was under the influence of the Witch, right Father?'

Griffin watched as doubt and disgust painted their way onto his son's face, for Garad had placed his father on a pedestal and idolised him from a young age. As well as this Garad was also obsessed with Merlin, a wizard world-renowned not only for his seemingly limitless power, but his will to use that power for good. The fact that his father could then use his own magic for an act of darkness filled Garad with both fear and anger. His father's actions went against everything he had ever believed in and had been taught.

'Garad, you must understand that in life we sometimes have to do things we may not wish to and, although it seems wrong to you now, greater things were achieved as a result of my actions.'

Garad went very quiet and very pale, his eyes were clearly welling up at the very thought of it – his father, a killer.

'Nelson became more powerful and, as he wished, ended the reign of Clinkhook Stumphammer, the tyrant who had killed thousands in his time.'

'Merlin would never kill anyone!' Garad snapped, wiping his eyes as he did so.

'Merlin?' said Griffin throwing his hands in the air. 'What does Merlin have to do with this?'

'He is more powerful than anyone! He could kill the entire world if he chose to but he only ever uses his power for good,' Garad barked, turning to stare at Griffin's old friends, who all wisely shrank back a few steps at the sight of the angered boy.

'And just where is Merlin eh?' Griffin asked rhetorically. 'Where is the greatest of all time? I think you have an unhealthy obsession with Merlin. You have every book and scrap of parchment about him, the walls of your room are peppered floor to ceiling with tapestries of him – what's next? Are you going to grow a long white beard?'

Garad did not reply straight away but instead stared coldly at the floor in front of him, trying with all his might to summon the courage to tell his father his true feelings, even if that meant upsetting him.

'I didn't want to believe the stories after you reappeared,' he began as his bottom lip wobbled, 'the whole town blamed you and so we were alone; me, Mother and Pereé. I had to look after them and I tried as best I could but we suffered months of torment.' A tear that had been stored for some time rolled down his cheek.

'Garad I…' But Griffin didn't know what to say and he stood awkwardly, feeling completely ashamed and embarrassed.

'Abuse in the streets,' Garad continued with a raised voice as his expression changed from sadness to anger, 'threats and closed doors were all we seemed to be offered in your absence. But school was the worst: "Baby Blackmouth" is what they all used to yell at me. "Baby Blackmouth" they'd shout in every lesson and down every corridor - sometimes even the teachers joined in,' he finished, gazing up at his father who himself was now welling up.

'But they were all right – you are evil.'

Griffin rushed forward and grabbed his son tightly by the shoulders, looking straight into his watery eyes.

'You don't mean that – please, let me make it up to you, you have to understand I had no control after I was taken.'

'And yet that aside you killed your friend, before you were taken – Merlin would never do such a thing.'

'Merlin is not your father!' Griffin exploded in a mixture of anguish and frustration.

'WELL I WISH HE WAS!' Garad thundered, 'Better a vacant old Wizard than a murderer like you!' he said, turning and running at full pelt out of the chamber, leaving Griffin flummoxed with his friends.

A fourth and final flash exploded into the chamber quickly followed by raucous laughter. But there was no smartly dressed Wizard or a pretty Witch, there wasn't even a half-dead floating necromancer – instead, smiling widely and dressed in a long, pristine-white cloak, stood what appeared to be a glittery blue pig. He had a flat snout and what looked like diamonds pitted into his skin.

'So, what have I missed folks?' the odd creature queried, smiling wider still, bearing two prominent tusk-like teeth.

'Blue – you made it!' Griffin cried, momentarily forgetting his son's grief.

'Of course I did – you know me, never one to miss a birthday – do we have cake? I like cake,' the blue pig chuckled.

'But…it isn't anyone's birthday Blue,' Griffin said, winking to his other friends.

'Oh well, happens to me a lot – coming here to an empty chamber, but this time you're all here!'

'Unfortunately…' Fineart mumbled sarcastically as he stepped forward to greet his blue friend.

'Hello Thomas, how are you?' Blue said, grabbing Fineart's hand and shaking it all over the place. 'Ooh do you still collect lightning? I caught one the other day…' he paused looking over his shoulder and around the room as if about to share a secret. Leaning in he whispered into Fineart's ear: 'Thirty three megasnips! Ooh she was a beaut – I've never seen one so big.'

'No Blue, my lightning days are done, I'm just too busy these days,' Fineart finished, stepping back having retrieved his hand.

The five friends spent the next hour or so gossiping and reminiscing about days gone by. Some had tales of adventure, others joked and laughed. Fineart was just telling the others about a new Witch in his life when he was interrupted by an almighty wail that came from the direction of the large blazing fire.

'Banshee!' Blue yelped, jumping to his feet. 'Quick, ready the nets – let's catch the beast!' he snarled as his diamond-encrusted snout grunted at the air.

'Calm down Blue,' urged Griffin, 'it's just Pereé, my youngest.'

Both Lizzi and Pereé had woken and, while Lizzi had met Griffin's old friends before, it naturally came as a complete shock for Pereé to wake to see a tall blue glittery pig-man and a floating dead ghosty-man in the chamber.

'She's a great screamer!' Blue yelped with excitement.

'Griffin she is so beautiful,' Lady Riveaux added.

Lizzi pulled Pereé close to her and scowled at the pretty Witch.

'Lizzi? Are you alright?' Griffin said looking puzzled.

'I will be…' she snapped, 'the moment she leaves!' Lizzi said, nodding in Lady Riveaux's direction.

'What's wrong Mother?' Pereé asked as she stuffed a soggy thumb back into her mouth.

'Oh nothing darling – just something your Father and I need to talk about.' Lizzi threw a glare in Griffin's direction.

Griffin, trying not to draw more attention to the situation, just stared back at Lizzi with a puzzled expression spread over his face.

The room fell awkwardly silent; Witch looked at Wizard and Wizard glared back at Witch until finally someone spoke.

'Mother what's wrong with that man's face?' Pereé squeaked with uncertainty, much to the relief of the rest of the room.

'He's nearly dead,' Lizzi said tonelessly.

'No Mother, the other one, the sparkly one – the blue piggy man.' Pereé said pointing as best she could while still clutching her bogey doll.

'Oh, he's a bit of a clumsy Wizard,' Lizzi began knowing she wouldn't offend Blue. 'He's very kind and funny but he sometimes gets his spells wrong and so he has ended up with a piggy nose and blue skin that grows diamonds all over it – oh and he doesn't taste very nice to monsters.'

Pereé giggled at which point Blue did too.

'He's pretty Mother!' Pereé said with Blue's reflection sparkling in her eyes, 'I like him.'

'And I like you too little lady,' Blue said with a grunt and a snort.

Lizzi quickly ushered Pereé and Garad to the sleeping chambers that ran off down a tunnel. Each chamber was crammed with cosy beds, food and floating teapots full of hot chocolate.

Meanwhile, Griffin spent some time explaining to his old friends what had been happening in Brickabrack over the last few months what with the deaths and sinister goings on at night. Once he had them up to speed they sat around the large table at the centre of the chamber; discussing and pondering, looking at maps and pouring over old scraps of paper. Some went researching to the archives in the upper levels but not Griffin.

He hadn't moved. He sat trying to make sense of Lizzi's actions for she was always so calm and collected. Why did she take issue to Robella's presence? Was she jealous of her natural beauty? Did she envy her power?

'It's the past,' Blue said patting Griffin on the shoulder supportively.

'But that was at school!' Griffin said raising his voice at Blue's suggestion. 'Robella and I have only seen each other a few times since and that was normally to overthrow some dark warlord or newfound terror – take the Beast of Blackthorn; hunting a creature so foul that flowers would wilt just from the smell of it – not exactly what I would call romantic,' Griffin finished with a sigh.

'Ah but this isn't about you is it my friend?' the sparkly blue wizard explained. 'Lizzi has her own reasons for feeling the way she does and as her husband you must be the one to help her see past them.' Blue picked a diamond from his warty blue nostril and flicked it on the floor.

'Feelings? What feelings?' Griffin said sharply. 'To my knowledge we are a happily married wizarding couple.'

'And there lies our problem my friend,' Blue whispered sympathetically before letting out a long sigh. 'Your knowledge, or memories for a better word, are in this case not entirely complete.'

Griffin stood quietly leaning on the desk, as his friends continued their desperate search to find something that could help Brickabrack – for it was now their duty to save it: 'Those who have the power also have the responsibility to do what is right and necessary.' That was the last thing Master Agar had said to Griffin before they entered the forest.

'Help me Blue, what am I missing?' said Griffin.

Blue looked up at him with a gormless grin, bearing stained teeth.

'You're missing…' Blue paused and for a few seconds the chamber fell utterly silent. He twitched and his head rocked a little then to Griffin's surprise he began to sing:

> *'You're missing and kissing,*
> *Witches that you shouldn't,*
> *You're hiding, confiding,*
> *In Wizards you normally wouldn't.*
> *So tell me, oh Blacky,*
> *What's your heart's desire?*
> *Is it Lizzi? The Children?*
> *Or rekindling an old fire?'*

'Oh here we go! I wondered how long it would be before we got Silly Blue out here,' Griffin said, watching his friend who was now happily spinning on the spot while laughing wildly and picking his snout with both hands; a grubby sausage-finger in each nostril. You see, following another mispronounced spell Blue developed two personalities; one, was wise, controlled and helpful while the other was funny, mad and often "unbearably annoying" as Fineart would say.

'Can I have Sensible Blue back out here again please – and what on earth was that song about? I haven't been kissing any Witches?' Griffin said, changing his tone as if he was talking to a child. Blue smiled even more naughtily before starting again:

> *'Not in real life,*
> *But talk to your wife,*
> *As I'm sure she'd like to say:*
> *Griffin my dear,*
> *Whisper truth in my ear,*
> *Of what you thought,*
> *While in court for a day.'*

Blue then sneezed sapphires and giggled as they went scuttling off in different directions. Meanwhile Griffin was certainly reluctant to try and make sense of anything Silly Blue was singing. His words echoed around his head and so he sat down, rummaging through his memories, or what was left of them, to try and understand Lizzi's upset.

'Me – kissing Witches? But not in real life? In a court room?' Griffin looked up with wide eyes at Blue as the answer hit him.

'My trial!' he said loudly.

'Indeed my friend,' Sensible Blue said, returning to the chamber in a more controlled state of mind.

'The truth orb,' said Griffin. Blue nodded. 'I said something or it showed something that Lizzi saw.' Blue nodded again. 'What did it show?' Griffin pleaded, feeling exhausted.

'The truth naturally – it's a truth orb, although most of us were as shocked as Lizzi.'

'What did it show?' Griffin shouted at his friend.

'It showed you falling from a great tree, remember, when you were taken. You were plummeting to what you thought was your death and your last thoughts were of your children and your beloved,' Blue finished.

Lizzi, who had woken up and, hearing her name mentioned had crept back to the main chamber. After listening quietly for a few moments, she stepped out from the shadows and began crying.

'B-but instead of me it showed her! You see her as your beloved; and she's 80 odd years older than me – I mean granted she looks younger but anyone can take youth pastilles these days – but I think it just looks fake…and…and…'

'Lizzi I…' Griffin began but she ran from the chamber, unable to face her once perfect husband. 'But I love Lizzi Blue,' he said honestly, 'she's my wife, my darling, the mother of my children for goodness-sake!'

'And yet you still hold onto your feelings for Robella,' said Blue.

'No!' Griffin insisted slamming his hand hard on the table. 'That was a long time ago. Besides, nothing ever came of it; Robella never wanted me, despite my advances.'

'Griffin, it's called a truth orb for a reason so I'm afraid this is something both you and Lizzi are going to have to confront and it has to start by you accepting the fact that you still, well –'

'Love Robella,' said Griffin.

# CHAPTER THIRTEEN

# The Wail of the Banshee

A few awkward days were spent in the secret place. Lizzi and the children spent their time in the sleeping chambers and only came out to eat, while the rest dedicated every waking hour to discussions and research.

Frustratingly, every time they thought they had the answer to the murderous riddle of Brickabrack it was shortly quashed by further investigation.

'We're getting nowhere fast!' said Fineart.

'Ooh is that like getting somewhere slow – but backwards?' Blue said, enthusiastically leaping to his feet, 'Because I can do that – watch,' as he started pacing, as if in slow-motion, backwards around the chamber – tripping on piles of papers and falling over furniture as he went.

'Any longer in here with him and I may find myself using a death spell,' Fineart said sharply, tossing another dusty and pointless scroll on the growing heap by the side of the large round table that they had spent hours at.

'Calm down Thomas,' Lady Riveaux said softly, 'at least he eases the tension. Besides, you cannot fault his determination,' she whispered, gazing over to see Blue once again in a heap on the floor after falling over yet another chair.

'Why are you whispering?' posed Fineart.

'I'm not,' she replied, raising her voice a little, but in truth she had been as quiet as a tacit troll (who are renowned for expressing themselves without even opening their mouths) since Lizzi's outburst. Rightly or wrongly Lady Riveaux had also been at Griffin's trial that day and was just as shocked to see her image being projected over the audience within the Council Chamber.

This had left her feeling angry for being made to feel guilty for something that was out of her control and for something that, some may say, wasn't even her fault. But she was a very wise Witch – she knew when to blow on a fire and when to pour a bucket of water over the flames and this was one of those occasions. So, she remained silent.

'He's just such an imbecile!' Fineart muttered as Blue was now doing headstands.

'At least he knows how to enjoy himself,' Lady Riveaux said glaring at Fineart, who did not take too well to her implication and as a result began to sulk like a spoilt child.

'I know how to enjoy myself but he isn't helping – we've been stuck in here for days with no glimmer of solving anything. We need help and…'

'You're right!' Griffin shouted from across the table to his handsome friend. 'We cannot solve this ourselves – we need help and I think I know who can help us.'

*

'ABSOLUTELY NOT!' Lizzi thundered, 'she's only four – Griffin what are you even thinking?'

'Lizzi we need to get Orbs back on side. He said it himself, the only one he feels will trust him now is Pereé and so she is the only one he will talk to. He won't even show himself to me.'

'How do we even know that he is still in his hollow?' Lizzi said, pacing up and down in front of the enormous fireplace. 'Say she does go all the way back through that monster-infested forest out there – he might not even be there.'

'He will be there darling.' Griffin said confidently.

'Don't call me that!' Lizzi snapped. 'Not now, not after what's happened.' Griffin closed his eyes and took in a deep breath. He knew that Lizzi felt betrayed and he himself was still shocked at what the truth orb had shown on the day of his trial – but now was not the time for it.

'Look,' he said sternly, staring straight into Lizzi's watery eyes, 'we have much to discuss; just us, alone, but now is not the time, we can get through this but our current predicament will not help us. Right now our only priority is saving the town and our children's future,' he paused as Lizzi offered him a reluctant smile, for she knew despite their relationship issues he remained a fierce father. 'We need Orbs to help us and sending Pereé is the only way.'

'But she's my baby – she'll be so scared out there on her own,' Lizzi whimpered, realising that as much as she hated the notion of sending their youngest into danger – it also made the most sense.

'She won't be alone,' said Griffin, 'you and Garad will go with her…'

'What, so you can be alone with *her!*' Lizzi boomed, while scowling at Lady Riveaux.

'For goodness sakes woman, no!' Griffin snapped. 'It's already pretty clear that if she braves the forest with you in tow nothing will try and snatch her; not now you've shown all the gribblies out there what a good rolling pin can do.' As he had expected, Lizzi's face looked a picture of emotions – joy one moment that she would be with Pereé but anger at the thought of travelling through the dense forest again. 'Also, Garad seems pretty handy with that wand so he will also be able to help.'

Lizzi still wasn't convinced. 'But say we get back to the temple and all the guests with the strange eyes are there – what will we do then? What if my father has become one of them?' she said, panicking at the prospect.

'Your father is exceptionally cunning Lizzi – granted he's madder than a box of frogs but he can outwit the best of us. I'm sure he'll be fine. As for Pereé – well let's just say she will have a few tricks of her own,' Griffin finished smiling like he knew something the others didn't.

\*

'Remember, only use your powers when you need to, okay poppet?' Griffin said patting Pereé on the head.

'Okay Father, I'll remember,' she replied sweetly.

'Lizzi, just as we discussed, get back to the temple. Take the route Thomas told you about; once there, provided there are none of the taken in sight, find Orbs and convince him to come back here and help us. We'll continue to search for clues while you are gone. Oh and avoid the river crossings; trolls normally like to wait for unsuspecting travellers as a light snack and, that aside, it may well be that the taken are patrolling them anyway. Just stay hidden and stay safe.'

*

It was night-time once more and Griffin hugged his family as the cool damp air of the forest tried to creep into the entrance of the secret chamber. Lizzi and the children waved a last time as the boulder under the pantree reformed again, concealing Griffin from sight and sound, leaving a deathly silence all around them.

'Right j-just us then,' Lizzi stuttered as she led them back into the dark of the forest.

'Mother I'm scared,' Pereé said instantly.

'There's no reason to be scared darling,' Lizzi said kneeling down and placing two warm hands on Pereé's cold cheeks. 'I'm here with my frying pan and rolling pin plus your brother has his new wand and best of all, you are here with all your lovely new powers.'

'Yeah, but why they gave them to her and not me is crazy,' Garad said snidely. 'I'm older and more powerful. I mean, has she even proved she is magical yet?' he said turning to his mother to argue his point for the third time since Pereé had been entrusted with these powers.

'Oh shush Garad!' Lizzi barked, 'You know perfectly well why – we can look after ourselves and besides…' Lizzi pulled Garad close so Pereé couldn't quite hear her, 'she feels less scared thinking she has powers, so stop your moaning and turn that oculus-thingy up.'

The family spent some time winding their way back through the forest. It wasn't long before the section with the large rocks and boulders was well behind them but, as Lizzi was to discover, an enchanted forest such as this left nothing to the imagination.

Trees moved, pathways disappeared and any distinguishable things like oddly-shaped roots or clearings had altogether vanished. They were lost again and Lizzi knew it.

'I think it's just up here,' she said, trembling.

'You're starting to sound like Father,' Garad said facetiously.

Moments later they entered a small clearing; the trees were old but appeared somewhat damaged as if recovering from an ancient fire.

'Garad, hold up your wand,' Lizzi whispered, 'something's shining over there,' she finished, pointing to an area of utter shadow that sat under a line of angry-looking trees.

*'Oculus Luxaurea Maximo!'* breathed Garad, creeping further forward into the clearing. 'Well I'll be...' Garad choked as he took in the sight before him. 'The Ogre Demon of Nazaroth!' he said in awe as Lizzi and Pereé joined him.

The three of them stood silently gazing up at the seventeen foot solid gold statue that was partially covered in ivy.

'You have to hand it to him,' Garad said, 'Grandfather must be pretty powerful not to mention brave to have beaten this guy.'

The ogre-demon was enormous; its bulky body, now frozen in time, still looked incredibly strong. Gigantic horns protruded from its angular head. Its mouth was wide suggesting it had been roaring at the point Lizzi's father had turned it into a statue; even the lines of saliva and spit dribbling from its mouth were solid gold. Then, oddly, Lizzi began to chuckle.

'What's so funny?' said Garad frowning at his mother as if she was going slightly mad.

'Do you remember the story your Grandfather told us about this ogre demon?' Lizzi said, giggling uncontrollably.

'Yes, why?' Garad replied.

'Look at his hands!' she said exploding into a fit of laughter, 'oh it's so funny!'

Garad had missed it at first glance, having been simply over-whelmed by the sheer monstrosity of the beast but as he looked harder he saw it: one of the ogre demon's hands was outstretched as if trying to grab something or someone, sporting claws that would skewer a wild pigdog. The other, however, was held tightly to the beast's chest and in it lay a fist full of solid gold poker cards.

'An enormous monster like this – getting all upset because he lost a game of cards – it's hilarious!' Lizzi spluttered.

The three of them stood giggling at the statue for some time – even Pereé, who in her mind still felt uneasy around the statue, was giggling loudly.

'What are we going to do Mother?' Garad said. 'We're lost again and we need to get to the temple, and fast.'

Lizzi slowed her laughter for Garad was right.

'Okay, let's look at this like your father would: what do we have to our advantage? Now my frying pan and rolling pin will not help us get unlost so Garad, you have your wand – do you know of any spells that could help us?'

'Not really,' he said contemplating all sorts that he wasn't really meant to perform outside the school walls. 'We've not really covered transporting or teleporting yet – really just the basics, you know – protection charms, healing potions and other sappy magic – nothing exciting like the Aura-curse,' he said, looking at his mother in the hope she knew what he was talking about. 'You know, the one where you separate an enemy's aura from their body and transform it into an enormous ogre or beast of your choosing and then set it on them – fun to watch I've heard as most of the time the Aura knows exactly what your enemy's next move will be.' Lizzi looked at her son with utter horror.

'Don't worry Mother, we don't get to learn about any of that stuff until my last year and that's ages away,' he finished with a huff.

'Well thank goodness for that!' Lizzi chortled. 'It sounds horrendous!'

'Okay Pereé – what gifts or tricks did your father and the others give you?'

'They're not tricks Mother,' Pereé said angrily, 'they're my magic!'

'Oh okay, sorry darling,' Lizzi said smirking at Garad, 'what magic have you got?'

'I bremembered them all off-by-heart just like Father told me to,' she said proudly. 'Father gave me this old stick and said it would bring my magic.' She pulled a tatty, crooked old wand (that looked more like a burnt twig) out of her pocket that had apparently belonged to Griffin's late mother. It was charcoal black and had faded markings etched on its surface – like some form of ancient writing. 'Mr Fineart taught me his *Imperatum* spell that he said could even make Merlin do as I say.' She stuck her tongue out at Garad who clearly took issue with this particular spell due to his fascination with the ancient works of the illustrious Merlin. 'So if Orbs doesn't want to play or won't do as he is told then I can make him.' She chuckled. Pereé liked the thought of this one – she thought she could use it on Garad so for once he would attend one of her bogey doll tea parties, complete with imaginary friends and invisible tea. 'That pretty Witch you don't like gave me her *Morphidius Cochlimus* charm that changes people and nasty things into snails. Then ghosty-man gave me a spell that undoes other spells and funny Mr Blue pigman gave me…'

'That's it!' Lizzi said, turning on the spot and eyeing the seventeen foot statue up and down.

'What good's her magic if we haven't even found Orbs yet?' asked Garad.

'We aren't going to use it on Orbs,' Lizzi said still staring at the golden ogre-demon statue.

'Then who are we…' Garad stopped mid-sentence and stared at his mother who was rubbing her chin with intrigue written all over her face. Then he stared at the beast, then back at his mother. 'Erm…should I be worried?'

'We're going to wake him up!' Lizzi said at last.

'WHAT!' the two children said in a somewhat united protest.

'Yes, that's it – wake him up and get him to fly us out of here and drop us home,' she finished with a slightly insane smile.

'And just how do you propose we do that? He's solid gold!' Garad barked.

Lizzi turned to both her children for she already knew exactly what to do.

'Pereé will use your Father's wand along with Nelson's spell to undo the spell your Grandfather did all those years ago. From there I will distract him by making lots of noise with my pan and rolling pin; then, as he comes for me you use that *Insanistultus* spell you do so well, leaving the beast confused and dazed. And then finally, once the ogre demon is chasing his own tail, Pereé, you use the wand again but this time use Mr Fineart's *Imperatum* spell and tell the beast that he is to fly us safely home and without any growly moaning. What do you think?'

'I think you're mad!' Garad said honestly, 'but I was right…'

'Right about what?' said Lizzi.

'You *do* sound just like Father.'

Lizzi smiled fondly at her eldest and offered a soft hand to his shoulder.

'Right, let's do this – ready?'

'Ready!' both the children replied who were stood with wands poised for action.

'Right Pereé, now!' Lizzi screamed.

Pereé lifted her dead grandmother's crooked old wand and aimed it at the enormous shiny statue. She then braved a last sharp look to her mother who gave a reassuring nod in return. Clutching tightly to her bogey doll she squealed loudly.

*'Expoverum'* – this was the spell Nelson had taught her and she had struggled to remember it what with being pre-occupied with grimacing at his half-dead skin. It reminded her of the skin that forms on gravy when you leave it in the pan too long - only his looked worse.

Within moments a line of solid gold spit glooped to the forest floor and evaporated. Droplets collected all over the statue as if it were sweating liquid gold and before long went trickling down the demon, gathering as a shiny puddle by its feet. With a crack like a small bone being snapped the ogre demon blinked before letting out an almighty yet confused roar.

Lizzi began beating her pan and rolling pin together in an attempt to draw its attention but to her amazement and concern the beast turned to the children.

*'Insanistultus!'* Garad wailed fearfully but nothing happened; the ogre demon stretched his wings wide and roared again.

'Hey ugly, over here!' Lizzi screamed at the top of her voice, banging her pan even harder, yet still he advanced towards the children. Then it hit her. She had missed one vital aspect of immense importance – her father's words suddenly rattled loudly inside her head: "Silence is golden."

Garad had attempted several *Insanistultus* spells with no results.

'Mother, I think my wand's broken!' he bellowed across the

clearing to where Lizzi stood.

'Make lots of noise children!' she wailed. 'Shout and scream now!' she insisted, at which point she shut up. The children wailed as loudly as they could at the advancing beast who miraculously turned to face their now silent, quivering-wreck of a mother.

She stood. Scared. Whimpering with fear under her breath.

*'Imperatum!'* Pereé shrieked as a dazzling purple light shot from the end of the old wand straight to the beast's head, knocking it to the forest floor right in front of Lizzi. The whole ground shook as trees uprooted and birds scattered. It felt more like a mountain had just been dropped from the sky into the little clearing.

'Now then you nasty beastie,' began Pereé in her bossiest tone, 'we need to get back to our temple and you're going to be the one to take us there, understand?' she said slapping the ogre demon across the cheek that must've felt like a fly had just landed on him. The ogre demon stood back up. It appeared somewhat dazed as if intoxicated and let out a little grunt that Pereé took as a *Yes*.

The great creature then bowed, as a jester would to his king, allowing Lizzi to climb onto his back while the children were carried in his colossal hands.

The forest looked very different from above, like an endless sea of leaves and waving branches. Every now and then the crisp moonlight would pick out a solitary Cherryberry that stood defiantly taller than the rest.

'If only your Father could see us all now eh!' Lizzi yowled from her perch on the beast's shoulders.

The creature soared high into the night sky and seemed positively joyous to be free of his golden prison.

As they began their descent through the dense canopies of the forest, with the temple now in plain sight, Lizzi thought that despite all Master Agar's tales of the fabled Ogre Demon of Nazaroth, being carried home by him was one of the more pleasant experiences of her life in the last few months.

After Pereé gave the ogre demon further instructions to be pleasant to everyone from now on and to never play poker again, they slipped through the last of the thicket, leaving the borders of the forest behind them. They then headed down the narrow path that led to the stairs at the foot of the less-used back door of the temple.

'Remember, quiet now – not a peep from anyone,' Lizzi commanded, with a firm finger pinned to her pursed lips. 'Once inside, and only if there are none of those funny people with the strange eyes to be seen, Garad, you and I will hide while Pereé creeps to the front door to find Orbs.'

The temple seemed empty. Each room they shuffled through was as dark as the last – all candles and lanterns had been blown out and the air was cold so their breath hung like a mist.

They finally entered the great dining chamber, which had been left in somewhat of a state. The plates were covered in mouldy food and a few chairs had been knocked over, suggesting that their crazy guests from the secret meeting several nights back had left in somewhat of a hurry. That is, all apart from Captain Shiverrs and Madam Croaker who were still frozen to their seats like statues.

'Okay, we'll wait here darling,' Lizzi said in a low whisper. 'Garad, let's float to the ceiling fireplace so we are out of sight should anyone or anything come back. Pereé, be careful darling and remember what to do if anything happens,' Lizzi finished, kissing Pereé on the forehead.

The corridor between the dining chamber and the kitchen was pitch black and Pereé was forced to literally feel her way along the warm stone walls, all the while praying that she didn't bump into anything or, worse still, anyone. She rounded the corner and knew instantly where she was – the air was always cooler in the main hallway to the temple and she, being clever for her age, had surmised that this was mainly due to the sheer scale of the entrance hall.

After gripping the handles of numerous umbrellas and the old scorched battle-axe she gauged the direction of Orbs' door as being diagonally across from her. Leaving the comfort and warmth of the stone wall behind she made for the black void in front of her. She had only taken a single step forward when she heard it – a sudden shallow breathing had entered the room. Pereé froze instantly, clasping both hands over her mouth to stop a terrifying scream from bellowing out.

Next, a faint purple glow appeared directly in front of her.

'Orbs?' she whispered towards the purple haze but there was no reply. Now terrified, she lowered herself to her knees and slipped slowly forward across the enormous slabs of polished stone. Moments later and with outstretched arms her fingertips touched the rough bark of the door.

The breathing had now become more erratic and louder. Pereé was dwarfed by the colossal door. She hoicked herself up from off her knees and began to climb as best she could towards the mushroom encrusted hollow. The further she climbed the more dazzling the purple light became.

'Orbs?' she whispered softly again, as her delicate fingers groped the rounded edges of the hollow. 'Orbs are you there?' and with a final heave she hauled herself higher and poked her head inside.

What she saw next would haunt her forever – Orbs was indeed in his hollow, his two orbs glowing fiercely above his head. His face was a picture of torment as expressions of pain, loss and anguish were complimented by his burning bright eyes and wide, twitching mouth. A strange purple lightning shimmered across his whole body but this was not the worst of it.

As Pereé stared on, trying to make sense of the horrific scene in front of her she saw it. There, among the painful expressions, purple lightning and erratic breathing something moved. At first glance it was hard to make out, but as she squinted in the darkness her greatest fear sprang into sight: eight legs and the same number of eyes now glared back at her.

Pereé's scream echoed across valleys, along every street of the town and pierced every gap of the forest until its petrifying sound began to resonate inside the secret chamber of the five friends.

'Ah an excellent wail!' proclaimed Blue in adoration, for that was the power he had entrusted to her, the infamous wail of the banshee and for a moment he sat there quite smug.

The others however, turned to him in utter disbelief that he had failed to contemplate the reason for her to wail in the first place.

'Something's wrong!' Griffin said, springing to his feet in utter panic.

'Nonsense Griffin,' Blue said, strolling casually over to the group of his now rather anxious friends. 'Why, she's probably just practicing, you know – having a bit of fun.'

'No Blue,' Griffin said shaking, 'I specifically told Pereé not to use the Banshee Wail unless one of them was in mortal danger.'

'But that's when you should use it,' Blue chuntered on, 'the last line of defence. You know as well as I that the Banshee Wail can leave an enemy near dead if used correctly.'

'We need to go now!' Griffin said frantically.

'We can take the Altering Path back to the temple,' Fineart suggested.

'No,' said Griffin.

'But it's the quickest route!' Fineart contested loudly.

'And I'm sure it will be patrolled; the normal routes are too dangerous, besides I told Lizzi that if they should be in danger and if Pereé had to use the Wail that they should meet us somewhere else.'

'And if they aren't there?' Fineart said abruptly.

'Then we must assume the worst and head back to town. It will still be the safest route for those of us left.' Griffin answered somberly.

'Where then?' his friends all grumbled as this was the first they had heard of it. Griffin looked up to see four puzzled faces.

'The only route that is now left for us to take - the only route that will allow us to get back into the town safely and unnoticed.'

'But Griffin the path is the only way…' Fineart argued.

'No…there is another.'

# CHAPTER FOURTEEN

# Ticklepenny Loch

'Right let's be off,' Griffin pleaded to Blue who was frantically rummaging through an untidy pile of weird and wonderful wizarding objects. They scattered off in all directions: some went in the fire but did not burn, some knocked over books and other objects, namely a mummified snot-goblin that smacked Fineart right between the eyes.

'OI! Watch what you're doing, you bumbling moron,' Fineart barked for what must have been the fourth time in less than a minute.

'Please Blue, time is of the essence!' Griffin now joined in at his glittery friend.

'Not without these!' he finally replied, holding up a pair of old pointy shoes that had tatty feathers poking out of the sides of them.

'Mercurial shoes!' Griffin exclaimed as he nearly choked on his own tongue. 'Where did you get those from?'

'My father left them to me bless his withered old soul,' Blue whimpered, wiping a few diamonds from his eyes as he did so.

'But…you don't have a father – you never knew your parents Blue, you're an orphan like me, remember?' Griffin said looking puzzled at his friend.

'Oh yes, yes that's right – must've been someone else then,' he said, shrugging off his previous comment.

'Blue…' Griffin began, 'why didn't you mention your shoes before? Lizzi could've used them to fly her and the children home.'

'No, no, I would've done Griffin but I remember Lizzi specifically saying she hated flying.'

'She doesn't hate flying,' Griffin said, 'she has a broom of her own - her only fear is of birds,' he finished angrily.

'That's it!' Blue said pointing at Griffin. 'I knew she wouldn't approve of these shoes. I mean, look at this plumage,' he said, ruffling the tatty feathers into a further state of disrepair.

The five friends took a few light provisions for the journey and began the ascent of the main staircase, leaving Blue's mess behind them. It wasn't long before they had reached the boulder at the entrance and could see the forest beyond.

'It's a strange thought…' Griffin offered.

'What is?' Fineart quizzed.

'That the last time we were all here together, and at the same time, we were at school. I wonder what age we'll be the next time we need to make use of our secret place.' he finished.

'Well, my birthday of course!' Blue proclaimed boldly.

'No one knows your birthday Blue, remember – we don't even know how old you are!' Griffin laughed.

'Oh yes, that's right…well, some friends you are!' Blue finished to which the rest of the group chuckled.

As the boulder with the Pantree on top began to reform the five friends stood, without speaking, offering each other looks of pride and nods of thanks to silently affirm their greatfulness of still being the same group of friends, working together, after so many years.

Griffin was the first to turn, leading the rest of the group away from the entrance and into the dense forest. He gazed back just once for a final glimpse of the entrance to their secret place. A place that had so many memories of easier times; a simple tree, sat on a boulder, in plain sight.

*

'So you're telling me we have to walk across half the forest towards the mountains until we hit this Loch and then travel all the way back up river into the town?' Fineart concluded.

'Correct Thomas,' Griffin said wearily. He found himself becoming aggravated by Fineart's constant moaning and felt as if he were a teacher addressing a cocky pupil that simply didn't know when to shut up. 'Well, I suppose Blue could carry us there using his magical flying shoes.'

'Afraid not Griffin,' Blue said defiantly, 'they're still sleeping, and if I wake them they most certainly won't take us anywhere.'

'What about the monster?' Lady Riveaux asked as she pushed brambles and thornsnickets out of the way. 'I've heard rumours recently of fishermen going missing again near those parts,' she finished, with a solemn stare towards Fineart.

'Don't be worryin' yaself Rowbella,' Nelson interrupted, floating forwards on a bed of green mist that smelled like rotting turnips and made the forest flowers droop and whither. 'No one has ever be seein de monsta since old Merlin paid it a lickle visit – an between us I tink he killed it once an for all.'

'It's a shame really,' Blue added.

'Why?' Nelson replied.

'Well I heard it was an incredibly magical creature. I mean, yes, it would drag you off the banks of the Loch to the depths to devour you or store you under a rock for supper, but it's a shame to just kill something because it's hungry and resourceful.'

'Resourceful? Blue maan, me heard dat at last count it be getting tru ten travellers a day. Now, you av a point maan but me tink dat be justification enough ta be killin' it.'

'How did it get here anyway?' Robella asked, looking to Nelson for the answer.

'Me heard dat some few hundred years back it climbed from de underworld up Mogg's Eye – de great maelstrom; and used de deepest rivers of dis world to find food before settlin' in de Loch.'

'Why though?' Robella said smoothly, 'Why use the rivers when I've heard it can travel on land?'

'I don't know lickle lady. Me tinks dat it wanted to stay hidden – ya know, like de killer we be huntin – if ya take a life ya best be making sure no one sees ya or ya be sure trouble be coming ya way.'

The friends continued through the night. Blue's Mercurial shoes never woke, much to the group's disappointment and as the hours dwindled so did the forest. At first the great river split the forest in two; a thick black snake, its treacle-like waters meandered silently like a cunning predator. Next, the ground became softer as the forest became less dense. Their feet squelched and slopped as they journeyed on. The hours ticked by seeing marsh turn to bog and bog turn to swamp.

The stars were still twinkling but dawn was fast approaching, silhouetting the mountains against an ethereal misty horizon.

'Ah, we're here!' Griffin said much to the delight of his soggy friends.

'Finally!' Fineart sulked, 'I'm sodden to my shoulders, another hour in this swamp and my top hat would've been dripping.'

The five continued down towards the shoreline.

'Ah look, the ruins of the once prosperous lake-town of Crunderdund,' Griffin said pointing at a row of old archways that adjoined a large crumbling castle. 'In its day it was quite the place to be, being referred to as: *"the ultimate destination of peace and tranquilit"* as written by the famous explorer Merekin Craggwiper.'

'Don't you mean *tranquility*' Fineart said, smiling at Griffin.

'No, no just *tranquilit…*' Griffin said confidently, 'you see he never finished writing the sentence – the monster plucked him straight off his deckchair and gobbled him up.'

'That's awful!' Robella cringed.

'I know!' Blue added, 'I hate it when I can't finish what I'm writing either – writers block: it's the worst,' he finished, snorting a little at the end.

'Well my friends,' Griffin began, scanning the edges of the Loch, 'there's no sign of Lizzi and the children – but we aren't alone – look…' Griffin pointed to a small island some way off from the shore and fishing happily on it was a fisherdwarf. They could hear him whistling merrily as he cast off again.

A little dwarven blunder-boat lay aground on the banks of the small island and the fisherdwarf's keep-net hung from a tree that swayed slightly from side-to-side.

'That's odd?' Griffin said watching the tree with intrigue.

'What is?' Blue said flicking diamonds from his snout into the Loch.

'That tree on the island, it's swaying oddly considering there's no breeze here – look at the water, it's still as stone.'

'Should we swim over to him? We could have a look at that tree too.' Blue suggested to the group.

'I'm not swimming in there!' Fineart grunted in protest, 'That monster could very well still be alive. Besides you may taste horrible to monsters Blue, but the rest of us would be simply delicious.'

'I'll go,' Nelson said enthusiastically, 'de water does wonders for me boils and rottin' parts.'

'Griffin? How about you? Fancy a dip?' said Blue.

'Well they do say swimming is one of the best forms of exercise.' Griffin said, pondering hard as to whether he believed anything was lurking down in the depths of the Loch.

'Poppycock!' Fineart laughed.

'It's true!' Blue said sharply, 'I've never seen a fish in one of those cartchair contraptions…'

The group's guttural laughs must have carried over the still waters of the Loch as moments later the fisherdwarf was merrily waving at them all.

Darker deeds, however, were unfolding below the water's surface. An enormous black tentacle, riddled with barbed spikes and a crab-like claw was hard at work teasing and groping at the fisherdwarf's hook. Moments later – he was gone – dragged straight from the small island and into the murky waters.

'Boy does he want that fish!' Blue said clapping in admiration.

The others, however, ignored this. They all stood dumbstruck.

'Erm…ideas?' Griffin posed to his friends, not taking his eyes from the shoreline of the little island.

Without hesitation, Nelson pulled a small glass pipette from his cloak that had 'MINI-MAXI' written down the side of it.

'Ere Griffin maan, I tink we might be needin dis.'

'I thought you had given all this up,' Griffin said taking it from Nelson's smelly decaying hand. 'I thought you were magically forbidden to make these anymore, that you had decided to devote yourself to accountancy.'

'Oh c'mon Griffin maan, did ya really be tinkin dat I would settle for being an accountant?'

'Well – I…'

'Sure, de money is good but dat, dat right dere in ya hand is my passion.'

Griffin offered an understanding nod at his half-dead friend before quickly turning and dipping the very tip of the pipette into the Loch.

'Just a lickle squeeze now Griffin maan – we don't be wantin' to suck de Loch dry – just aim to take half.'

Griffin pinched the rubber teat ever so slightly and watched in awe as half the Loch was sucked into it – it was an odd sensation as rather than the water level seeming to drop, it appeared more as though the mountains and land around them was rising up high into the sky.

'I guess you were wrong then Nelson –' Fineart said staring out to where the island with the tree had been.

'Yeah maan,' the necromancer replied, staring at the same spot. 'Merlin didn't kill it after all.'

The five friends stood, side by side on the bank near the Crunderdund ruins, unable to move, unable to speak, frozen with pure fear at what was in front of them.

The small island with the tree began to rise but this wasn't because the water level was still dropping; the island, it turned out, was the top of the monster's head.

An enormous fish-like head reared skyward. It had three mouths, one on top of the other, crammed with teeth as large as the blunder-boat that was now nowhere to be seen.

Next came its body – dark and segmented; similar to that of a beetle which had strange vents, dotted along the length of it. A large mouth-like opening gaped at its underbelly that had angular limbs resembling sharp black fingers surrounding it. They all poked and twitched as if trying to grab and shove things inside.

Glaring past this hungry opening the monster's body thinned to an enormous eel-like tail that coiled deep into the Loch.

Higher and higher it rose, dwarfing the tallest towers of the nearby ruins. It didn't look out of place between the mountains that ran boldly either side of the Loch.

Lastly came six dark tentacles, hundreds of feet long covered in lethal spikes with a claw at the end of each of them. They whipped and snapped through the air – looking to catch the next morsel.

'WANDS!' Griffin screamed, staring hundreds of feet into

The five friends take on the infamous

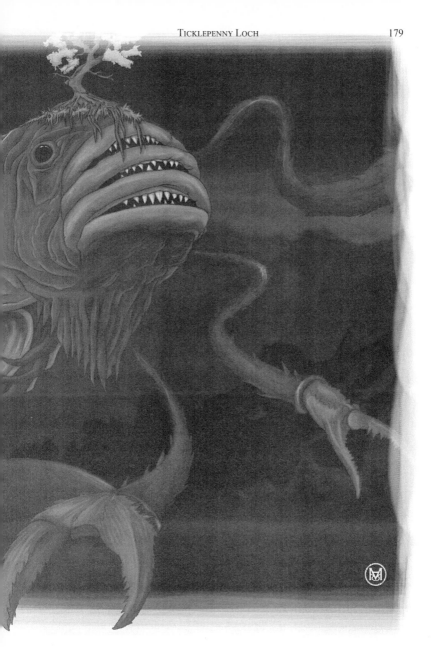

Ticklepenny Loch monster

the air where the monster's head had now finally come to a stop. He himself was still without his magic and so was relying on his friends to protect him.

Blue took aim first.

*'Flammahastam,'* he wailed as a jet of flame poured from the end of his battered wand that firstly scorched the ground in front of him then arched up and struck the Ticklepenny Loch monster beneath its lower jaw. Seconds later one of its barbed tentacles came thrashing down separating the group and smacking Griffin through the air.

'Flame spears?' Fineart bawled. 'We need to kill it Blue not tickle it!'

'The laws!' Griffin said clambering from the mud and back to his feet. 'Killing as a last resort.'

'THE LAWS?' Fineart bellowed in utter disbelief. 'This creature, this monstrosity of the ancient world, will scoff the lot of us for its breakfast if we don't kill it first, right here! RIGHT NOW!'

Griffin looked up at the towering mass of teeth and tentacles. 'Agreed…' Griffin said turning back to Fineart, 'but it'll take all of us.'

'Then let's do it,' Fineart wailed.

As the monster swayed in the misty morning light the tentacles came snapping at them once more. Four of the friends remained on the banks of the Loch, three of which bombarded the monster with lightning bolts, clouds of flame and piercing spears of light. Griffin stood firm, but was nothing more than a powerless spectator.

Blue, however, was now soaring through the air.

'And about time too!' he said to his well-weathered Mercurial shoes that were flapping like mad as he dodged spiky tentacles and ferocious snapping claws. As he neared the beast's gigantic head its lowest jaw fell wide, letting out a deep thunderous belch, releasing a reeking odour that bellowed past row after row of jagged teeth.

Its enormous eye that resembled a giant black marble but was as tall as a man – spied the sparkly Wizard and instantly Blue was plucked from the sky by one of the silent tentacles.

'*Multicreptis!*' Blue wailed in agony, as the tentacle tightened its grip to the point of breaking bones. A beautiful bombardment of blue spheres pulsed from the end of Blue's wand, each of which exploded on the seemingly impenetrable surface of the monster's beetle-like body.

Nelson had now taken to the air as well, levitating to within a few feet of the monster's gaping underbelly – the dark angular limbs grabbed for him but he was cleverly just out of their reach.

From the banks Fineart and Lady Riveaux continued to fire every spell at it – as well as destructive curses and death curses they tried the less impressive *Ludemortis, Insanistultus* and *Morphidius* spells but to no avail.

Suddenly, to Nelson's surprise, two fleshy pipes sprouted from near the monster's underbelly and shot searing bolts of orange lightning at him. Try as he might, there was no avoiding them and he was struck hard, battering him deep into the Loch's grim waters.

'That's it!' Griffin said excitedly, having noticed something the others hadn't.

'What?' Fineart said, firing more spells at the beast.

'Its weakness!'

'What, its lightning pipes?' Fineart said, looking hard at the beast – what was he missing?

'No, its underbelly, that's its weakness – that's why it hit Nelson. Robella you go and get him. Thomas you help Blue. I'll keep an eye on the underbelly from here.'

Fineart went running to the nearest tentacle until he was within reaching distance.

'*Gladiolignum,*' he shouted, and his cane instantly turned into a sword that glowed bright white. The tentacle with its claw splayed wide came storming at him. He jumped high into the air as the claw went scuttling underneath. He fell hard onto it, driving his white blade deep through its crunchy exterior and into softer flesh.

Meanwhile, Lady Riveaux was sprinting over the rippling water of the Loch – a natural power she had discovered as a child. She soon reached the spot where Nelson had been thrust under and as of yet, hadn't resurfaced. She aimed her wand beneath her feet and chanted:

'*Amicis Retrivo.*' A fluttering of bubbles rose to the surface shortly followed by an almighty splash that erupted all around her. Nelson, looking more worse-for-wear than usual, suddenly sprang out of the Loch and into her arms.

After laying a spluttering Nelson on the shoreline she turned to see Blue still trying to free himself from one tentacle while Fineart stabbed and slashed at another.

Finally she turned to Griffin who was stood, silent and still, looking at his hands.

'Griffin!' she screeched in despair, 'Griffin what are you doing? Help us! GRIFFIN HELP US!'

He turned to her, smiling darkly with a fresh sparkle in his eyes.

'What is it?' She shouted at him, now desperate for a response.

'My magic,' he said laughing wildly, 'I have my magic back! That crazy old fool did it!'

'What crazy old fool?' she said hurriedly.

'Master Agar - the old man found a way!'

Robella smiled and nodded at him knowing that this changed things, for Griffin, despite his gaunt appearance, was the strongest of them. He was the only one of them whose magic could be manifested from within him. It meant that at his most powerful he didn't need a wand and this wasn't something you could learn or be taught, it was pure. It coursed through the very veins of the Witch or Wizard fortunate enough to possess such powers.

And he felt powerful. It was as if he had been half-asleep and half-drunk since the Council elders had revoked his powers. He had never felt more powerful – it was almost as if he had been granted additional potency.

Just by thinking it he rose from the muddy bank, floating up towards the belly of the beast. The tentacles that weren't pre-occupied with his friends came for him.

'*Invictacorum Maximo,*' he said softly, now fearing nothing. His friends watched in both shock and amazement as he floated without aid underneath the monstrosity.

The tentacles came snapping and thrashing at him but grabbed nothing. Each attempt was thrust back by the protective and quite invisible bubble in which Griffin had placed himself.

Blue had become less important to the beast and was subsequently tossed to one side as the tentacle then headed for Robella.

Fineart, seeing this, shrieked at Griffin to kill it.

Finally, Griffin raised his hands as if paying a final homage to the ancient creature.

'Griffin no!' Robella cried as the snapping tentacle advanced towards her hungrily, 'Thomas! IT STILL HAS THOMAS!'

Fineart tried to free himself from the beast's claws but it was hopeless. Griffin turned to Fineart who caught his eye and, accepting his fate, nodded to Griffin.

'NO!' Robella wailed, seeing this, as the claw attempted to chomp down hard on her leg.

Griffin smiled fondly back at Fineart before finally aiming his hands at the monster's gaping underbelly.

*'FACTUMORTIS!'* He roared.

An almighty blast of green light and sparks radiated out from his entire body, seeping into the monster's writhing underbelly. Moments later the same green light beamed out of each of the fleshy vents along the full length of the beast.

A lasting roar bounced off the mountain sides as the dark creature plunged dead back into the Loch with Fineart coiled underneath it in a mass of quivering black tentacles.

Then – silence.

# CHAPTER FIFTEEN

# Riveaux and Fineart

'THOMAS!' Robella shrieked at the still waters before breaking into a mess of wails and crying.

Griffin along with Blue floated back to the shore where Lady Riveaux and Nelson were consoling one another.

'You killed him!' Robella spat wildly like a venomous snake as she charged at Griffin with clenched fists and white knuckles.

'Robella I had no choice, it was him or you, and *he* chose you – it was his decision.'

'No.' she barked, 'it was yours, you could've waited…'

'By which time you would have been dead,' Griffin snapped back in protest, not entirely appreciating her reaction. 'He told me to kill it to save you – you should be proud of him for being so brave and for being a fierce friend.'

Lady Riveaux threw both hands up to her face, sobbing again as she did so.

'But that's just it…'

'Just what?' Griffin said wearily, as a feeling stirred in his gut like he was about to be told something he wouldn't like.

'He wasn't just my friend…' she said, her bottom lip quivering uncontrollably with emotion, 'and you let him die, my Thomas, my true love.' She turned from the group to stare at the murky, silent waters once more. 'My last great adventure…' she whispered before dropping to her knees as more silent tears fell.

'Your true love? You two?' Griffin sneered with disgust and jealousy. 'After all these years? You two – together?'

'Yes,' she said proudly. 'He tried to tell you all in the secret chamber but you kept interrupting him.'

'That's why you arrived on your Henge Stones together,'

Griffin said sharply, now making sense of it all. 'You were living together!' An old rage swelled within him.

'What gives you the right to be upset? You have Lizzi,' Robella said angrily. 'Nelson has his corpse-bride and Blue is happiest talking to himself so were we not entitled to be happy, to be allowed to love and be loved?'

'Loved?' Griffin barked, 'Thomas Fineart didn't know how to love! He's never loved anything in his life but himself!'

'You're wrong!' she wailed tearily. 'He loved me more than words can say. But none of that matters now, b-because he's dead and it's all your fault,' she screamed, scrambling to her feet to face Griffin.

'I wouldn't be so convinced...' Griffin snapped back. 'Thomas always did have a good poker face.'

Lady Riveaux's face went from rosy pink, through red to purple.

'How dare you speak ill of him, how dare you – he always spoke so fondly of you. He thought of you as a brother!'

Griffin stood silently in front of her. She gazed, watery-eyed up at him and without warning slapped him hard around the face. He made no cry nor sound but took a moment to accept the pain. He turned back to her as she made for a second strike but this time his hand stopped hers.

She spat in his face.

'Well done Griffin,' she said with a vicious tone, 'first Emillia Brull at school and now Thomas.'

'I didn't kill Emillia Brull!' Griffin bellowed.

'Really? Who was it then?' Robella said sarcastically.

'I can't remember.'

'Ha. How convenient. Your memory always eludes you when it suits Griffin, like when you forgot how to be a decent wizard, becoming the vile Warlock you are now.'

'That wasn't my fault!'

'No, nothing ever is,' she said coldly. 'But I have news for you Griffin – this is! This is entirely your fault.' She paused and shot him a look of pure hatred that Griffin felt deep inside him. It felt somewhat like his heart was withering as a flower would after spending too much time in the sunshine.

'Yes, well done Griffin,' she said, narrowing her eyes to a scowl, 'you just killed your best friend.'

Griffin hung his head and turned from Lady Riveaux.

'Actually he didn't…' came a deep manly tone from behind them all. There, stood bold as brass was Thomas Fineart, albeit dripping wet and covered in weed.

'Thomas!' Lady Riveaux wailed, flailing herself forward, wrapping her arms around him and frantically kissing every inch of his slimy face.

'I – I thought…'

'You thought wrong Robella – didn't you notice it?'

'What?' she said, looking confused.

'Griffin's protection charm.'

'Yes I saw it.'

'He cast it for me at the same time. I'm sorry to admit the beast had the better of me and was ready to claw me in two, but Griffin's charm saved me and then kept me from drowning. Without him I would've been a gonner,' Fineart finished, wringing out his fine waistcoat that now looked rather more like a dirty dishcloth.

'Griffin – oh Griffin, I'm so sorry, please…' Lady Riveaux began.

But he was gone. The group argued among themselves as to whether in the confusion of Fineart's return from the grave Griffin had quickly sloped off on foot or whether his new-found powers allowed him to vanish unaided. Blue wasn't one for arguments but instead wandered around the group speaking to thin air saying things like: 'it's okay, you can come out now.'

The truth was that Griffin had sloped off very quickly – sprinting to one of the old Crunderdund towers and it wasn't because he was upset by Robella's hurtful words or the sharp slap round his face. He ran off as he couldn't cope with the notion of Robella being with another Wizard. And in his heart what made matters worse was that she had chosen Fineart – his best friend and not some distant equally good-looking traveller or magician.

It was an odd place to be. He loved his wife – he would die for her just as he would his children – and yet he couldn't suppress his desires for Robella. This was a different kind of love. She had been his first love and as such owned a small piece of his heart, buried deep, hidden, like that last treat or treasure you save for yourself, stored in secret until you are at your most desperate.

Deep down he had always yearned to rekindle that magical spark they had shared together so briefly in their youth. He loved his family unconditionally, yet his love for Robella was irrevocable.

'Sorry you had to hear that Griffin,' Blue said, plonking himself down next to his friend. 'I know you still hold…feelings towards Robella.'

'How did you know where to find me?' Griffin asked in a tone that suggested he didn't care much for the answer.

'I didn't,' Blue said. 'I was actually hoping I might find a toilet around here somewhere – I've kind of needed to go ever since the old monster reared its ugly head. Can't think why though?' he finished, snorting loudly.

'I want to be left alone,' Griffin said coldly. 'Besides I think the toilets are down there,' he said, pointing to several pits cut deep into the floor of the ruins.

'Too late now,' Blue said, as a shower of diamonds and glittering sapphires trickled from under his robes.

Griffin burst into laughter.

'That's actually one of the most disgustingly beautiful things I think I've ever seen – disgusting, oh yes, but beautiful. I've seen you sneeze diamonds a good few times you see and I've always thought: I wonder how he – you know…'

'Huh, that's nothing. It's when the geodes hit the deck – that my friend is when it's time to really wonder.'

The two Wizards sat chuckling for a while, laughing at all of Blue's various odd bodily functions.

'Have you ever felt it Blue?' Griffin said, turning the conversation back to serious. 'That aching in your heart and the following worry that you may never feel it again?'

'Erm no, is it like indigestion?'

Griffin smiled.

'Do you know I first danced with her at the Blindman's-Buff

Ball at school?'

'Ooh, was that the one where the old blind caretaker…tut, oh what was his name?' Blue paused, gazing up and rubbing his diamond-encrusted chin.

'Mr Buff?' Griffin said rhetorically with a smile.

'Yeah, that's the one. Was he the same caretaker that would randomly select a couple to dance in front of the whole school?' Blue asked, scratching his head.

'Yes, that's the one,' Griffin chuckled.

'Yeah, now I remember,' Blue said. 'When we were at school some scrawny kid got picked as well as his ridiculously stunning dance partner. Always thought she was way too good for him.'

'Erm, Blue…'

'Yeah Griffin, what is it?'

'It was Robella and I that got picked.'

'Oh, well…right…damn caretakers eh, out to make fools of us all.'

'Anyway, that's when I first felt it.'

'Embarrassment?' Blue said quickly.

'No.' Griffin said frowning.

'Shy and like you wish you'd practiced the dance a little bit more?' Blue added a little too eagerly.

'No Blue. I'm referring to the relentless ache of love. A single dance with her felt like an eternity.'

'Yeah, I had a dance partner like that once,' Blue added.

'And as the dance finished I felt heartbroken and bereft,' confided Griffin.

'Your friends love you Griffin, all of us, and I feel that now you must confront your emotions. Tackle your fears head on.'

'I can't,' he said. 'Not at the moment. We need to find the killer and save the town before there is no town left to save.'

'Then let's be off!' Blue said, jumping to his feet. 'We'll find Lizzi and the children together – five friends forever!'

'No. Not now,' Griffin said with a somber tone.

'What do you mean?'

'Riveaux and Fineart are to go home.'

'Griffin you must accept that they are together now.'

'I have, not that I like the idea but that is why they must go, we cannot risk their lives further.'

'Don't do this to protect Robella, Griffin, she can look after herself.'

'I'm not,' Griffin said convincingly, 'I'm doing this to protect them both. Besides, the atmosphere would be unbearable and we need to be focused when we reach the town.'

# CHAPTER SIXTEEN

# The Dark Command

Several days had passed since the secret gathering at the temple although to Master Agar it felt more like several months had transpired.

While Griffin, Lizzi and the children had sloped off into the darkness of the forest he had been tasked with pretending to be "taken" which involved walking with a limp, staring like a mad man, drooling and making the odd twitch or funny noise. His eyes had been constantly streaming as he was fearful of blinking and being exposed. He had spent days barking like a rabid dog, drooling like a goblin with no teeth and had near enough invented a new demented language, which the rest of the taken seemed to understand. It mainly comprised of talking to himself as if possessed, with long periods of sinister whispering that were only broken up by the occasional psychotic outburst.

Following his family's departure from the dragon temple, those remaining had spent days at the Tongue-tie table (including Madam Croaker and Captain Shiverrs frozen to their seats, with rumbling bellies) before finally venturing towards the town.

Naturally Master Agar's desire to find the killer meant that, after a lot of squawking and odd staring he had joined the group of "taken" friends and colleagues and headed for the town's limits.

As they limped, twirled, skipped and in some cases crawled up the slope that led to the entrance of the town, he had expected a flurry of guards to cascade down the winding path towards them, but they never came. As they drew nearer he spied the walls and gantries but no Brickabrack guards were patrolling them. In fact, as they approached the large lanterns he noticed they were extinguished, swaying sadly in the darkness. Once inside he saw that all

the many street lanterns were unlit too and a strange and disconcerting silence was present – where was everyone?

Master Agar quite sensibly decided to make a dash for it,
leaving the rest of the taken to amble and trip down the desolate streets. He skipped along cobbles, slipped through archways
and climbed spiral stone staircases before reaching one of the
normally heavily-guarded wall turrets that led to the great town
walls. For some time he ran along the rampart, meeting no one but
being very aware of himself. Every now and then he would stop
to catch his breath and check the dark streets below for any signs
of activity. But there was none – all the windows were frosty and
unwelcoming, the sea of chimney pots were smokeless – the town
had only darkness and silence to offer.

The only sign of life was an eerie glow that he could now see
coming from the middle of the town by the marketplace. Granted
the marketplace was usually well-lit at this time of night, but
something felt different. Anyone else may have fobbed it off as
the moon playing havoc with their eyes, but Master Agar felt
unnerved by it and so naturally wanted to get a closer look. The
issue with this was being able to get close enough without being
seen. Master Agar's cloak and robes were, after all, famous in their
own right; why some say they were woven from pure moonlight
as they seemed to shimmer like a cluster of stars in the darkest of
nights, and so, for now, he remained loyal to the wall.

As he continued, lightly skipping along the huge stones, he
approached the grand tower of the school library; a monolithi-
cally beautiful tower cut into a huge shard of stone that extended
up from the Spitwind Cliffs. As he gazed high into the night sky,
being momentarily bedazzled by the scale of the tower's silhouette
against the evil moon, he had an epiphany: his old broomstick. It
was in his office in one of the upper towers of the school and, even
though it didn't exactly fly straight anymore (following the battle
with the Ogre Demon of Nazaroth), it would be the only means
possible to get nearer to the marketplace. In no time at all, for
an arthritic knee-knocker with a bad case of Wizard-flick elbow,
the old Master found himself whistling over rooftops and dodging
chimney pots as he had done so often (and without his parents'

permission) in his youth.

As he soared closer to the town centre he could hear a commotion unfolding.

In order to maintain a safe distance but also get a better view of the town centre, he decided it would be wiser to land on the roof of the colossal Council Chamber Two. After a somewhat bumpy landing he hopped off his old battered broom, giving it a pat like you would a well-behaved puppy. Master Agar squinted and focused his eyes but he was struggling to make out just what was going on in the marketplace. So, summoning what bravery he had left he got down on his knees and climbed down onto a ledge that was spattered not only with dragon dung but also rows of enormous stone statues. Not being the fondest of heights he made for the nearest one, a giant grotesque statue of some foul creature that, once his eyes had become accustomed to the darkness, he realised was a statue of Fonzo Fidrib. He stared at the statue for some time feeling he preferred it when he thought it was a foul creature.

A large noise suddenly erupted from the marketplace that shocked the old Master so much he now found himself hanging from Fonzo Fidrib's nose – a place no one would want to find themselves really.

After a lot of climbing and panting Master Agar sat happily on Fonzo's shoulders gazing down into the marketplace, where an enormous fire was burning fiercely. The flames themselves were nearly as high as the surrounding buildings.

What looked like half a forest's worth of wood had been stacked around the old well and was now roaring high into the midnight-blue sky.

Suddenly and without warning shadows began to flood into the marketplace – only shadows for Master Agar couldn't define any features because of the monstrous fire. All he could see were thousands of eerie and in some cases, gargantuan silhouettes swarming to the light of the fire.

In a matter of moments the town had gone from deadly silent to being very much alive. Doors flew open, windows were smashed, even a wall adjoining one of the Imperial Guards' quarters was destroyed as something huge came thundering through it.

Master Agar could do nothing apart from hold his breath and look on. As the shadows advanced nearer the fire he was now able to identify some of them: trolls, ogres, bogies, Dogdyke were-wolves, demons and unclean abominations such as he had never seen before and all of them with varying masses of horns, teeth, tentacles and entrails. It was as if all the world's evil had come to gather in Brickabrack, as if they had decided this was now their home. Master Agar wondered just how long they had all been lurking, unseen and undetected within the walls of the town.

As more and more crammed their way forward in an untidy mess he saw something that turned his stomach and made him nearly fall from the stone version of the ginger Councillor again. To his horror, the townsfolk now began to pour into the market-place, lining the streets in every direction and all of them looking ravenous, drooling with wide glassy eyes that shone brightly as the grim moonlight caught them.

The huge creature that had moments earlier destroyed the wall of the Imperial Guards' quarters slithered forward on heavy, writhing tentacles. It had a grotesque face with an enormous tooth-laden smirk that did nothing but conjure thoughts of sadness and misery as Master Agar looked on.

'Silence!' the enormous creature began. 'You all know why we are here, so stop your wailing and wait for her.'

The evil army fell utterly silent all at once. As this happened the enormous fire turned from warm orange to puce green, drenching the surrounding area and its occupants in a sickly bile colour. It was an odd sight as the townspeople now resembled the creatures around them. It was as if they all had the same coloured skin and so Master Agar found it hard to distinguish who was truly evil at heart and who was not.

The fire billowed high, almost to the height of the Council Chamber, as a piercing cackle carried over the entire town.

The surrounding crowd lurched back as a hooded figure stepped straight out of the roaring green flames.

Master Agar gawped on in disbelief. The hooded figure held out a manky hand and thrust it back into the inferno. In an instant, the blaze zipped down into a tiny ball that the figure clenched in its claw-like palm. It held it up to its face and with a swift blow a thunderous jet of the same puce-green flame went roaring around the entire town lighting every lantern, candle and lamp as it went.

An evil green haze now hung over Brickabrack like mist at a harbour.

'That's better!' the cloaked figure wailed, pulling back its hood.

Master Agar saw an old hag turn to the mass of beasts that surrounded her. She glared at the watchful crowd.

'Well tickle my bones,' she cackled, 'we did it! Years of preparation and hard work and just look at us, here, in this place.'

Every beast howled, roared and hissed with merciless glee.

'Look. Even the townsfolk have decided to join us,' she joked, gesturing to the streets filled with the taken.

'And what is your plan my Witch Queen?' questioned the enormous unclean beast, as its thick hanging tongue licked the boils on its belly.

'We begin with my revenge! Next we destroy this town, wipe it from the memory of the world; the town that time forgot, we scrub it out.'

'Yes my Queen, and then…?'

'Then, like a flood we shall wash over these lands until all the joy has been eradicated from it, sunk, like a ship never to be found again.' The hag burst into a frenzy of sour laughter that could crack glass and soon had the whole army of beasts joining in.

'And then?' asked the great unclean beast once more. 'Once we have left these lands to ruin, what next?'

The Witch turned to him and smiled with an evil glint in her eye.

'Bring out my prisoner!'

A huddle of foul things dragged another creature forward: it was bound and had a collar round its neck with thick ropes attached to it. The mass of beasts in the marketplace all snapped and barked at the bound creature as it was led towards the Witch.

Master Agar who was still sat on Councillor Fidrib's stone shoulders could not make out what was being led forwards.

'Tut tut,' the Witch began, 'this won't do, release his wings.'

A small bogey crept forward with a crooked knife and slashed a rope behind the creature. Moments later, impressive wings were outstretched, silhouetted against the green mist of the besieged town.

'Kestrell!' Master Agar whispered to himself loudly.

'Kestrell isn't it?' the Witch snapped. 'Yes, I have heard of you. A once great thunderclapper warrior if the tales are true, and yet you are fallen, banished for treason to your kind.'

'Not all stories are true,' Kestrell replied.

'That aside *bird,* once we have destroyed these lands I have another place I wish to visit – the Great Realm of the Lasting Light, and you'll be the one to tell me how to get there.'

'Never!' Kestrell replied, thrashing his wings violently.

'You will talk bird, oh yes, I will make sure of that,' the Witch said turning her back to him. 'You see, I will start by clipping your beautiful wings, after which my minions will have some fun with you.'

'And if that fails?' Kestrell asked.

The Witch turned to face the thunderclapper.

'I will hunt down and kill your family.'

Kestrell's feathers ruffled for the first time out of fear.

'Yes bird, I know your secret. You see the stories tell of four falling from the Great Realm. Yes – oh how does the song go:

> *Four fell, but only one was Kestrell,*
> *Yet they shared his bright plumage,*
> *His courage and will.'*

'You'll never find them!' Kestrell squawked.

The Witch bared her grim smile once more.

'We already have,' she said malevolently.

'LIES!' Kestrell exploded with fury. 'They are far away, safe from here.'

'My dear bird, there is no safe place from me, no rock nor shadow defy my gaze. I see everything.'

'I don't believe you!' Kestrell yelled.

'Then maybe this will help,' the Witch said, hobbling forward before touching him on his feathery forehead.

In an instant an array of horrible images were thrust into his mind like memories that did not belong to him. They were of his wife and two fledglings. He could see them safe in their shelter, a nest perched high up in distant mountains but then a horde of creatures found them, snatched them and dragged them away in cages. The last image he saw was of them all in a horrifying dungeon, the like of which this earth had never seen before.

The moment her fingertips left his feathery forehead he knew the Witch was telling the truth. She had his family.

'They shall suffer pain like none before them if you do not tell me where the hidden gate lies,' the Witch screeched.

Kestrell's feathers danced in the breeze before ruffling once more with sadness. An uneasy lump rose in his throat as he spoke.

'Their pain will echo through the ages and all will know of their sacrifice; that the few stood against a tyrant and died to protect the many.'

'Off with his wings!' the Witch boomed. 'Bring forth the clipper.'

Kestrell's beak fell wide as a horde of goblins dragged an enormous torture contraption forward. Wooden wheels squeaked and jerked over the cobbles as cold steel glistened and clanged out loud. The torturous device had a wooden frame with many sharp objects dangling from it, but even more terrifying were the lines of gribblies strapped to the frame, all savagely snapping away, hungry for their own little taste of him. He could see how the contraption worked. The blades were for the rest of his body whereas the gribblies would be the ones to remove his wings – they would chew their way through them.

'I could end your life in a second with my powers bird, but that would be too easy, too…quick. No, I want you to feel every crunch, every chomp as my minions have their fun.'

Master Agar decided he had seen enough and been silent for too long. He whistled for his broom which came whizzing over in an instant, albeit wobbly and the wrong way up.

As several creatures fought Kestrell into the giant contraption Master Agar came hurtling down Westgate, his staff outstretched in front of him, screaming as if charging into battle.

All manner of beast turned to face the old Wizard, grabbing high into the air with sharp claws and whipping tentacles. Snarls and dark wails were ignored as Master Agar whistled straight over their heads with only the Witch in his sights.

As he entered the marketplace he raised his staff high above his head.

*'Iaculis Luxulgor,'* he bellowed, as a bolt of lightning erupted from thin air straight to his staff which he then aimed at the Witch.

*'Dimittulum!'* he belted, as lightning shot from his staff straight at the Witch, who was thrown backwards into the onlooking crowd of creatures, bowling several of the smaller ones over.

Silence fell over the marketplace as the Witch got back to her feet.

'Very good Luther,' the Witch spat. 'I wondered how long it would be before we saw your face.'

'How do you know my name Witch?' Master Agar quizzed as a little trickle of fear crept up his spine.

'Why Luther, we have known each other for years, and for a time I was one of your greatest students; "a natural", that's what you used to say as you smiled at me from your self-scribbling chalk board.'

'I never forget a face Witch, and I remember every student that I have ever taught, evil or pure, and you my dear hag are not among them.'

'Then look again!' the Witch screeched. She placed a black feather with a ruby crystal tip to her temple.

*'Revelare Veritas.'*

Before the old Wizard's eyes the impossibly old-looking hag twisted and writhed, her bones cracked and snapped as she yelped with pain. Her mottled see-through skin turned soft and warm like buttercream. Young, beautiful eyes now stared back at the old Wizard as well as a youthful, familiar face.

'E-Emillia Brull!' Master Agar stuttered in utter shock. 'You're behind all this chaos,' he mumbled, with a vexed expression embossed onto his face. 'You died. At school, long ago. How has your soul returned and even more intriguingly your body?'

'That is of no concern to you Luther. However, what you should be concerned about is your family as well as the residents of your precious town. What is so special about this place anyway? All I see is an untidy mass of old bricks and chimney pots that would be better served as breakfast at a rock troll banquet.'

'This is home Emillia,' the old Wizard said gently. 'You see bricks and chimney pots but when I think of Brickabrack it conjures great memories of adventure and all those loved and lost.'

His last word struck a chord with the Witch as her face turned sour once more.

'Enough talk Luther,' she said, aiming her feather-wand straight at the Wizard. 'As of tonight your precious town, along with all your memories, will be nothing more than a pile of old rubble and ash.'

'My dear Emillia, you know I cannot allow you to do that,' he said, staring deep into her vengeful eyes. 'It ends here,' he finished softly.

Emillia's eyes widened with fury.

'Ha ha ha,' she cackled loudly, 'this will not end Luther. Tonight you will bear witness to the dawn of a new age, an age of darkness and sorrow. It begins with Brickabrack and, as my legions spread across these lands, a new order will rise. A Dark Command,' she finished proudly.

'Emillia this is madness. Listen to yourself, all this talk of death and your *Dark Command* – you will have many that will oppose you,' Master Agar said wisely.

'Of course I will!' Emillia shrieked in a joyous fashion. 'I welcome it, in fact I'm relying on it. You see, the brave who defy me shall simply perish, and the weak, well they shall join my ranks, after a few *modifications* first – like your townsfolk here. And as my army of darkness grows none shall stand in my way.'

'And then what Emillia? After you cast the world into darkness and all is lost, what next?'

'That my dear teacher is where the bird comes in,' she said, turning to Kestrell once more.

'Kestrell? What does he have to do with this? He's just a thunderclapper?'

'Exactly!' she said enthusiastically. 'That bird will show me the way to the Great Realm of the Lasting Light.'

'Emillia, there is no such place,' said Master Agar, exasperatedly.

'It's there Luther. And this feathery trickster is going to take me there,' she said, jabbing Kestrell with one of her fingers.

'Emillia, I have read nearly every scroll there is to read on hidden gates and mysterious realms and I can assure you there is no such place. Kestrell, tell her,' the old Wizard said, turning to his beaked friend but Kestrell did not move. He just stared ahead blankly, thinking only of his imprisoned family.

'Well Kestrell?' Emillia barked. 'Tell me.'

'It exists,' he began. 'It has been a secret entrusted to every thunderclapper since time first started ticking. And to this date only four outsiders know of its existence – the Witch and you makes the count six.'

'I don't believe it,' Master Agar said, stunned.

'I don't care what you do or don't believe. My Dark Command has work to do and lives to ruin. You'll have to excuse my rudeness but you need to die now Luther.' Emillia cackled like a naughty child at which the rest of her followers joined in.

'Emillia, if you do go through with this I must know two things before you finish me off.'

'Oh really Luther. Well, I suppose I am a merciful killer so what might they be?'

'Firstly, when you were alive your magic never reached the levels of power we have seen. You were still at school when you died and so your capabilities were limited. So how has your magic strengthened in death?'

'I'm afraid that one will just have to remain a mystery Luther.'

'Lastly then – the killings? How did you infiltrate our town, undetected and murder our residents as well as turn those left into these crazed, wide-eyed maniacs I see before me – this I must know.'

'Oh, my dear Luther, still trying to solve the riddle. You really are a poor excuse for a Headmaster and just to think, how many people look to you as the Master of Wisdom.'

'Emillia please…' Master Agar begged.

'Oh very well. Time is short so here's a clue, ahem:

*You walk on two, though I have eight,*
*I scurry around when dark and late,*
*I spin a home and wait for flies,*
*I'll pierce your soul with my beady eyes,*
*I'll bite your head with fangs of black,*
*You won't see me coming for my silent attack,*
*Let chaos unfold and the fear spread wider,*
*For none can defend from the evil Hair Spider.'*

# CHAPTER SEVENTEEN

# The Flight
# of the Thunderclappers

Griffin, Nelson and Blue arrived back at the temple to find only Lizzi and Garad.

Lizzi was beside herself.

'Oh Griffin, she's gone, our baby's gone.'

'Gone? What d'you mean gone?' Griffin asked, as a sickly wave of fear washed over him.

Lizzi's crying was hysterical and Garad was silent as stone – he just stared at the ground and wouldn't even look at his father. They had scoured the temple high and low looking for Pereé and Orbs but they had altogether disappeared.

'Well?' Griffin demanded, 'what happened? Did you lose her in the forest?'

'No,' Lizzi wept, 'the Ogre Demon brought us all here.'

'Ogre Demon?' Griffin said, nearly falling over. 'How?'

'We were lost and luckily stumbled on the golden statue in the woods and decided he was the best option to bring us here – then we crept around the temple…' Lizzi began to cry again.

'Go on,' Griffin insisted.

'Garad and I stayed back and let Pereé go alone to Orbs' door as we thought it might be best if it was just her, what with her being the only one he would trust…'

'Yes…'

'All we heard was a brutal scream that must've knocked us both out cold and when we came to they had both disappeared. Oh Griffin, we've searched everywhere: the temple, the clearing, we even spent half the night in the forest screaming her name…' Lizzi said sobbing and breathing heavily between words. 'Where's our baby gone Griffin?'

'We'll find out darling,' Griffin said reassuringly, taking Lizzi by the shoulders and pulling her close. Despite her fears she felt momentarily comforted as Griffin ran sensitive fingers through her hair. It reminded her of when they had first met and he used to hold her tenderly for hours, and they would just talk; not about anything in particular, just hours of chit-chat. But those days now felt like a distant memory. How she wished she could go back to them. Back to when she felt loved.

'We need to be off,' Griffin said softly to her.

'Then let's go maan,' Nelson enthused, 'me could do wid some more action.'

'No. Nelson, Blue – I need you to head back to the secret place and quickly. We're going to need some help. Lizzi, we're taking a different path.'

'Where?' Lizzi replied mopping her tears up.

*

'Spiders!' Master Agar spluttered while at the same time nearly swallowing his own tongue. 'But I haven't seen...' he stopped. What had vexed him oh so cruelly for months now stared back at him with menacing, beady black spheres for eyes.

As several of the taken townsfolk limped and twitched forward he saw them; some were tiny that scurried along single strands of hair, some were huge with legs that hung like dread-locks. One woman had two that at first glance looked like a pair of earrings but were actually dangling from her ears on silvery shimmering wisps of web.

'All this time! Spiders! But how?' the old Wizard asked in astonishment.

'Hair spiders are renowned for their stealth.' Emillia boasted, 'I just gave them the power to control – one tiny bite to the head and they control their victim,' she finished with a tone of smug arrogance.

'How did you come to give them these powers?' Master Agar pleaded.

'I had some help from a friend and that is all you need know,' she snapped with a noticeable level of uneasiness.

'But how did all these spiders infiltrate the town without being noticed?' the old Wizard asked, squirming at the thought of thousands of spiders all scurrying about.

'That was the easy part. GREED!'

'Greed? What do you mean?'

Emillia turned from Master Agar and began wandering between the ranks of her Dark Command.

'Your huntsmen been doing well in the old forest of late?' she began as the old Wizard stood silently pondering. 'Has no one noticed that the butcher's shop has been stacked to the hilt with venison in recent months? Hmm?' she went on, smiling wickedly as she patted a bogey and then stroked a werewolf.

'No,' said Master Agar.

'Exactly!' she exploded, waving her finger at the old Master. 'Everyone in this stinking town failed to notice what was literally under their noses the whole time – even as they were eating it! Blinded by greed they were, all of them!'

'The meat?' Master Agar asked, 'But how?'

'That's the clever part,' Emillia beamed, without showing an ounce of modesty. 'I began by hiding my special eight-legged assassins in beautiful flower-parcels. Next, I lured the majority of the forest deer to me and fed the flowers to them. The parcels were bewitched you see, sending the deer somewhat dopey while at the same time making life for your huntsmen a whole lot easier. So, once the butcher took his daily delivery and set about the carcass with his cleaver the spiders were released; free to roam the town as they saw fit.'

'That's how poor Mr Proofgrease's son died,' whimpered Master Agar through his long white beard. 'They were attacked first.'

'Naturally…' Emillia said darkly and without remorse, 'and as the finger-pointing began and the greediness continued the rest was easy. Why, some evenings I would go, unchecked, and literally slip my little friends out of my cloak pockets and straight under the doors of these filthy houses.'

Master Agar was dumbstruck. He had no quibbles nor remarks

to make. All the while the town had been searching for one murderer, thousands of tiny eight-legged ones had been scurrying along floorboards and dangling from ceilings.

'Though I have to hand it to you Luther, you had the master stroke – inviting your old friend Blundell here and throwing him and the entire town a party. Everyone got a taste! Even better was sneaking into your secret meeting and leaving some very well prepared cuts of meat – oh yes, I was there too! Don't feel bad though Luther – you tried, but unfortunately some things are meant to happen and so here we are.'

The old Wizard didn't budge. He gawped hard at the cobbles by his feet, taking a deep gulp before speaking.

'I cannot allow this Emillia, I cannot allow you to destroy something so beautiful.'

'Hah! Beautiful?' Emillia said turning her nose up. 'Granted the old Library Tower is impressive but this town of yours is nothing more than a stain on these lands. The world will be better off without it,' she finished, glaring at the old Master with disgust.

'Emillia…' Master Agar began coolly.

'I've heard enough Luther, the time has come for you to die.'

'Emillia…' Master Agar said again.

'What!' she barked.

'I wasn't talking about the town.'

'W-What? But…' she began but Master Agar had the better of her. In a flash he aimed his staff at Kestrell.

*'Amica Domum,'* he chanted as the glorious thunderclapper vanished with a pop leaving nothing more than a puff of smoke and a few feathers that fluttered slowly to the ground.

'You fool!' Emillia screamed as her face turned a deep shade of beetroot. 'Do you realise what you have done!' she wailed. 'You will die old man,' she said, raising her wand at him again, 'you and that stupid bird's family.'

Her eyes burned green with fury as she screamed.

*'FACTUMORTIS!'*

Master Agar closed his eyes, waiting for the imminent pain to start. He knew it would be useless to try and compete with Emillia as he could feel deep inside that she was more powerful. He didn't understand how but he just knew that it would all be over soon. He would leave the fleshy shell that he had resided in for all his long years and finally be reunited with his wife among the stars.

But the pain didn't come.

He opened his eyes to see the back of a dark figure standing before him, silhouetted against a halo of green. It was Griffin.

'Not tonight Witch,' Griffin thundered, as green flames poured from the end of Emillia's feather-wand but did not pass beyond his outstretched hands.

As her spell dwindled Griffin was met with a face he hadn't seen since school. A face that had haunted him most of his life.

'Emi? Is that you?' he said, almost trembling with fright.

'Surprised to see me Griffin, or should I say Blackmouth?'

'It was you? You did this to me? WHY?'

'Simple really Griffin – revenge.'

'*Revenge?* For what?'

'Poor Griffin, no memories, banished, but I see you have your powers back,' Emillia smirked. 'And by the looks of things you have acquired some new ones,' she said, aiming her wand at him once more.

'That's right Emillia. Now let's see how you get on without your wand – *Magicum Oblitero!*' Griffin said confidently as Emillia's feather-wand turned to ash in her hand.

'You were foolish to come back Griffin,' Emillia snarled. 'I made you who you are, remember? Blackmouth the mighty Warlock. P'ah! After I kill you tonight you won't be remembered. You have no friends, no one that loves you, not even your wretched wife and children can bear the look of you. You are alone.'

'Then if you speak the truth, that is something we have in common,' Griffin said quickly.

'Silence!' Emillia spat, her voice wobbling with anger. 'I'll be remembered alright. None shall forget the name of the Witch who destroyed the world.'

'Until there are none left in the world to remember it.' Griffin said coolly. 'Like I said, if what you say is true, being alone and unloved is all you have to look forward to' Griffin finished, enraging Emillia further.

'I have an army of companions who would die for me. Look at them –' she said frantically throwing her arms off in all directions, pointing at the worst looking of them all. 'Each and every one of them loyal to the end,' she said, again gesturing to the slobbering ranks that were now closing in on Griffin. 'And what do you have?' she asked sharply.

'I have these…' Griffin said pointing to the stars.

*'And?'* snapped Emillia, 'They could be fireflies for all I care.'

'Look again,' said Griffin with a grin.

Creature, beast, Wizard and Witch all gazed up as four shooting stars streamed overhead, twirling over one another before crashing down into the marketplace, scattering the crowd of creatures.

'Pretty stones falling from the skies will not help you here Griffin,' Emillia hissed, who was clearly less than impressed.

'These aren't pretty stones,' said Griffin sincerely, staring straight into Emillia's eyes. 'These are Henge Stones!'

'IMPOSSIBLE!' Emillia roared, as a blinding white light erupted from a stone near her feet.

When her vision returned a funny blue pig creature in white robes stood proudly smiling like a witless wonder in front of her.

'Happy Birthday,' Blue said warmly.

'It's not my birthday,' said Emillia, full of confusion.

'Ah right, yes, I do need to work on that,' Blue said snorting loudly. 'Well nothing else for it then,' he said, leaning forward as if puckering up for a kiss but what came next shocked the Witch and all her minions.

Blue slowly opened his mouth wide as the most powerful scream charged out at all who were sinister. The deafening noise began by sending the startled Witch flying back several feet into a mass of tentacles and teeth who were then themselves bowled over. As the wail vibrated through the marketplace, row after row of goblins, trolls, werewolves, bogies and the taken were knocked clean off their feet.

After several seconds the entire gathering of evil in the marketplace had been toppled. Blue finished his wail, at which point a small burp crept out from the corner of his mouth.

'Oops, pardon,' he said, turning deep blue with embarrassment.

'ATTACK!' roared Emillia, clambering back to her feet so angrily that several huddles of her minions went scurrying off whimpering.

'CHARGE!' joined in the great unclean beast.

Suddenly, another white flash erupted from a different corner of the marketplace followed by thick green plumes of smog.

'Ah – playtime,' Nelson smirked, as he lifted a staff with a large skull at the end high into the air. *'Rigidum Quasilapis,'* he said confidently as three charging goblins turned to stone.

Another two flashes and Riveaux and Fineart were standing bold as brass holding hands. Her wand flicked elegantly here and there while Fineart's cane jousted and thrust as they both chanted spell after spell. All of this saw the ranks of the Dark Command being turned into snails and frogs while others were turned to dust or blown high into the night sky, never to be seen again.

The marketplace had been transformed into a battleground. Legions of dark creatures and the taken rushed forward as the brave friends sent colourful streams of sparks, flames and light off in all directions - fending off their advancing enemies.

'Black, you fool!' shrieked Emillia suddenly, pushing her way through her minions.

'Luther!' Griffin wailed to his Wizard-in-Law, 'Lizzi and Garad are hiding in the school, you must get them to safety,' he finished frantically.

'Where's Pereé?' the old Master said, with a heightened sense of concern.

'Safe with Orbs – hopefully,' Griffin replied heavily.

'She's too powerful Griffin,' Master Agar said stiffly, 'can you not feel it?'

'Of course I can Luther – she's too powerful for me – but not for someone else.'

'Who?' said Master Agar.

'No time Luther, she's coming, get my family to safety.'

'Your *family* – right,' said Master Agar with an odd expression on his face. 'Before I go Griffin tell me one thing.'

'Quickly then…'

'Madam Croaker and Captain Shiverrs, are they still at the

temple?'

'No. Why?' Griffin asked, wondering why that was relevant at this very moment.

'Well where are they my lad?'

'We released them of Blundell's spell and brought them with us, they are hiding with Lizzi and Garad. Why?'

'Good!' the old Wizard said. 'Keep them all busy.'

'B-But Luther I don't understand –' but Master Agar had already darted off in the direction of the school.

'Black!' came a shriek from behind him. He turned to see Emillia standing ready, her hands held high and her eyes burning green. 'You were foolish to think you were the only one who had magic beyond the wand. You won't be so smug after I split your skull.' She aimed a delicate and youthful index finger at Griffin and yelled. *'Cranius Contundito,'* by which time Griffin had his hands raised to defend himself. The ground trembled and a large crack formed between them.

'You have great magic at your command Emillia, I grant you that, but your army I find somewhat lacking – why, my friends are just having fun with them.'

'Oh poor Griffin, don't you remember we used to play chess together at school?' she said coldly. 'You know full well you always start with the little ones – maybe I should introduce you to someone more impressive.' She looked to the sky, giving a short sharp whistle that carried like a howling wind. 'Griffin Black, let me introduce you to Riptail – chiefest of dragons and son of none other than Spineback, oh and trust me, he makes his father look like a pussycat.'

Griffin glanced up to see an enormous shadow momentarily blot out the stars. He gazed back to Emillia who smiled wickedly.

'Meow,' she muttered.

'Blue!' Griffin shrieked.

'Yes. I'm here darling!' came a strident voice.

'Time to use those shoes of yours,' said Griffin, his eyes still fixed on the night sky.

'Griffin is that you? I thought you were someone else, what did you say about my shoes?'

'LOOK UP!' yelled Griffin.

At that moment Riptail landed heavily on a nearby rooftop destroying its chimney stack. Riptail, being a dragon hatched with a natural lust for treasure and shiny things, found the sight of a six and a half foot, blue diamond running around in the market-place, the most tantalising sight he had ever seen, and something no dragon could resist.

'Hello ugly!' Blue snarled to the dark monstrosity that was now lurching over him with jaws so wide it could have swallowed an entire house. 'Let's fly!' said Blue, darting instantly high into the air as the small, tatty wings on the sides of his pointy shoes flapped furiously.

Back in the marketplace, as Griffin and Emillia continued their duel, Riveaux and Fineart had fended off the remainder of the taken (whom they had simply sent to sleep) and scared off, destroyed, killed or squashed everything else. Just one now remained.

It squelched forward as rolling tentacles coiled and groped the floor. Its enormous tongue would still every now and then lick fresh boils on its sagging stomach.

'I shall enjoy turning this one into a snail,' said Lady Riveaux with a slight sneer.

'Oh it's snails you want is it my dear?' the great unclean crea-ture said, baring thousands of wicked teeth like pins. 'Be careful what you wish for,' he finished, smirking.

'AAAARGH!' Fineart yelped as he doubled over in pain. His legs suddenly shortened and his back rolled and hunched. Slime dribbled from his mouth and stalks sprang up from his forehead.

'THOMAS!' Lady Riveaux screamed in utter horror. Moments later a snail with a brightly coloured shell was leaving slimy trails where Thomas Fineart had moments earlier been standing.

'Be careful where you stand now my dear,' the obese creature cackled.

Lady Riveaux scrambled over and quickly plucked the snail from the ground.

'You have magic beyond any troll or ogre – what are you?'

'I'm different,' the creature proclaimed mysteriously.

'You are one of the Witch's followers are you not?' she said, whimpering as she tucked the colourful snail into her cloak pocket.

'Yes…and no,' the creature said, thrashing his tentacles wildly as an angry octopus might. 'I am not of this world my dear. I come from somewhere much fouler; a greater realm where the air is not sweet like daisies but rank and suffocating.'

'Then you can go back there then!' Lady Riveaux said, pointing her elegant wand at the unsightly creature.

'Ha! Your powers are pathetic girl,' snarled the creature. 'When I'm done with you…'

THUNK!

The creature was hit with such a force it laid him out cold on the cobbles.

'SORRY!' wailed Blue as he whizzed overhead closely followed by the biggest dragon Lady Riveaux had ever seen. 'It's this dragon!' Blue went on. 'It's making my tummy do somersaults!' he finished as another geode hit the deck on the other side of the marketplace and smashed open revealing purple quartz.

Lady Riveaux turned to face the creature whose tentacles were still writhing and twitching. With a swift flick of her wand, the creature was gone.

Nelson had now taken to the skies. Levitating high over the town he pursued Riptail, who was still chasing Blue. They soared high, then low; scraping rooftops and weaving in and out of the tall, beautifully crafted chimney stacks that rained rubble on the streets below as Riptail passed. Huge jets of flame thundered hungrily behind Blue.

As they passed the marketplace for the eleventh time Blue gazed down to see Griffin still duelling with the Witch, smoke, sparks and lightning bounding off in all directions. Their riotous voices bounced and echoed off all the houses in the town as spell met chant and curse met hex.

Blue had been chased by dragons before. In fact they were always after him; swooping down and interrupting a picnic or tea party to glare greedily at the odd-shaped blue diamond that moved. Not that he knew it, but Blue was actually etched into dragon lore. They had made growl-like songs about him and believed that the dragon who could catch the fabled walking diamond would live forever, feasting on fresh maidens in a land made of gold. Of course Blue had been quite good at concealing himself and even better at evading any would-be winged guests. And they had all been different, ferocious yes, wise – well mostly – but Riptail was in a league of his own. Blue had once taken a short holiday to the Plundertoft Mines to read the ancient scrolls of Spineback, Riptail's father, and he could say that Riptail was more menacing, brutal and clever.

Perhaps this was because his enormous muscular jaws were agape not ten feet behind him. This thought made blue feel funny, his stomach lurched again and he felt sweaty. Then –

SMASH! SMASH! SMASH!

'Oh no! Not again!' Blue winced as geodes began to rain down from beneath his pristine white robes, clanging off roof tiles and smashing open on the misty streets below.

Naturally Blue couldn't help it but Riptail was in awe – a moving giant diamond that made other precious stones. Riptail went berserk, hell-bent on catching this famous treasure of all treasures.

Blue could hear the beast's wings flapping more ferociously, like a horse changing from trot to gallop. He glanced back to see teeth slam shut so close they nearly ripped off his backside.

'Blue!' yelled Nelson, trying desperately himself to catch the jet-black terror.

He fired all manner of lightning spear and firebolts at Riptail's behind but nothing could stop him. It was hopeless.

'Blue watch out maan!' he wailed again.

'Nelson!' Blue screamed back as more geodes plummeted over the town. 'Nelson help!'

Jaws full of crooked teeth surrounded Blue before – SNAP!

'NOOOOO!' Nelson shrieked, still giving chase. 'Not my friend – you're mine now beast!' said Nelson, with a rage that even turned his manky rotten flesh slightly rosy.

But all of a sudden the beast started jerking and flapping around in the sky like a wounded bird. It gagged and gargled like it was about to be sick.

'What be up beasty?' said Nelson tauntingly. 'My friend givin ya a lickle belly ache hmm? Well good! Dat'll teach ya to be eatin my friends ya greedy, black, terror of de skies.'

Riptail seemed oblivious to Nelson's shouting as he now began to choke and splutter as if he had something stuck in his throat.

Without warning a beautifully sharp axe that glistened in the dim light of the moon went whistling past what was left of Nelson's gammy ear. The blade had intricate scripture and markings on it and attached to the leather-bound handle was a rope.

Riptail let out an agonising roar as the axe tore through his left and favourite wing.

Nelson watched as the dragon flapped clumsily higher and higher. He then traced the rope down from the axe, and there, holding on tight, skimming the rooftops below was a brightly-dressed dwarf.

'ARR! FINALLY REVENGE WILL BE MINE!' Captain Shiverrs boomed as he bounced off another chimney stack.

# CHAPTER EIGHTEEN

# A Disappearing Act

'*Revenge?*' Garad called over his shoulder to his mother as they sprinted down Westgate, shortly followed by a panting Master Agar and a wheezing Madam Croaker. 'What does he mean revenge?'

'Maybe the dragon beat him at a game of poker,' Lizzi suggested as they passed Council Chamber Two.

'Wrong,' Master Agar said, pointing to the colourful dwarf who was still dangling from Riptail like a worm on a hook. 'Look at the sash hanging from his belt,' he finished, heaving in another lung full of air.

At first it was hard to make out, but as Riptail flapped higher the cool night air caught the sash, flicking it wildly for all to see. It was a beautiful piece of cloth, no doubt silk, and emblazoned onto it was an emblem Garad had seen before: an iron fist holding a tankard with a "D" on it.

'Dithers!' Garad exclaimed with excitement.

'No,' Master Agar said assuredly, 'his son.'

'The Flag-bearer,' Garad gasped. 'Captain Shiverrs is the Flag-bearer?'

'Indeed, and it is a curious thing,' Master Agar said, scratching his head, 'that both Spineback and Dither's sons should now be engaged in battle – as if they were destined to the same fate as their fathers. And as father fought father, now son fights son.'

The small group of dragon watchers finally passed the Tipsy Toad storming their way towards the marketplace.

Emillia and Griffin continued their duel, using their magic to the best of their abilities. Fire was transformed into great hulking beasts that charged on Griffin and that were coolly extinguished with a swift clap. Next, loose sections of wall and boulders were fired at the Witch as Griffin frantically swished and swooshed his hands through the air.

She retaliated with crackling green bubbles that whisked their way speedily towards Griffin. He fashioned a floating defensive wall from more nearby rubble and as the bubbles popped against it they exploded violently, sending dirt and debris showering off in all directions.

Griffin suddenly spun himself into a vortex that skirted around the Witch, darting back and forth. In an instant he stopped, shocking Emillia as he grabbed her by the shoulders.

'Emillia this must stop!' he pleaded.

'Ha. You still think you are more powerful than me,' she cackled wildly.

'I've never thought that. There was a time when I thought a great deal about you Emillia. We were good friends once were we not?'

'Yes we were once. Both orphans. Dealing with life together. I loved you Griffin and you killed me.' Emillia finished with sadness in her eyes.

Griffin's expression turned from courageously determined to sorrowful at hearing this.

'*I* killed you? That's what you think?'

'There was no one else it could've been,' Emillia spat.

'But I have no memory of your death,' Griffin said honestly, 'you just disappeared.'

'WELL I REMEMBER!' yelled Emillia in protest. 'I remember it well – it was after the Blindman's-Buff Ball at school. You had declared your love for your precious Robella and she didn't even bat an eyelid before she walked away in disgust. Not like me – I was *always* there for you, always ready to listen and talk. It was as I comforted you that my life was ended – tell me Griffin – was it the denial of her affections that fired the rage within you? Is that why you killed me?'

'I TOLD YOU I DIDN'T KILL YOU!' Griffin thundered.

'Actually you did,' came the warm gravelly voice of Master Agar as he stepped from the shadows into the ruined marketplace.

'*Luther?*' Griffin said, turning to see the wise old Wizard step forward. 'What do you mean? I have no memory of killing her. She was my friend, why would I do such a thing?' Griffin asked, feeling even more confused than he ever had, as large tears welled in his tired eyes.

'B-Because –' stammered Master Agar, his lip wobbling at the same time, 'b-because we made you,' he finished, as his face sank.

'*YOU!*' Emillia bellowed, 'WHY? WHY KILL ME AND ALLOW GRIFFIN TO TAKE THE BLAME?'

'It was not just myself Emillia – all the Councillors deemed it necessary and using Griffin was the only way. Believe me child, it was no easy decision for any of us,' the old Master finished.

'MURDERERS! ALL OF YOU!' Emillia screeched with anguish written all over her face. 'BUT WHY?'

'To protect me,' Madam Croaker wheezed through broken teeth as she too stepped from the shadows.

'And who might you be?' Emillia demanded. 'Are you not simply the town drunk?'

The old hag looked long and hard at Griffin with sad eyes set deep into pale wrinkly cheeks. 'Luther, it is time,' she said turning to the old Master. He offered her a smile before softly muttering.

'*Bellarune Adversus Veritatem.*'

The magic was painful. The hag fell to floor with a yelp. She writhed and rolled around screaming in agony as her bones cracked then snapped back again in a different place.

'What are you doing to her?' Griffin yelled. 'What was that spell? I've never heard it before.'

'And, my dear boy, it is unlikely you ever will again,' Master Agar said boldly as he nodded to where Madam Croaker lay. As the noise stopped she lay face-down, a quivering and trembling wreck.

Griffin knelt down and placed a gentle hand on her shoulder.

'Madam?' Madam Croaker are you alright?' he asked, full of concern.

'I am now Griffin,' came a gently spoken, sweet voice from where Madam Croaker was laying.

'You sound different,' Griffin said in a shocked fashion.

The old hag slowly turned to Griffin who's jaw fell wide.

'Goodness. You look different too!' he said, becoming more and more puzzled by each passing moment. 'I've known you my whole life and you have always looked and sounded the same – who are you?' he finished, almost forgetting he was still holding Emillia, who was just as keen for answers.

'Griffin…' she said, which was followed by a long pause, 'my name isn't Madam Croaker, that was just a name picked to conceal my true name.'

'So what is your true name?' Griffin said, his heart fluttering with anxiety.

'My name is Bellarune Black,' she said as the town seemed to fall completely silent. 'I'm – I'm your mother.'

Griffin stared at the gentle-looking Witch before him. She had a warm face and a soft smile, her teeth were straight and there wasn't a wart in sight – even her hunched back had gone.

'Griffin doesn't have a mother!' barked Emillia in blatant protest. 'He was orphaned like me. Cast aside like a piece of left-over meat, left to fend for himself and be raised by the murderous Council elders – that's why we ended up friends, our similarities: both unloved, both abandoned,' she finished, spitting near Bellarune's feet. The spit hissed like acid as it hit the ground.

'Not abandoned!' Master Agar said boldly. 'Griffin your mother had to do what no mother had ever done before – she was forced to abandon you.'

'But why?' Griffin said with tears in his eyes.

'To protect you and her,' the old man said, 'Griffin, you and the name of Black are special. Throughout history all Witches and Wizards, your mother included, going by the name of Black have been hunted by a dark evil.'

'Hunted?' Griffin said curiously. 'Hunted by what?'

'A terror like no other. A terror that knows of a prophecy that pre-dates this very town and tells of a day when a Black family member will rise up and defeat the purest of evils.'

'And when is this day?' Griffin asked in a somewhat bewildered tone.

'It is coming, and soon according to Merlin,' the old Wizard explained.

Griffin let go of Emillia. What he had just been told had alto-gether exhausted his mind. A thousand questions now raced through his head. In a few brief moments he had discovered he was forced to kill a friend, his mother was actually alive and she had not abandoned him, but instead had spent her life in disguise as the town drunk, and he may be in line to destroy the purest of evil. His legs suddenly felt heavy as he slumped to the ground and buried his face in his hands. It was just all too much.

\*

Meanwhile as the revelations unfolded below, Nelson gave chase after Riptail who still had a Wizard in his gullet and a dwarf hanging from his wing.

'Get down here beast!' Captain Shiverrs grunted loudly from below as he smashed through yet another roof. 'Oh I've had enough of your games dragon,' he wailed, pulling a beautiful double-barrelled flintlock from his broad belt. Still clutching to his father's rope-axe with one hand, he took aim and fired true, straight into Riptail's chest.

Riptail gave a colossal roar as two bullets made of diamond cut through his scales and buried themselves deep into his flesh. The flapping of his wings slowed as he tumbled heavily towards the town.

When Captain Shiverrs came to he was surrounded by rubble and the debris from what used to be two houses off Upgate; the street that future generations of Witches and Wizards would argue over as to whether to rename Riptail Row or Shiverrs Street.

As he got to his feet, which didn't take long, it was clear the dragon had vanished – disappeared without a trace, save for two blood-stained diamond bullets.

'So that's how it works!' Captain Shiverrs said loudly.

'How what works? He he!' came a spluttering, grunty voice.

Captain Shiverrs turned to see an odd-looking creature that had blue diamond-encrusted skin – its white cloak was soggy as if it had just been for a swim in a river of spit.

'That's no business of yours, creature!' the disgruntled dwarf barked.

'BLUE! You's alive maan,' Nelson cheered, as he floated to the ground on what Captain Shiverrs would later describe as a green cloud that smelt of trumps.

'Yes, I'm fine!' Blue began, wandering around looking rather delirious. 'Not a scratch, good as new – that's me! NOBODY PANIC!!' he garbled before fainting in an untidy heap.

*

'So, let me get this straight,' Emillia started, waving her hands about frantically as if she were conducting an invisible orchestra. 'The Councillors forced you,' she said pointing to Griffin's mother, 'to abandon your son and you,' she said pointing to Griffin, 'to kill me – so, the Councillors are to blame for my death.'

'No!' Master Agar said sternly. '*You* are to blame for your death Emillia; you meddled with dark magic beyond your control, or ours. A magic that saw you coaxed into submission by the very evil we were trying to protect Griffin and his mother from.'

'You do talk codswallop Luther!' said Emillia, looking a tad flustered as she did so.

'You can stop pretending now Emillia,' Master Agar said, 'you know of whom I speak.'

'LIES!' she shouted, 'I came here tonight for revenge, to kill those responsible for my death and it's you Luther, you were the Headmaster at the time, you were the Council leader, and now you must die.'

As Emillia raised her arms to cast a killing spell the puce fire that had been burning fiercely around the well exploded into a thousand-foot shaft of flame that stretched high into the night sky, knocking all those in the marketplace to the ground, including Emillia.

As the group of Witches and Wizards got to their feet a deep sinister rumbling voice echoed throughout the town. It simply said three words.

'KILL THE BLACKS!'

Griffin recognised it instantly as the same voice that had been present when Emillia turned him into Blackmouth. It sent an icy-cold reminder of fear coursing through his body.

'They are not to blame for my death Master,' Emillia said

shakily, 'Agar is to blame, he must die,' she finished.

'KILL THEM NOW OR RETURN TO THE FLAMES YOURSELF!' came the deep, thunderous voice again.

Emillia wearily turned to Griffin, raised her arms and screamed –

*'FACTUMORTIS!'*

'NO!' Griffin wailed, as his mother jumped in front of him. Her scream would haunt Griffin for the rest of his life. Master Agar, Lizzi, Garad, Blue and Nelson all rushed forward as Emillia raised her hands to Griffin once more.

All of a sudden, time slowed. Griffin looked around as all his friends and family charged in slow-motion towards him – it was like the day of the trial, following their banishment, when Lizzi and him were given a brief, but much needed, moment to themselves.

A dazzling white light emerged as if from nowhere.

'We're here Father!' said a magical voice from behind him that Griffin had missed more than words can say – it was Pereé and stood next to her, holding her hand, was Orbs.

'Hello Blacky,' Orbs said, 'funny how times can be flying sometimes hmm?' The little forest gnome smiled. 'But sometimes we's be needing to slow things down.'

'It was you,' said Griffin as the truth struck, 'that day in the street, you gave Lizzi and I that moment –'

'And before we had even met!' Orbs replied, beaming from one pointy ear to the other.

'How?' asked Griffin.

'Ah Blacky, still so much to learns and I shall teach you's in good times,' Orbs said hurriedly, 'other things must be coming first.' The forest gnome reached into his small leather satchel and pulled his faithful orbs from it; one golden, the other purple. Without request they floated above him and began to twist and spin.

Griffin turned and looked at his family and friends who continued their less-than-steady race towards him. He then looked to Emillia whose mouth was moving at a sluggish rate. Shortly after this a green light trickled slowly from her fingertips towards him

A lonely bogey doll

– she had cast another death spell.

The two orbs span quicker and quicker above Orbs' lemon-shaped head.

'Mother!' Pereé squeaked, seeing her mother drifting slowly forwards and who then proceeded to run, at normal speed, towards Lizzi, still with her favourite bogey doll clutched tightly in her hand.

'PEREÉ NO!' Orbs shrieked. The purple orb then settled above his head as a deep thunderous laughter filled the air.

In a flash time returned to normal. Griffin closed his eyes expecting to die. It did not come but in that instant the purple orb pulsed energy that deflected the curse back at Emillia - killing her instantly, but at the same time knocking Pereé into the puce column of flames that had engulfed the old well.

Instantaneously the flames disappeared and Pereé was gone.

Lizzi collapsed at the sheer sight of this. She hit the cobbles hard, shaking and retching at what she had seen. She screamed at the blackened well for her daughter but received no answer. A lonely bogey doll lay on the steps leading up to one of the pillars that supported the well's domed roof. Lizzi, unable to stand, dragged herself to it and after frantically turning it over noticed that it was badly scorched down one side and its other button-eye was now hanging off.

Pereé was gone – she had altogether disappeared.

'WHERE'S MY BABY?' Lizzi yelped. 'Griffin where's our baby gone?' she said, crawling clumsily back to the silently grieving group of familiar faces.

'Orbs what happened?' Griffin said with tears streaming down his face. He cleared his throat. 'Orbs where's Pereé?'

For the first time since they had met him, the small forest gnome they had invited into their family remained silent.

No smile. No jovial comments.

In all honesty Orbs had found a friendship in Pereé as like he had never experienced before and for this reason he remained quiet and solemn.

'WHERE IS SHE? WHERE'S MY BABY?' Lizzi wailed hysterically, like any parent would given the circumstances.

'She has been taken,' said Orbs finally and much to the relief of all those present.

'Taken?' said Griffin urgently to make sure he hadn't misheard, 'taken where?' at which point Lizzi stopped her crying to listen.

'She's not dead?' said Lizzi.

'No,' Orbs replied, 'not being dead – she is being taken. Taken to a realm beyond this one, to an evil place of fire and terror.'

'How do we get her back?' Griffin said instantly, forgetting all he had just been through.

Orbs looked around him. At a ruined town and a huddle of hopeful Witches and Wizards who were ready to brave the unknown. He looked up at them and offered them a smile.

'We must be going on a journey. Together. As a family.'

# A Note from the Author

Dear Reader,

In purchasing this book you have actively chosen to make a difference to the lives of children all around the world.

A percentage of the proceeds from the sale of this book will be donated to UNICEF.

For the avoidance of doubt, UNICEF is the world's leading organisation for children, working in over 190 countries. They do whatever it takes to make a lasting difference to children's lives. In everything they do, the most disadvantaged children are their priority.

All their work is based on the UN Convention on the Rights of the Child, which sets out the rights of every child, no matter who they are or where they live, to grow up safe, happy and healthy.

Thank you for reading.

Kindest regards,

A. M. Richardson

For further information please visit www.am-richardson.com